BARK TO THE FUTURE

**Other Books in the
Chet and Bernie Series**

BARK
to the
FUTURE

Spencer Quinn

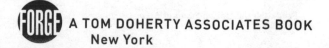

FORGE A TOM DOHERTY ASSOCIATES BOOK
New York

This is a work of fiction. All of the characters, organizations, and events portrayed in this novel are either products of the author's imagination or are used fictitiously.

BARK TO THE FUTURE

Copyright © 2022 by Pas de Deux

A Forge Book
Published by Tom Doherty Associates
120 Broadway
New York, NY 10271

www.tor-forge.com

Forge® is a registered trademark of Macmillan Publishing Group, LLC.

Library of Congress Cataloging-in-Publication Data

Names: Quinn, Spencer, author.
Title: Bark to the future / Spencer Quinn.
Description: First Edition. | New York : Forge, 2022. | Series: A Chet &
    Bernie mystery ; 13 | "A Tom Doherty Associates Book."
Identifiers: LCCN 2022010452 (print) | LCCN 2022010453 (ebook) |
    ISBN 9781250843272 (hardcover) | ISBN 9781250843289 (ebook)
Subjects: LCGFT: Novels.
Classification: LCC PS3617.U584 B37 2022 (print) | LCC PS3617.U584
    (ebook) | DDC 813'.6—dc23
LC record available at https://lccn.loc.gov/2022010452
LC ebook record available at https://lccn.loc.gov/2022010453

Our books may be purchased in bulk for promotional, educational, or
business use. Please contact your local bookseller or the Macmillan Corporate
and Premium Sales Department at 1-800-221-7945, extension 5442,
or by email at MacmillanSpecialMarkets@macmillan.com.

First Edition: 2022

Printed in the United States of America

0 9 8 7 6 5 4 3 2 1

For Anthony

BARK TO THE FUTURE

One

"Let's see what this baby can do," Bernie said.

And there you have it. Bernie's brilliance, lighting up the whole oil-stained yard at Nixon's Championship Autobody. *Let's see what this baby can do.* Can you imagine anyone else saying that? I sure can't. I wouldn't even try, and who knows Bernie better than me? Sometimes humans talk to themselves, as you may or may not know. Humans have a lot going on in their heads. Too much? I couldn't tell you. But I wouldn't trade places. Let's leave it at that. The point is that when they're talking to themselves they're trying to dig down through all the too-muchness and get to what's at the bottom, digging, as it happens, being one of my very best things. Maybe we'll get to that later. For now, the takeaway is that Bernie talks to himself in front of me. So I know what's at the bottom of Bernie, way down deep, case closed. Closing cases is what we do, by the way, me and Bernie. We're partners in the Little Detective Agency—Little on account of that's Bernie's last name. Call me Chet, pure and simple. Our cases usually get closed by me grabbing the perp by the pant leg. Although there were no perps around right now and we weren't even working a case, my teeth got a funny feeling.

Nixon Panero, owner of the shop and our good buddy, patted the hood of our new Porsche. We've had others—maybe more than I can count, since things get iffy when I try to go past two—but never one this old. Could I even remember them all? Perhaps not, although I have a very clear picture of the last one in my mind, upside down and soaring through snowy treetops, the windows all blasted out and me and Bernie also in midair, although slightly closer to the ground. I'd miss that Porsche—especially the martini glass decals on the fenders—but this one, with an interesting black and white pattern, as though a normal PD squad car was rippling its muscles, if that makes any sense, looked none too shabby. In fact, and in a strange dreamlike way, a thing of beauty. And to top it off, my seat—the shotgun seat, goes without mentioning—couldn't have been more comfortable, the leather soft and firm at the same time, and possibly quite tasty. A no-no, and I forgot that whole idea at once.

"One last thing," Nixon said.

Bernie, hands on the wheel, ready to go, glanced up at him.

"All parts guaranteed original and authentic," Nixon said. "Excepting certain aspects of the engine."

"No problem," Bernie said. "You're the expert."

"Thanks, Bernie. But what I'm saying is in horsepower terms authentic might be stretching it the teensiest bit. So my advice would be to take it on the easy side at first."

"Sure thing," Bernie said, sliding his foot over to the gas pedal.

"On account of what we've got here," Nixon began, "is kind of a—"

Beast? Was that what Nixon said? I couldn't be sure, because at that moment Bernie's foot—he was wearing flip flops, one new-looking, the other old and worn—touched the pedal, just the lightest touch to my way of thinking, but enough to get our new engine excited in no uncertain terms. It roared a tremendous roar and this new dreamlike ride of ours shot out of Nixon's yard and into the street. I felt like my head was getting left behind, meaning that shooting out doesn't really do the job here. Was it possible we were actually off the ground? I believed we were.

"Woo eee!" Bernie cried as he brought us safely down, all tires on the pavement. "Woo eee, baby!"

As for me, I got my head and body properly organized, sat up straight, and howled at the moon, although it was daytime and cloudy to boot. We had a beast on our side. No one could touch us now, although the truth was no one ever had before. I felt tip-top, or even better.

"My god," said Bernie as we came off a two-laner that had taken us deep into the desert and far from the Valley, where we live, and merged onto a freeway, the tops of the downtown towers visible in the distance, their lower parts lost in the brassy haze. "Can you believe what just happened?" We slowed down to what seemed like nothing, although we were zooming past everyone else. Bernie patted the dash and glanced my way. "Rough beast, big guy, its hour come round at last." That one zipped right by me, but Bernie laughed so it must have been funny. "Did we hit one forty? Next time I'll snap a picture of the speedometer. You'll have to take the wheel."

No problem. That had actually happened once, if very briefly, down Mexico way, where Bernie and I had had to leave a nice little cantina in somewhat of a hurry, following a misunderstanding between Bernie, a very friendly lady, and a late-arriving gentleman who turned out to be her husband and also the head of the local cartel. Bottom line: Bernie could count on me.

Not long after that we were winding slowly down the ramp at the Rio Vista Bridge, close to home. There's always a backup on the ramp, and at the bottom a few leathery-skinned men holding paper cups or sometimes cardboard signs are waiting. Today there was only one, a real skinny barefoot guy, wearing frayed cargo shorts and nothing else, his shoulders the boniest

I'd ever seen. He was mostly bald, but had a ponytail happening at the back, a gray ponytail with yellow-stained ends, the same yellow you see on the fingertips of smokers. Also—and maybe the first thing I noticed—a small but jagged scar across the bridge of his nose. A cigarette was hanging from the side of his mouth but its tiny fire had gone out. Traffic came to a stop when we were right beside him. He looked down at us, his eyes watery blue. I was pretty sure I hadn't seen him before, and certain I'd never smelled him. My nose is never wrong on things like that. In this case it wasn't even a close call. Had I ever picked up a human scent so . . . how would you put it? Complex? Rich? Over the top? You pick. As for me, I was starting to like this dude a lot. Meanwhile Bernie dug out a few bills from the cup holder and handed them over.

Except not quite. Yes, Bernie held out the money, but the dude made no move to grab it. Instead he shook his head and said, "Can't take your money, Bernie."

"Excuse me?" Bernie said.

The dude took the cigarette out of his mouth, plucked a little twist of something from between two chipped and yellowed teeth, and said it again.

Bernie gave him a close look. "Do I know you?" he said.

"Guess not," said the dude. He glanced down at the money, still in Bernie's outstretched hand, and his lips curled in a sort of sneer, like that money was way beneath him. "But I'll take a light," he said.

Bernie stuck the money back in the cup holder, fumbled around inside, found a book of matches and held them out. The guy took the matches, broke one off, but he couldn't get it lit, his hands suddenly very shaky. In front us traffic started moving. From behind came honking, not easy on my ears. Bernie pulled off the ramp, getting us mostly onto the narrow dirt strip next to the bridge supports. He opened the door, put one foot on the ground, and looked back at me.

"Better stay, Chet."

Too late. Meanwhile the traffic from behind was on the move, perhaps still slightly blocked by us, but hardly at all. A truck driver leaned out of his window, an unpleasant expression on his face. He opened his mouth to say something, saw me, and changed his mind.

"Here," said Bernie, holding out his hand.

"Here what?" said the dude.

"The matches."

The dude handed over the matches. Bernie lit one, cupped the flame. The dude leaned in, got his cigarette going. For a moment, his face—so weathered, wrinkled, with little blotches here and there—was almost touching Bernie's hand, so perfect. The dude straightened, took a deep drag, let it out slow, smoke streaming from his nostrils.

"Waiting for me to say thanks?" said the dude.

"No," said Bernie.

"Then get back in your super-duper car." He glanced over at me, turned away, then gave me another look. "The both of you."

"In a hurry to get rid of us?" Bernie said.

The dude was silent for what seemed like a long time. Then came a bit of a surprise. He smiled. Not a big smile, and lots of teeth were missing and the tip of his tongue was yellow-brown, but he no longer looked quite so messed up.

"You haven't changed," he said. "Always those goddamn questions."

"For example?"

The dude thought for a moment or two. Then he stiffened and shouted at Bernie, a shout with a sort of whispery, ragged edge, so not particularly loud, but real angry. "You makin' fun of me, Bernie? That's another question you just asked. Think I'm nothin' but . . . but . . ." Whatever it was, he couldn't come up with it.

"Sorry," Bernie said, "I didn't—"

The dude's eyes narrowed down to two watery slits. "You was always an asshole but not mean. What the hell happened?"

"Look," Bernie said, "I—"

"Aw, the hell with it," the dude said, his anger vanishing all at once. He waved his hand—fingers bent, nails thick and yellow—in a throwaway gesture. "You stood up for me. I don't forget things like that. Well, I do. I forget . . . you name it." He laughed a croaky laugh that got croakier until he finally spat out a brownish gob. It landed at the base of one of the bridge supports. I moved in that direction. At the same time, the dude took a very deep drag, blew out a thick smoke ball, peered through it at Bernie, then wagged his finger. "But I sure as shit remember that time with Raker."

"Coach Raker?" Bernie said.

"Who the hell else are we jawin' about?" said the dude. "He was gonna bench me for showin' up late to the game against Central Tech and you said hey coach bench me I forgot to pick him up on the way to school. Which wasn't even true. No way you don't remember that. You were on the mound and don't deny it. Two outs, bottom of the ninth, bases loaded, up one zip, and some dude hits a scorcher in the gap and who runs it down?" The dude tapped his skinny chest. "Game over. Took us to the state, uh, whatever it is."

Bernie has wonderful eyebrows, with a language all their own. Now they were saying a whole bunch, but amazement was a big part of it.

"Championship," he said softly.

"Yeah, state championship, what I said," said the dude. "Next year you guys won it but I was . . . was . . . like movin' on."

"Rocket?" Bernie said. "Rocket Saluka?"

The dude—Rocket Saluka, if I was following things right—nodded a slow, serious kind of nod, and stood very straight before us, there in the bridge shadows, his shoulders back, his scrawny bare chest rising and falling. He and Bernie had played on the same team? Had I gotten that right? Baseball, for sure, bottom of the ninth and bases loaded being baseball lingo, but how was it possible? Rocket was an old man.

Traffic on the ramp was now mostly stop and not much go, meaning folks had plenty of time to check us out. Rocket didn't seem to notice them, and neither did Bernie. He and Rocket were just standing there, Rocket smoking his cigarette, Bernie watching him. At last Bernie said, "I could use a burger."

Rocket nodded another slow, serious nod.

"How about you?" Bernie said.

Rocket took one last drag and tossed the butt away. Bernie ground it under his heel. I took a good close-range sniff of Rocket's brownish gob, lying in the dirt. Was actual tasting necessary? I was leaning in that direction when Bernie made the little chkk-chkk sound that meant we were out of there. Burgers or brownish gobs? Burgers! Burgers for sure! But that was Bernie, always the smartest human in the room. Just follow him—especially from in front, like I do—and you can't go wrong.

There are many Burger Heavens in the Valley—just one of the reasons it's the best place on earth—but our favorite is the one between Mama's Bowlerama and Mama's Kitchen, Bath and Fine Art, mostly because Mama owns it, too, and Bernie's a big fan of Mama, has told me more than once that she's what puts America over the top. Perhaps a bit confusing—I had a notion that Bernie and I were Americans and that was pretty much it—but it didn't matter. Mama's burgers were the best I'd ever tasted. I was enjoying one now just the way I liked it at a picnic table on one side of the Burger Heaven parking lot, on a paper plate, no bun, no nothing, and over in a jiff. Bernie sat on one side of the table, dipping fries into a ketchup cup. Rocket sat on the other side. He'd polished off his first burger real fast, taken a little more time with the second, and was now working his way through the next one, the number for what comes after two escaping me at the moment. Except for ordering, no one had said a thing. Now and then, Mama glanced our way from the kitchen window of the hut, her huge gold hoop earrings the brightest sight in view.

Rocket burped, sat back, searched the pockets of his cargo shorts, pulled out a switchblade knife, not an uncommon sight in my line of work, but it seemed to surprise him. He shoved the knife back in his pocket. The top of the handle, rounded off with a green-eyed human skull decoration, peeped out from inside his pocket.

"What you got there?" Bernie said.

"MVP," said Rocket.

"Most valuable player?"

"Close, real close," Rocket said. "Most valuable possession."

"What makes it valuable?" Bernie said.

Rocket shoved the knife deeper in his pocket, the green-eyed skull now disappearing from view. "Let's keep that between the two of us, me and me," he said. "Keep on keepin' it thataway." His hand was still in his pocket, rummaging around. It emerged with a bent cigarette. "Smoke?"

"Sure," said Bernie, meaning he was about to take one of those breaks from giving up smoking.

Now would be when most folks would be expecting Rocket to produce another cigarette, but that didn't happen. Instead he broke the bent one in two and handed half to Bernie.

"Thanks," said Bernie, striking a match.

They smoked in silence for a while, Rocket taking quick glances at Bernie, Bernie looking nowhere special. I got the feeling something might be going on in Bernie's mind, but whatever it was he was in no hurry. I was about to settle down under the table for a little shut-eye when the Burger Heaven back door opened and Mama stepped out with a package in her hand. She came over to the table. Rocket didn't seem to notice her until she was right there. Then he looked startled.

"What the hell?" he said. Rocket's hand went right to his cargo shorts pocket, the one with the flip knife inside.

Two

Bernie rose, so smooth you might have missed how quickly he got himself between Mama and Rocket. I was right beside him, goes without mentioning. As for looking alarmed or anything like that, we did not. We were just two casual dudes on our feet.

"Always the gentleman," Mama said. "But you don't have to get up for me, Bernie. How about introducing your friend?"

Bernie turned to Rocket, whose hand was kind of trembling, not quite in the cargo shorts pocket.

"Mr. Rocket Saluka," Bernie said, "meet Mrs. Pedra Cruz."

"Nice to meet you," Mama said. "But everyone calls me Mama."

Rocket blinked a few times but didn't call her Mama, or anything at all.

"Never met a Rocket before," Mama said.

"Huh?" said Rocket.

"Is it a nickname?" she said.

"Yeah," said Rocket. And then he shouted, "Like Mama!" He turned and made a bow, like to a big audience, although there was nothing in front of him except a dumpster. "Live from New York, it's . . . it's . . ." Rocket stood facing the dumpster, rocking back and forth.

Mama and Bernie exchanged a look. Bernie gestured at the package with his chin, a sweet human move they maybe don't get enough credit for. She came over to him and whispered. I can pick up whispers from far away. This one was a piece of cake, although cake isn't really my thing. Have I eaten my share, including the entire top layer of a wedding cake, where the tiny bride and groom dolls—totally made of frosting, by the way, sweet enough to make you pukey surprisingly soon—stand? Let's not go into that, but just stick with Mama's whisper. "No shirt, no service, Bernie. It's the rule."

Bernie nodded and reached for the package, but Mama didn't hand it over.

"I'll do it," she said.

She headed over to Rocket. Bernie took a step to follow but saw I was already beside her and stayed where he was. We're a team, me and Bernie.

"Got something for you, Rocket," Mama said.

He turned away from the dumpster. "What're you talkin' about?"

"A present." She held out the package.

He didn't take it. "Not my birthday." Then his forehead wrinkled up. "Upsy-daisy—is it January ten?"

"No," Mama said.

"I was born January ten, Mama. In the godforsaken panhandle of Oklahoma. You know Oklahoma?"

"A little."

"Where the wind comes right behind the rain." He snatched the package from her, tore it open, and took out a black-and-gold T-shirt. "What's this?"

"Is it your size?" Mama said.

"Someone's giving me a T-shirt?"

"I am," said Mama. "But there's something in it for me, too."

"Like, an angle?"

"Si," Mama said. "Read what it says on the back."

Rocket turned the T-shirt around and read out loud, "'Mama's Bowlerama. The one. The only.'" He squinted at Mama. "So what's your angle?"

"You'd be advertising for me," Mama said.

"Don't get it."

"I own the Bowlerama."

There was a long pause while Rocket thought that over. "Own," he said at last.

"That's right," Mama said.

"Okey-dokey," said Rocket. "We're on the same pageroo. I bowled a three hundred at your place once."

"Congrats," said Mama.

"Tell her, Bernie."

"Tell her what?"

"Huh? Not listenin'? That's rude, Bernie. Tell her I bowled a three hundred."

"Never bowled with you, not that I remember," Bernie said. "But I can believe it. You were a fine athlete."

Rocket's free hand moved back toward his pocket. "You never used to be rude. Now I'm guessin' you'll deny I snagged that ball."

Bernie smiled and shook his head. "Nope," he said. "I can see it like it was yesterday."

"I'm not following this very well," Mama said.

"Rocket won us a big game back in high school. They don't call him Rocket for nothing."

Rocket closed his eyes tight. "They don't," he said. "They don't call me Rocket." Bernie and Mama exchanged another glance. My guess was it meant something but I had no idea what. Rocket's eyes flew open and he started putting on the T-shirt real fast. "Gonna advertise the shit out of this, big Mama. Easy peasy for me—I love your Bowlerama."

"Thanks. And just Mama is fine." Mama went back inside the Burger Heaven hut.

"Where can we drop you?" Bernie said when we were all done eating.

"Back where you found me, where else?" said Rocket.

"At the ramp?"

"Didn't I already say where else?" Rocket said. "Gotta work."

"I'm going to ask you an intrusive question," Bernie said.

"Huh?"

"How much do you make in a day?"

"What are you, the government?" Rocket said.

Bernie laughed. "I told you it was intrusive."

Rocket gave Bernie a long look. First I thought he was real angry, and then I didn't.

"I always liked you, Bernie," he said.

"Right back atcha," said Bernie.

For a moment Rocket's eyes seemed to fill with tears, but maybe it was one of those tricks that light plays out here in the desert.

"But the reason I ask," Bernie went on, "is I could make up what you'd be taking in the rest of the day and you could knock off early."

"Knock off?"

"And go home."

"Home?" said Rocket. His eyes cleared. He was angry. Maybe I'd been right all along. "The ramp, Bernie, and hustle up."

One thing about this new Porsche, and all our other Porsches: it's the perfect ride for two, with a nice roomy driver's seat for Bernie and a nice roomy shotgun seat for Chet. So if you want to ride with us—even if you're Stilts Wilton, former basketball star, if I got the story right, who'd had an issue with a bunch of trophies stolen from him, although in the end it turned out that he'd forgotten which mansion was his, a complicated story, but not the point, which was even Stilts Wilton rode on the little shelf in back, as Rocket had on the ride over to Burger Heaven, no problem. Only Charlie—Bernie's kid, living mostly with Leda since the divorce, and let's not leave out her new husband

Malcolm with the very long toes although he has nothing particularly interesting going on in the foot smell department,
but has grown a bit buddylike with Bernie, kind of a surprise
and . . . and . . . Back to Charlie! Whew! Funny how the mind
can sometimes take off on its own like . . . like it needs a leash.
Uh-oh. An uneasy thought. Perhaps, sitting beside the picnic
table at the Burger Heaven parking lot, I squirmed around a
bit. I'm sure you do the same when an uneasy thought pops up.

Bernie glanced my way. "Chet? Not worms again!"

Worms? Me? What a strange idea, especially coming from
someone of Bernie's brilliance. Why would worms pop into his
mind? There's a feeling that comes from worms, my friends, a
feeling that leads to a visit with Amy the vet, followed by pill
pockets and a little game Bernie and I play, all about scarfing
up the pockets but spitting out the pills—the fun we have with
that! It never gets old! But not the point, all about not feeling
that wormy feeling at the moment. Uh-oh! Was . . . was Bernie the one feeling wormy? That would be a first. I gave him
a close look, saw no sign of any squirming, and wasn't paying
attention to anything else, so I was too late to put a halt to a
very disturbing development, namely Rocket opening the passenger door of the new Porsche and plunking himself down on
the shotgun seat.

I ended up—you may not believe this—on the little shelf in
back. The tiny little shelf in back, I might add, and I myself am
a hundred-plus pounder, as I know from the time Bernie got
the idea of weighing me on the bathroom scale, which I very
much did not want to sit on, so he first weighed himself and then
picked me up and . . . well, let's just say that one of the wonderful things about Bernie is how often he finds new games for

us to play. And if we no longer have an actual bathroom scale, meaning a bathroom scale in one piece, who even remembers stuff like that? The takeaway is that I was on the tiny little shelf in back—all except for my head, perhaps poking through to the front a bit—and Rocket had the shotgun seat. I was forming a plan, still hazy in my mind but action-packed, when I felt the beast rumbling beneath me, somehow much more present here on the shelf, and my plan faded away.

"You lose track of people," Bernie said, as we drove along a street with warehouses on one side and the Rio Vista, dry except for the weakest muddy trickle in the middle, on the other.

"Speak for yourself," Rocket said.

"I meant one," Bernie said. "One can lose track of people."

"Huh?" said Rocket.

I was with him on that.

"Me," Bernie said. "I can lose track of people. I lost track of you."

Rocket shrugged, his bony shoulder, rather near my muzzle, making a knobby bump in his new T-shirt. "So what?"

"So do me a favor. Fill in the blanks."

Rocket shook his head. "Already doing a favor. That's enough favors for one day."

"What favor is that?"

"Wearing the damn T-shirt. Aren't you paying attention?"

"Then how about doing me tomorrow's favor in advance?" Bernie said.

"Tomorrow's favor in advance? Then what goes down on the very last day?"

Bernie shot him a quick glance.

"Day of judgment, Bernie my amigo. When we all get put on the golden scale. When there's no goddamn tomorrow, come hell or high water."

Whoa! Scales were back in the picture? One thing for sure: I wasn't getting on any scale with Rocket, not now, not ever, even if a scrawny guy like him could lift me, which I very much doubted.

We stopped at a red light. All at once the whole Valley went quiet, a strange thing that sometimes happens. And when Bernie spoke his voice, too, was strangely quiet, actually kind of gentle. "What did you do after high school?" he said.

Rocket was silent. The light turned green. Sounds rose up again. We started moving.

"You know what my lovebird always said?" Rocket said.

"Who's your lovebird?"

"Was. Who was my lovebird?"

"Okay," Bernie said. "Go on."

"No going on. She took the long fall, as I should know."

"But who was she?"

"Tormentor in chief. Well, not in chief. We all know who that was."

"Who?" said Bernie.

"Come on, Bernie, the one who beats your mama. You never had a tormentor?"

Bernie shook his head.

"Then you're a tormentor." Rocket rubbed a thin, jagged gap he had in one of his eyebrows. "Tormentor or tormented—them's the choices."

"I don't believe that," Bernie said.

"You're like, what? Three days old?" Rocket's watery eyes went very dark in a way that reminded me of the lake on Ponderosa Mountain on a night that had gone wrong for some people, although not me and Bernie. Then he laughed, a brief, harsh laugh, not easy on my ears. He twisted in his seat and pointed at Bernie. "What did *you* do after high school?" And when Bernie didn't answer he laughed again, even harsher this time. "Ha! Gotcha! Gotcha good! Right between the ribs, pally!"

Whoa! Didn't Rocket realize that my teeth were right there, practically touching his bony shoulder? Or was it possible he didn't understand what these teeth can do? There's a certain kind of human you get to know in my line of work who always ends up on the receiving end. Rocket turned out to be that type. We had nothing to fear from him. The truth is we have nothing to fear from anyone. Some I have to keep an eye on, that's all.

Meanwhile Bernie was nodding his head. "Fair enough," he said. "After high school I caught a real lucky break and got into West Point."

"Bang bang shoot shoot," said Rocket.

"That came later. After I got out I went into law enforcement, like lots of ex-military. It turned out I was more suited to private investigation, especially after I teamed up with the right partner."

"You got a partner?" Rocket said.

What a question! There I was, right in his face!

Bernie's eyes brightened in the way they do when something fun starts up, but I had no idea what it was.

"Very much so," he said. "Partner slash boss. Anyhow, that's my story."

What was this? We had a boss? That was very confusing. I was suddenly thirsty.

"Where's the bang bang shoot shoot part?" Rocket said.

Bernie shrugged. "I was overseas for a couple of tours." After a long pause, he added, "Three."

Rocket's lip turned up in a sneer, not the best human look, exposing a chipped tooth, another tooth so yellow it was closer to brown, and a gap, the gum bleeding a bit. "So you want me to thank you for your service?" he said.

"Nope," said Bernie.

"I coulda served too, you know."

"Sure thing."

"I'm handy with my fists. Remember the brouhaha on Halloween?"

"Doesn't ring a bell," Bernie said.

A bit of a surprise, since at that moment church bells happened to be ringing all across the Valley, the way church bells do every day, out of the blue but all at the same time, for reasons unknown to me. I have no problem with that. My problem is with Bernie's ears—not small, certainly not for a human—but what do they do, exactly?

"Sposta be smart, Bernie," Rocket said. "Sposta remember."

"Fill me in," Bernie said.

"Fill yourself in," said Rocket. We came to the bottom of the Rio Vista ramp. "My stop," Rocket said. He felt for the door handle, couldn't find it.

"What was your lovebird's name?" Bernie said.

"Tryna get out," said Rocket. "Do not disturb." His fingers wrapped themselves around the handle. He tried it a few ways, opened the door, got one foot out, and then turned back. "Private investigations—like you're a private eye?"

"Yes."

"What dya charge?"

"It depends."

"On what?"

"Lots of things—the nature of the case, how much travel's involved, the ability of the client to pay. Why?"

"No reason," said Rocket. He tapped his pocket. "Most valuable possession!"

"Maybe you should sell it," Bernie said.

"Out of your mind, hijo?"

"Hijo?" said Bernie.

"Means sonny, down in Mexico."

"You've spent time there?"

"Mucho," said Rocket. "Too mucho." He walked off toward the ramp. A shirtless guy wearing an eyepatch was going from car to car, coffee cup in hand. Rocket ripped off his new T-shirt, balled it up, and threw it at the coffee cup guy. They began yelling at each other.

Three

"Where'd you go to high school?" Bernie said.

We were out on the patio behind our place on Mesquite Road, the sun going down and the sky all wild with fiery colors, reminding me of an incident involving Charlie's paint set and Leda's new white couch, on my very first visit to the huge house she and Malcolm had in High Chaparral Estates, the fanciest part of the whole Valley. Leda's always had a special way of looking at me. I saw it that day, big-time, and it stayed in my mind for ages and ages, finally fading just before I made my next visit. You won't believe what happened on that one, so let's not even go there.

"Freshman year was at Navajo Hills," said Weatherly, sipping her drink, a drink with bourbon—Bernie's a big bourbon fan—and also some other stuff in it that he'd learned to make just for her. "When I moved down here to live with Grammie I went to Northside High. Why do you ask?"

Bernie didn't answer right away, possibly on account of the rather large flames that suddenly leaped from the grill, licking over the top of our very high back gate, so high it's hard to believe it's actually leapable not just by shooting flames but also by a certain member of the nation within the nation—which is what Bernie calls me and my kind—that leapability leading to a complication or two in my life. Maybe we can get to that later, but right now is a chance to fill you in on Weatherly Wauneka—Bernie's girlfriend, unless I'm missing something. Which can happen, by the way, but probably not for someone like me in a situation like this, where the scents of the man and woman involved change so obviously whenever they catch sight of each other. Obviously to me, that is. Not long after they met, Bernie said, "I wonder what she thinks of me."

Come again? There's so much to like about humans but at times you have to feel a little bit badly for them, and even worry. At that moment—we were working a case involving a tortoise named Torquemada, as I recall, although I wish I couldn't recall anything about it, starting with Torquemada herself, Torquemada being a she, which took me quite a bit of sniffing around her to establish, tortoise smells being somewhat unusual—I gave Bernie a long look. Bernie! Don't you know from her smell? Can't you hear it in her voice? And it was while I was distracted with those thoughts that Torquemada tried to bite me. The fury in her eyes! Snaky-type eyes, by the way. It might have been scary if it hadn't been happening in slow motion. But what was her problem? Something about me? Or was she annoyed by us trying to boost her up into the bed of a pickup with the tire jack, Bernie working the jack and me encouraging him to the best of my ability? One of our worst cases. Did I mention that Torquemada was a runaway? Yes, I know what you're thinking.

Meanwhile Bernie, all done with the fire extinguisher, turned to Weatherly and said, "Ran into an old high school buddy today."

"Yeah?" said Weatherly. "What high school?"

"Chisholm," Bernie said.

"Go Bears," said Weatherly.

Bernie laughed. What was funny? And why were bears suddenly in the picture? Tortoises were stubborn and hard to move, but if given a choice I'd prefer to deal with them rather than bears any day. Once we'd somehow gotten between a mama bear and her cubs, me and Bernie. There was nothing funny about bears, as he had every reason to remember.

He sat across from her at the little table in front of the swan fountain—the only thing that Leda didn't take with her when she left—and topped up their glasses. Down underneath the table, where I've seen plenty of action in my career, many humans under the impression that what happens under tables is invisible, Weatherly slipped off her sandal and laid her foot—not the biggest foot you'll see, but strong and kind of broad, with dark red-painted nails—on Bernie's. Bernie himself was wearing sneakers, his bare feet, the best there are, hidden from view. But in a strange way I got the feeling that her bare foot and his were . . . how to put it? Communicating, maybe? Communicating through the sneaker material. Meanwhile, up above the table top, Bernie was sipping his drink and Weatherly was watching him.

"The girls must have loved you," she said.

"Huh? What girls?"

"The Chisholm girls, of course. They had a reputation back in the day."

"Oh? Like what?"

"A reputation, Bernie," Weatherly said. She ran her bare foot under the hem of his jeans. "Capisce?"

"Um," said Bernie. "I, uh . . . well, in retrospect, maybe . . ." His voice got strangely thick and he came to a halt.

"Plus what with you being the big flamethrower and all, dot dot dot," Weatherly said. She seemed to be having lots of fun all of a sudden, for reasons I didn't know but felt quite nearby, possibly even in my eventual grasp. And that didn't happen often! All of a sudden I was having lots of fun, too! Imagine that! Just lounging on the patio and doing zip could be a tip-top experience.

"Flamethrower?" said Bernie.

"Up there on the mound," Weatherly went on. Then came a long pause, "mound" somehow staying around for a bit. "Dishing out the heat," she added after a while. "What did you like better? A windup or pitching out of the stretch?"

"Stop," Bernie said.

"Stop?" Weatherly's eyes, deep and dark, opened wide. "Stop what? Stop with the inside baseball?"

Bernie laughed. Weatherly joined in. They laughed together, laughed and laughed. It turned into a kind of music. I came very close to prancing around before the laughter died out. Weatherly slipped her foot out from under the hem of Bernie's jeans, picked up her glass, clinked it against Bernie's.

"Okay," she said, "tell me about your high school buddy."

"Rocket Saluka," Bernie said. "I wouldn't actually call him a buddy. More like a teammate. He was a year ahead of me, very fast, which was why they called him Rocket."

"What was his real name?"

"If I ever knew, it's gone now. What I do remember is a catch he made against Central Tech. A game saver. We carried him off the field. They were our big rivals—this was my sophomore season and we hadn't beaten them for a few years before that and . . ." He shook his head, looked down. "Crazy to think how intense it all was."

"I don't think so," Weatherly said. "Let's hear the game saver story. I love baseball."

"You never told me that."

Weatherly smiled. "We've got time."

Bernie sat back. I could feel his body relaxing. His face changed, looked for a few moments a little younger, and Bernie's already the most young-looking man around, for his age. All this youngness just because we had time? We had loads and loads of time—didn't everyone know that? Time went on and on forever, day after beautiful day, if you leave out monsoon season which, by the way, can kind of sneak up on you.

Bernie gazed into his glass. "Bottom of the ninth, up one-zip, winner goes to the state championship. Bases loaded, two outs, my pitch count probably getting up there."

"You'd pitched the whole game?"

"Coach Raker was a throwback, didn't go in for pitch counts. No one questioned him. Partly because of his temper, but mostly because of his credibility—rock solid."

"Let me guess," Weatherly said. "He had a cup of coffee in the majors."

Bernie glanced at her. "You're way ahead of me."

"Want me to slow down?"

"How would you do that, exactly?"

"Touché," Weatherly said, losing me completely. "Tell me about Coach Raker's cup of coffee."

Bernie nodded. "Career minor leaguer. Rode the buses for ten years, maybe more, making peanuts. But on the last day of his last season he got called up. Pirates or Phillies, can't remember which. Game went into extra innings and they emptied the bench except for him. Finally they sent him in to pinch hit."

"And he hit one out?"

"Nope. Safe on a fielder's choice. But that one at bat gave him the status to manage any way he liked. And he didn't like pitch counts. The funny thing was that Danny Feld, the kid who took care of the equipment and also kept score, did keep track of pitch counts. In fact, he was a math whiz, developed all sorts of stat models kind of like what they have now. He always sat at the far end of the dugout, as far from Raker as possible, and when you came off the mound at the end of an inning, he'd air draw the number for you, backward so you could read it. One day Raker figured out what he was doing and almost canned him on the spot. So I don't know the number I got to in the Central Tech game. I was still throwing pretty hard but when I tired I lost control of my changeup—my only off pitch back then—which was how I ended up with the bases loaded. Walk, ground out, runner to second, walk, sac bunt, runners advancing to—" Bernie went silent. "Sorry. This must be pretty boring."

"Shut up," Weatherly said. "Go on."

Which was kind of confusing. All I'd really understood so far was the part about working for peanuts. Once I'd palled around—well, maybe not palled around, more like attempted to herd, actually—an elephant, name of Peanut. This was deep in the desert, maybe down Mexico way. But before that Peanut had worked in a circus for peanuts, just like this Raker dude. I knew one thing for sure: if he was like Peanut, herding him was off the table.

Bernie shrugged. "Don't remember what count we got to, but the catcher—this was Herschel Brock, our best player—called for another changeup. I was scared I'd bounce it and the runner would score, so I shook him off and went with the fastball. The batter—Ed Torres, a fireplug type I actually served with overseas years later and got to know—hit a screamer into the left center gap, a sure bases-clearing double, but Rocket made a full-stretch diving grab, game over."

"Wow," Weatherly said. "Did you guys talk about it today?"

"Kind of—it meant a lot at the time. But Rocket's in a bad way."

"How so?"

Bernie started telling her. I was all set to listen my hardest, but that was when the back door of the house opened. You open it from the inside by pressing down on the little thumb thingy, but a paw works just as well, meaning I can open the back door. So can Bernie and also Weatherly. Trixie, supposedly napping under the ceiling fan in the living room as she does on every visit, cannot. And yet here she was, ambling out.

"Well, would you look at that," Bernie said.

"She must have figured it out from watching Chet," said Weatherly.

Bernie looked my way. "Hey, big guy. How's it feel to be a mentor?"

Weatherly laughed. Mentor? A new one on me. And not the point, which was that everyone seemed to be taking this outrage very lightly. How annoying was that? Have you ever noticed that one bothersome thing is often followed by others? For example, the way Trixie had her tail held up so high. So high and mighty! What could I do but hold my own tail up even higher and mightier? That made a difference right away and I was just about back to my normal self when Trixie went by in that light-footed way of hers that always reminds me of how fast she is. Not as fast as me, amigo, don't go thinking that for one second. Still, it was another annoyance, although not even the worst one. The worst annoyance was that aroma I detected on her breath—the aroma of a Slim Jim, one of a kind and unmistakable. How had she gotten hold of a Slim Jim? The Slim Jims in our house have been kept in many places, Bernie finally settling on the meat compartment in the fridge. I've taken a number of swings at opening the fridge door, none successful. So far. Was it possible Trixie had done what I . . . whoa. I didn't want to go there. And then came a really hideous thought. Some time ago I'd managed to corral a Slim Jim on a little neighborhood excursion of my own that . . . well, the details aren't important. In fact, I'd forgotten the whole episode, including the most important part, namely that I'd hidden that Slim Jim in the . . . in the . . . oh, please! Where? Where? Where?

Then in hit me: in the living room! In that dustbally space behind the TV, a tangle of cobwebs and cables, the perfect hiding place! I ran into the house, down the hall—perhaps hearing Weatherly say, "What's with him?" and perhaps not—into the living room, around the TV and—

And my Slim Jim was gone.

＊ ＊ ＊

I faced the living room wall, stood motionless, doing pretty much nothing. Pretty much nothing except . . . why Trixie? I had no answer to that question. All I knew was that Trixie was out of control. Had things started that way? Far from it. We'd rescued Trixie from a cave or abandoned mine, me and Bernie. So far a normal day at the Little Detective Agency. Then it turned out Trixie had been kidnapped from Weatherly. Was that how Weatherly came into our life? When did normal begin to slip away? All I know is that Weatherly loved us for finding Trixie. No problem there, I suppose. The problem is that Trixie and I—this is from what I've heard, not really seeing it myself—look alike. Why would anyone think such a thing? Just because our coats are the same—shiny black except for one white ear? Didn't my being so much—or at least somewhat—bigger count for anything? One little irritation was another fact, namely that aside from the she-ness of her scent and he-ness of mine, they were rather similar. But who knew that, other than Trixie and me and every single member of the nation within? Certainly not Bernie or Weatherly. So how had they arrived at the strange idea that Trixie and I must have been puppies together? Strange and unacceptable.

I remained in the living room for some time, refusing to accept. Then I gave myself a good shake and trotted out to the patio. The sky had darkened and the moon was up, but dim and sort of smeared by a thin cloud. Bernie and Weatherly were sitting side by side, gazing up at it, Trixie curled at their feet.

"That whole Rocket story makes me feel so lucky," Weatherly said. "Does it make you feel lucky?"

"I feel lucky for lots of reasons," said Bernie.

"What do you think happened to him?" Weatherly said.

The thin cloud drifted away and the moon brightened and got very clear, turning Bernie's face a stony color. "Good question," he said.

"But whatever the answer is it won't be good," said Weatherly.

Bernie gave her a look. I'd seen that look before, but always directed at me. It meant hey, glad we're on the same team, buddy. The team was me and Bernie, as I hope you know by now. So Bernie had given Weatherly that look by mistake. No one's perfect.

"Therefore," Weatherly went on, "most folks would just leave things right there."

"Yeah," Bernie said.

Another thin cloud slid over the moon. Then came thicker ones. It got dark out on our patio.

Four

First thing the next morning we drove to Burger Heaven. That was new. Donut Heaven first thing? No surprise there. But Burger Heaven? I felt uneasy. Then Bernie bought a bag of burgers, and took one out, which we split. My uneasiness disappeared just like that.

"Gotta be gradual," Bernie said, chewing thoughtfully, a ring of fried onion sticking out from between his lips and then licked inside. What a beautiful eater he was! As I'm sure you can imagine. "He won't take money but he will take burgers. So that's where we begin."

Whatever this was began with burgers? Was it a case? Cases usually begin with the appearance of a client. They end, of course, with me grabbing the perp by the pant leg. In between we kind of . . . what is it we do, exactly? We . . . we . . . we sniff around! That's it! That's what we do! Wow! I finally figured it out. And what a lucky break that sniffing around is our thing, because sniffing around is right in my wheelhouse! Wow! Just wow! I can't believe—

"Chet? A little space there, buddy?"

Ah. I seemed to be—well, not quite in Bernie's lap, but mostly on the driver's seat for sure, with Bernie maybe even craning his head a bit to get a clear view. In short, a reasonable request on his part. I shifted over to the shotgun seat and looked around. What a beautiful day, the sky a brownish haze and the smell of pee on every breeze, the breezes already hot even in the morning. Lots of tequila had gotten drunk in the Valley last night, an interesting fact I filed away. You never knew what would turn out to be important in our line of work.

Bernie pulled over and parked by a boarded-up warehouse on Rio Vista. He grabbed the Burger Heaven bag and we crossed the street and headed for the off-ramp. Traffic coming off the highway was light and there was only one dude standing on the oily dirt to the side. His back was to us but he was wearing Mama's black-and-gold Bowlerama T-shirt.

"Rocket?" Bernie called.

The dude turned toward us. An old leathery dude with watery eyes, like Rocket, but not Rocket. We walked up to him. He rattled his coffee cup at us.

"Change, mister?"

"We're looking for Rocket," Bernie said.

"Who's we?"

"Me and Chet."

"Chet's the dog?"

"Correct."

"He fixin' to bite me?"

"Why would he do that?"

Bernie was making a good point, except oddly enough and quite suddenly I had an urge to do that very thing! But I'm a pro, and pros always think to themselves, Is this a good time? I was going back and forth on that when the dude rattled the cup again.

"I'm peaceable," he said. "Got any change?"

"Maybe," Bernie said. "What's your name?"

"Jersey. Short for New Jersey, which is where I'm from."

"Nice to meet you, Jersey. I'm Bernie and you've already met Chet. We're looking for Rocket. Just tell us where to find him and we'll be out of your hair."

"Ain't got none."

"It's just an expression."

"Maybe to you. Chemo burned mine away."

A gust of wind blew down on us, one of those real hot ones from the desert. I smelled fire, far far away. Bernie spoke gently. "Rocket Saluka, Jersey. He's usually here at the ramp."

"Don't know no Rocket whatever it is."

Bernie smiled. He has lots of smiles for when he's having fun. This wasn't one of them. "Nice T-shirt," he said.

Jersey pulled at the sleeve fabric and squinted at it. "Yeah? Thanks."

"Where'd you get it?"

Jersey kept squinting, but now he turned his squint on Bernie. "You a cop?"

"No."

"You look like a cop." Jersey blinked a couple of times and stopped squinting. "I ain't done nothin' wrong. And the mayor says we can work this ramp all we like, what with the politics and all."

"We don't care about any of that," Bernie said. "It's just the T-shirt."

"You want it or somethin'? The shirt offa my back?"

Bernie gazed at him and said nothing.

"I got it fair and square."

"Who from?"

"Pirate. Swapped him some meds."

"Who's Pirate?"

"Asshole with the patch. Who else? Pirate? Patch? Come on, fella."

Bernie nodded. "Gotta up my game."

"For sure."

"So what I'm going to do is describe Rocket. Then you tell me how to find him."

"That sounds tough."

Bernie took out some money, stuffed it in the coffee cup.

"Shoot," said Jersey.

"Rocket's a skinny little guy, probably barefoot, wearing cargo shorts. He's mostly bald, except for a gray ponytail, has a scar on his nose, maybe from getting hit with a bottle or something like that, and is missing a few teeth."

Jersey shrugged. "Could be anybody."

"Take your time," Bernie said.

Jersey's face twisted into an angry shape. "I hate when people say that."

"No offense intended," Bernie began, "I only—"

"I hate that whole mentality, unnerrstan'?"

"I do," Bernie said.

"Well then," Jersey said. "Well, well, well." He gazed down into the coffee cup. "What's so important about this Rocket guy?"

"We've got some breakfast for him."

"What kinda breakfast?"

"Burgers. Want one?"

"Burgers for breakfast? Hell, no. Got any waffles?"

"No."

"I like waffles. You can fill up all those little squares with syrup. But you don't have any syrup. I can feel it."

"Sorry," Bernie said.

"Pirate could help you with the burgers."

"Yeah?"

"He's a burger freak—gets them out of this dumpster back of a restaurant. Restaurants throw out lots of food at night. Maybe that's news to you."

"What restaurant?" Bernie said.

"Huh?"

"Where Pirate raids the dumpster."

Jersey's eyebrows, one with a jagged gap in the middle, rose. "Pirate raids. Jesus. I never thought of that. Pirate raids. Almighty

God." He picked his nose for a moment or two. Human nose-picking is a huge and fascinating subject so I'm sorry there's no time to go into it now. "Is there all this meaning out there? We don't even see? Ever wonder about that?"

"Oh, yeah," Bernie said. "You and me both. Where's this restaurant?"

Jersey pointed up the ramp. "Cross the highway, brother. Sign of the bull."

"That's the name of the restaurant?" Bernie said. "Sign of the bull?"

"That's the sign, for crissake. Did I say anything about names? You always this slow? Must be a cop after all." Jersey backed away and stuffed the coffee cup with the money in it down his pants.

We took the underpass and entered a neighborhood with the same kind of warehouses and strip malls as on the other side of the highway except that the hipsters were moving in and fixing things up. Bernie has a special frown for when he sees that happening, and he was frowning it now.

"Sign of the bull?" Bernie said as we drove up and down street after street. "Or just bullshit?"

That sounded like a tough one, way too tough for me. I spotted a cat in a window, lounging beside a potted plant, actually a potted plant of a pot plant, as I could smell even though the window was closed and we were just passing by. At the same time I let that cat know what was what, and in no uncertain terms.

"Chet? Something wrong, big guy?"

Wrong? Were cats somehow wrong? Yes! Yes, that was it exactly! Why had it taken me so long to understand how simple it was? What would I do without Bernie? I didn't even want to go there.

"Hey!" Bernie laughed and got us back on the right side of the road. "What was that about?"

I didn't understand the question. And then it hit me that I'd just given his face a nice big lick, possibly leaning his way just a bit, or perhaps more. Nothing beats riding around in cars, as I'm sure you know. Maybe we could spend the rest of the day—and the rest of every day to come!—just zooming around in the—

"Bingo," said Bernie, pulling over and parking between two delivery vans. "Toro Contento."

Overhead hung a sign with a big black bull who seemed to be charging right out of the frame. An all-black bull, except . . . except for one white ear. I've had some experience with bulls, none good, but I was starting to like this bull, although I had no idea why.

Bernie grabbed the Burger Heaven bag. We got out of the car, went to the door, and peered through the glass. Inside was a restaurant, not yet open for the day, the chairs all upside down on the tabletops. From under the door drifted smells of different cleaning products, and mice. I came close to rethinking the whole cats thing, but didn't quite let myself get there.

We walked down the block, me and Bernie, side by side. Who would even dream of messing with us? A surprising number of dudes, most of them now breaking rocks in the hot sun. We turned down an alley, came to another, turned down that one and arrived at a dumpster I'd been aware of the whole time. The lid was open, the dumpster filled to the brim, and a guy wearing an eyepatch stood on top of all the trash, tossing stuff this way and that. He saw us and paused, a toilet plunger in his hand.

"What's your problem?" he said. His one eye looked angry, reminding me of certain birds I'd seen, namely buzzards.

"No problem," Bernie said.

"Gonna bust me for scavenging?" He shook the plunger at us like a weapon.

"It would have to be a citizen's arrest," Bernie said. "How are the burgers at Toro Contento?"

"I've had worse."

"Say compared to Burger Heaven?"

"Better than Burger Heaven."

"But these are fresh, Pirate," Bernie said, tossing up the bag. It fell at his feet, Pirate—if I was following things right—making no move to catch it.

"Do I know you?" he said.

Bernie shook his head. "But we have a mutual friend. His name's Rocket Saluka."

"He ain't no friend of mine," said Pirate.

"Why not?"

Pirate reached down and picked up the bag. He made a move to open it with his other hand, seemed to realize he was still holding the toilet plunger, and spun it over the side. Then he pulled a burger from the bag, took a tiny bite, chewed it slowly and thoughtfully, and nodded down to us. "Fresh is how to go," he said. He took another bite, bigger this time, and got to work on the rest of the burger, taking his time. When he was done he reached down into the trash, picked up a scrap of paper, and wiped his mouth. "You don't know Rocket if you can ask a question like that," he said. "He's one mean son of a bitch, and dangerous, too. Carries a switchblade twenty-four seven and he knows how to use it. Take it from me."

Bernie gazed up at him.

"Nope," said Pirate, tapping his eyepatch with his finger, none too gently. "He had nothin' to do with this. Cost of doing business, back in the day."

"What kind of business?" Bernie said.

"Right to remain silent," said Pirate. His one eye narrowed. "You the one in the big red car?"

"What big red car?" Bernie said.

"Late last night, down at the ramp," said Pirate. "You and another guy, even bigger. Rocket saw 'em coming and took off. What's the word for when you're even more than real surprised?"

"Shocked," Bernie said.

"Naw. That's for when you touch a wire with the juice still on."

Pirate put his hand to his chin and seemed to be thinking. After that had gone on more than long enough, in my opinion, Bernie said, "Did Rocket say anything?"

"Nope. Just vamoosed. But maybe for some other reason. Or no reason. A lot that happens is for no reason, in case you don't know."

"What make was the car?"

"Big. Red."

"Can you describe the two men in it?"

"One was big like you." Pirate squinted. "But maybe not so dark, more of a blondie. So maybe you're right."

"About what?" said Bernie.

"That you're not him. And you're for sure not the other guy. He was real real big, wore a desert kind of hat." Pirate raised his hands and made motions around his head. At that moment he noticed me for the first time. Most humans spot me from the get-go, but there is that other group. Here's a surprise: some of my best human buddies end up coming from that other group.

Pirate lowered his hands. "That your dog?"

"We're partners," said Bernie.

"Smart," Pirate said. "Dog like that'll have your back." He reached in the bag for another burger. "You know Padre Plum-tree?"

"No."

"Spanish for Father."

"Don't know him in either language."

Pirate blinked a couple of times and said, "He's got a church. Back of the church there's this tent camp. You can try that but nothin' good'll come of it. Not with the likes of Rocket. I knew him back when."

"What do you mean?" Bernie said.

"Before he vamoosed down to Mexico. He got worse down there, way worse. Shoulda never come back."

Pirate sat down on the trash heap and got to work on the burger, his back to us.

"Why did he?" Bernie said.

"Mmm mmm good," said Pirate, rocking back and forth a bit, his mouth full.

Five

We have some tough parts of town here in the Valley—South Pedroia, for example—but the Flats, between the old railroad yard and the Arroyo Vano culvert, always dry—is the toughest. The broom closet case, our very worst although we did solve it, only too late, began in the Flats, in a horrible walk-up overlooking the culvert. But now we were on the other side, driving slowly down a potholey road that backed onto the railroad yard. Apartment blocks, some wooden and some stucco, none very tall, passed by on both sides, all windows dusty, broken, or covered in plywood. The sun was strong now, the air still and dusty. We stopped in front of the only building with a tree outside, a building no bigger than any of the others, but made of brick. Bernie read the sign outside.

"Church of Saint Kateri, Doug Plumtree, Priest. All welcome."

This was a church? Then where was the bell tower? Churches have bell towers. That's how you know it's a church, from the sound and the sight of the bell tower. If we'd been working a case I might have been a bit worried, but how could we be? There was no client. I felt better and worse at the same time. We went inside.

Churches have high ceilings in my experience, but this one did not. Also it wasn't very big, with just a few rows of benches leading up to an open space where a vase of flowers stood at the base of a small wooden cross. Except for a snake somewhere under the floor there was no one around except a guy in jeans and a sweatshirt with cut-off sleeves, up on a ladder screwing in a light bulb. He turned our way, a longhaired, bearded guy maybe around Bernie's age.

"Can I help you?" he said.

"We're looking for Padre Plumtree," said Bernie.

"Look no more. And call me Doug." He finished screwing in the bulb. "Mind trying the switch?" He gestured toward the wall.

We went over and Bernie flicked the switch. The light went on. "And then there was light," Bernie said.

That must have been one of Bernie's jokes—he can be quite the jokester—because Doug laughed as he made his way down the ladder.

"What can I do for you?" he said.

"I'm Bernie Little and this is Chet," Bernie said. "I understand you've got a tent encampment behind the church. We're looking for someone who might be there."

Doug eyes lost their sparkle. His gaze went to me and back to Bernie. "Chet has a K-nine look about him. Are you with law enforcement?"

"No," Bernie said.

K-9? Why had Doug brought that up? I'd come oh so close to being K-9, flunking out the very last day. On the leaping test! Can you believe that? When leaping is my very best thing? A cat was somehow involved and there may have been some blood—so little it's hardly worth mentioning—but that was the day I met Bernie, so right there is the kind of thing that makes you think, which we had no time for now, Doug tilting his head back in a way that was unfriendly for sure.

"Do you have some way of proving that?" he said.

"Like handing over a non-badge?" Bernie said.

Doug turned his eyes on Bernie, clear blue eyes and very big, not a single sparkle in evidence. Was he starting not to like Bernie? I got ready for anything.

"My time is not my own," Doug said. "So I have a duty not

to waste it. If you're here about our ongoing situation please contact Mr. Pickersly at Pickersly and Nunez."

"Whose time is it?" Bernie said.

"Excuse me?"

"This time that isn't your own."

Doug closed his big blue eyes and took a deep breath. Once I happened to interrupt one of Leda's yoga classes, the details not important now. Doug wasn't wearing yoga pants and I'm sure there were other differences, but the expression on his face reminded me of hers on that occasion, just before . . . before a certain amount of action that must have made sense at the time.

The big blue eyes opened. "I know your type," he said.

"Oh?" said Bernie.

"The type who won the West, as they used to say," said Doug.

"What type is that?"

"Big on justice, less so on mercy."

"Have we met?" Bernie said.

If we'd met Doug, I'd have known. Once I get a whiff of you, you're in my nose forever, if that makes any sense. Doug's smell was one of the weakest human smells I'd run across, reminding me again of Leda, specifically of a kind of cracker she liked to eat when she was on one of her diets, possibly called a wafer.

Doug placed his hand on his chest. "That was out of line on my part. I apologize."

"No need," Bernie said. "I think we're in a misunderstanding of some sort. What's the ongoing situation you mentioned?"

"You really don't know?"

"Correct."

"Come with me," Doug said.

We followed him to a side door. He opened it and made an after-you gesture but I was already outside, preferring to be in the lead when it came to doorways. Was it possible that I brushed Doug aside on my way, even knocking him somewhat off-balance? Bernie says there are some things that can never be known. That had to be one of them.

We stood outside this strange unchurchlike church and gazed out over the railroad yard with rusty criss-crossing tracks, piles of broken bricks, and the remains of an old train engine lying on its side. Scattered through all that were tents in faded colors, a few porta-potties, and lots of trash, some in plastic bags and some just drifting around in the breeze. There were also a few people, some lying on the ground, a few sitting in lawn chairs. A woman passed a thick rubber tube to a man. He tied one end around his arm.

Doug gestured at this whole setup. "The bone of contention," he said.

Ah ha! I understood at once why we were here. One sniff of the air and—oh, yes, for sure. There were bones buried out here in the old rail yard, bones on bones. Digging them all up was going to mean a lot of work, but I'm a hard worker and always will be.

"In what way?" Bernie said.

"You don't follow the news?"

"Maybe not religiously."

Doug didn't like that, whatever it was. His head went back again, like he wanted to be farther away from us. "What you see is a tent sanctuary. It's the finest work the church has ever done in the Valley, but the city—and the state, for that matter—consider it a blight."

"Is it illegal?"

"Illegal?"

"Who owns this land?"

"Do we really need to get into that? Mr. Pickersly is sorting things out, and it's going to take time." Doug's voice rose. "I intend to make it take as much time as—" He cut himself off and took another one of his deep breaths, his eyelids fluttering but not quite closing. "The point is every human being needs a home. Don't tell me you dispute that?"

"My opinion doesn't matter," Bernie said.

"You can do better than that. You're clearly an intelligent man."

Doug had gotten that right. Was he making sense at last? Bones, yes. Bernie brilliant, yes. I began to feel better about whatever this was.

Bernie gave Doug a long look. Uh-oh. Not an angry look or ugly in any way, not even unfriendly—especially if you didn't know Bernie. But I do so take it from me: he wasn't liking Doug a whole lot. Would I end up grabbing Doug by the pant leg, which was how our cases ended? Whoa! So therefore this was a case? Wow! I'd done a so-therefore, straying into Bernie's territory, just as . . . just as him grabbing Doug by the pant leg would be straying into mine! All at once I wanted to make that happen, so so badly. I gave Bernie a little push in Doug's direction, tiny really, nothing the least bit obvious.

Doug backed up a step. "What's your dog's name again?"

"Chet," said Bernie. "We're more like partners."

Doug nodded. "I don't think your partner likes me," he said.

"I'm sure it's not that," said Bernie. "He likes things to move along, that's all."

Hey! Why hadn't I realized that? It was so true! You had to love Bernie, and of course I did.

Doug's eyes went to me, back to Bernie. He smiled a small smile, there and gone, but in that moment looked like a happier guy. "Who is it you're looking for?"

"Rocket Saluka," Bernie said. "Word is he's out here somewhere." He gestured at the rail yard.

Doug went still. "What do you want with him?"

"Nothing, really. We were in high school together. I ran across him yesterday and . . . well." Bernie shrugged.

"He's not in any kind of trouble?"

"Not from us. We'd like to help him, that's all."

Doug thought for a bit and seemed to relax. He nodded a quick little yes, took out his phone, and started tapping away. "This may look haphazard—which I don't mind at all." He gave Bernie a sharp glance. "Organization being a false god." After that came a pause, maybe for Bernie to say something, which he did not. Doug turned his attention back to the phone. "Nevertheless, all tents are plotted here on this grid, along with the names of their residents. And here—C-seventeen—is Mr. Saluka, although I have the first name as Martin, not Rocket."

"Rocket's probably a nickname," Bernie said. "He was fast."

"In what way?"

Bernie looked surprised. "On his feet," he said. "Running."

"Ah," said Doug. "I'll have to remember that."

"Why?"

"I make it a point to know something about all our residents, especially the newly arrived, like him."

"Newly arrived?" Bernie said.

"Mr. Saluka has only been with us for a month or so."

"Where was he before?"

"It seems he spent considerable time in Mexico." Doug's eyes got an inward look. "But I'm not sure what was fact and what was fantasy in our conversation."

"When was that?" said Bernie.

"Quite recently," Doug said. "But it was in the form of a sacramental confession."

"Meaning?"

Doug smiled a friendly smile. "Meaning I've already told you too much."

"I take it," said Doug, as we walked across the rail yard, "that the two of you weren't close, you and Mr. Saluka."

"Why do you say that?" said Bernie.

Nearby lay a man in his underwear, half in and half out of his tent. His eyes followed us as we went by but he made no other movement.

"Isn't it obvious? You didn't know his real name."

"Play any sports growing up, Doug?" Bernie said.

"No."

"Teammates can get to know each other pretty well," said Bernie. "Just through action."

"Action meaning playing games?" Doug said.

"It's a way of life for some kids," said Bernie.

Doug shot Bernie a quick look, then another, longer one. Bernie missed both of them. Doug stopped before a tent like all the others—big enough for me to stand in, although maybe not Doug and certainly not Bernie—the canvas faded by the sun, and the whole thing leaning sideways a bit.

"C-seventeen," he said. The tent flap was closed. Outside lay the remains of a small fire. I smelled chewing tobacco in the ashes. "Mr. Saluka?" Doug called. "Martin? You there? It's me, Doug."

No answer. No one was in the tent—obvious to me from the get-go, but maybe not to Doug, who said "Martin" and "Mr. Saluka" a few more times.

"I'd like to take a look inside," Bernie said.

"I don't know about that," Doug said. "Well, in fact, I do. This—" He gestured at the little lopsided tent. "—is a home. We don't enter someone's home without permission, do we?"

"The law allows it in certain circumstances," Bernie said.

"But you and I aren't the law," said Doug.

Oh? Not Doug, of course, but weren't we the law, me and Bernie? Wasn't the law all about rounding up perps, snapping on the cuffs, hustling bad dudes into orange jumpsuits in no uncertain terms? Doug seemed like a smart guy but who can know everything? I entered the tent, pushing aside the flap with my shoulder in one easy shrug. I'm at my best on the move, if you don't mind my saying so.

"Now just one sec—" Something or other, Doug began. Too late, whatever it was. I was already inside the tent. After all this fuss there wasn't a whole lot to see, in fact, nothing, the tent being completely empty.

"Where's all his stuff?" Doug put a hand to his chest. "I don't understand."

"Did he have any friends in the camp?" Bernie said. "What about visitors from outside?"

"We don't intrude on their personal lives," said Doug.

If Bernie had anything to say about that I missed it, on account of how the hardpacked dirt floor was starting to interest me, or rather interest my nose, if that makes sense. I sniffed around a bit. Have you ever noticed how often sniffing leads to digging? Skipping ahead—but not very far ahead—I'd soon dug up Rocket's switchblade knife, the one with the human skull decoration, buried not too deep at all.

All the color drained from Doug's face. He even swayed slightly, as though he might faint. "Good God," he said, placing his hand over his chest. "It's really—" Doug went silent, actually biting his lip.

"You know something about this knife?" Bernie said.

Doug shook his head real hard, almost like he was trying to shake it right off. "Weapons are absolutely forbidden. It's the one thing we won't tolerate."

"That's not what I asked," said Bernie.

Doug looked down at the little hole I'd dug and said nothing.

"What did Rocket tell you about the knife?" Bernie said.

Doug tried to meet Bernie's gaze but could not. "Anything

anyone may or may not have con—may or may not have told me under the sacrament of confession is privileged," he said. "Perhaps I hadn't made that clear."

Bernie blew the dirt off the knife. A ray of light came through the open tent flap and shone on the skull. For a moment it looked like the skull was smiling, but light can play tricks, especially in our part of the world.

"Even if the confessor is the one who ends up getting hurt?" Bernie said.

Doug looked up. "I assume you don't realize that the confessor is the priest," he said. "The person doing the confessing is the penitent."

"And it's fine if the penitent gets hurt on account of your silence?"

"There are questions we can't answer," Doug said.

"That's too easy," said Bernie.

Doug gave Bernie an angry look. Bernie pocketed the knife.

"That doesn't belong to you," Doug said.

Bernie ignored him. He turned to me and said, "Good boy."

Six

Otis DeWayne turned the switchblade knife in his hands. His eyes went to Bernie, then down to the knife again. We have experts for everything, me and Bernie. For example, Prof over at the college is our go-to guy when it comes to money, except for how to get some. Otis, a big dude with hair down to his shoulders and a beard down to his chest, is our weapons expert. He lives in Gila City, which is maybe in the Valley and maybe not—always a tough call since the Valley goes on forever in all directions—and has wide open country in the hills behind his house, just one of the many nice things about visiting Otis, another being that guns often get fired out back for testing purposes, the kind of fun that pops up in our line of work.

But right now a lot of time seemed to be passing with nothing going on. Finally Bernie said, "A tough one, huh? Anything at all you can tell us about it?"

Otis slowly looked up. He wasn't one of those ripped big dudes, but not the flabby kind either. Have you ever noticed that big dudes of his type often move kind of slow? This looking up he was doing now hit me as extra slow. Should I mention that we were out at the work bench behind his place, and that Otis wore faded overalls with no shirt? Probably not. It will only slow things down even more. But one more quick thing. Otis has a deep, rumbly voice. "You first," he said.

"Meaning what?" said Bernie.

"Meaning you tell me."

"About the knife?" Some people's voices rise a whole lot

when they're surprised, Bernie's just the slightest bit. "Well, it's one of those switchblades where the blade springs straight from the front."

Otis nodded. "OTF—out the front."

"Better than the side-flip-out kind?" said Bernie.

"Apples and oranges," Otis said. "What else?"

"I don't know, Otis. You're the expert. But I'd say it looks high quality."

"That's a start," Otis said. "High quality considering the age of the maker. Where did you get it?"

"Considering the age of the maker?" Bernie said.

"Fourteen," said Otis.

Bernie sat back. "You made it?"

"You're quick, Bernie. Do folks get that about you?"

"Well, um, uh," Bernie said.

"I'm guessing they do not, no sir. You're probably making hay off that disconnect, someone in your line of work."

The conversation had taken an odd turn. Cash was always best at the Little Detective Agency, but we'd also accepted a pair of boxing gloves once worn by Joe Frazier, or perhaps someone who'd once sparred with Smokin' Joe, plus a real oil well with a real working pump and real oil way down deep, enough to fill both of our jumbo sized gas cans before it ran dry, and there's no forgetting a private performance of—what would you call it? A sort of dance? Close enough. A private and surprise dance performance down Mexico way by a friendly young lady named Senorita Montez, after we'd sprung her boyfriend from lockup, or possibly gotten him locked up. Not important. What's important was that we'd never been paid in hay. Good or bad? Bad, I suppose, if we had a horse, which we did not. Was a horse somewhere in our future? I didn't want to think about that and lucky for me a sun-whitened bone lay in the dirt within gnawing distance. I got started on a nice session with that bone, all the more pleasant because I knew whose bone it was, the bone owner's scent all over the place out back at Otis's, although he himself was not.

"Blacksmiths and farriers," Otis was saying, "going way back. I had a great-great—not sure how many greats—granddad who forged horseshoes for the Arizona Rangers."

"I had a great-great of my own who rode with them," said Bernie.

Otis thought about that. "And now here we are."

Bernie nodded.

"Ever think," said Otis, "if you could just brush all this away and we'd be living back then?"

"I try not to," Bernie said.

"Like I said, you're smart." Otis's gaze went again to the knife. "My great-uncle Zel—I inherited this place from him— was the one who taught me. This particular blade was the first I ever forged all on my own." He held up the knife. "You're looking at my ninth-grade science project."

"You got an A?"

"Only one of my academic career. And then Mr. Kepler, the science teacher—"

"Whoa! You went to Chisholm?"

"Just the one year."

"But I went there, too!"

"I know."

"You've never mentioned this."

"Never came up," Otis said. "Long before your time and who cares about high school? Do you want to hear about the knife or not?"

"Did you play any sports?" Bernie said.

"So the answer's no? You don't want to hear?"

Bernie laughed. "Go on."

Otis cleared his throat, sounding for a second or two like a big engine getting in gear. "Mr. Kepler bought this here knife off me for twenty-five bucks, a fortune for me back then." He shook his head. "My older brother—also named Zel—and me drove down to Nogales and spent it all at a cathouse."

"I didn't know you had a brother," Bernie said.

"Long gone," said Otis. "And he did the spending. I sat outside."

That made total sense. A cathouse—actually something I'd never seen and had no desire to—would be kind of small. Otis, even as a kid, could never have squeezed inside. How nice to be following the conversation so well! Was it possible I was . . . was getting smarter? Whoa! Clear the decks!

Otis tapped the knife on his palm, both hands so big but the movement very gentle. "Haven't laid eyes on this little baby since then. You found it at a campground?"

"More like a homeless encampment."

"You're not saying that's where Mr. Kepler ended up?"

"Nope. A man named Rocket Saluka had it last. That's who we're looking for."

"Never heard of him. What's he done?"

"Just fallen on hard times," Bernie said. "Why the skull?"

"Immaturity. I was fourteen, like I said. Were you mature at fourteen, Bernie?"

"Still not there," said Bernie. "Those green eyes are amazing."

"Wyoming jade," said Otis. "Dug it up myself on a hunting trip with the old man."

Otis was the digging type? I'd always liked him and now liked him even more. I was considering jumping up onto his lap when General Beauregard, owner of the gnawing bone, appeared. The General, who lives with Otis, is one of my best buddies, or at least a buddy. He's one sizable dude and surprisingly fast, although now, as he topped the rise and came through the scrub between rolling hill country and their backyard, he was kind of lumbering along. But what was this? Dangling from the side of his enormous mouth was a rabbit. A floppy sort of rabbit with its head at an impossible angle and blank blank eyes. In short, a dead bunny. He took no notice of the bone in my mouth and came closer, showing me the bunny. I had no interest whatsoever in the General's dead bunny, until he brought it right up to me, practically within touching distance. And then I did! I had interest! Big time! I dropped the bone and . . .

Not long after that—although come to think of it, which I actually did not, the sun had moved quite a distance across the sky—the General and I returned to Otis's place from an excursion in the rolling hill country. Neither of us was in possession of the dead bunny, although we both had had possession, once even at the same time. All we ended up bringing back were a few jumping cholla needles, stuck in our tails. Otis turned out to be very good with tweezers. After that, for being such good boys, we each got a steak tip, me and the General. Mine was bigger. I tried to take my time with it so I'd still have some when the General did not. I came so close!

"Chisholm High, Chet." Bernie took a deep breath. His eyes got a faraway look. "A kind of madhouse, in retrospect."

What was that about? We were parked by a playing field that lay alongside a brick building, not tall but big and sort of heavy-looking. Madhouse sounded bad but nothing bad seemed to be going on. All I saw was a bunch of boys in football uniforms, many of these boys on the large side, standing around a red-faced bald little dude with a whistle hanging from his neck.

"It can't be," Bernie said. "Coach Raker? Shouldn't he be dead?"

All at once I was finding Bernie a bit hard to understand. I made up my mind then and there not to let him out of my sight for the rest of the day. We hopped out of the car—me actually hopping and Bernie not, although he can, as he proved beyond doubt the day a diamondback slithered out from under the driver's seat and started wrapping itself around the gear shift—and headed across the field.

"Uh, a little space there, big guy?"

I tried to give him a little space. He shot me an odd look. At that moment, the little red-faced dude blew his whistle, real loud, the harshest whistle blast I'd ever heard. Shoot him, Bernie! Oh, no, what a terrible thought. That was my ears doing the thinking, not me. And besides, we weren't even carrying, the .38 Special locked up in the office safe back home, along with the single shot .410 and some World War Two grenades that recently came into our possession following a case I hadn't understood from beginning to end.

Meanwhile the boys had taken off on a trot around the field. The little red-faced dude's eyes followed them closely, narrowed and mean.

"He used to be much bigger," Bernie said quietly. "At least twice the size."

That one zipped right by me. We walked up to this dude, little and no doubt about it.

"Coach Raker?" Bernie said.

He turned toward us real quick, and not just quick for an old guy, which is what he was. Some old guys—and lots of old gals—have ways of making parts of themselves look younger, although the red-faced dude hadn't done any of that, which wasn't where I was going with this at all. Where I was going was that nobody ever does anything to make themselves smell younger. Old folks smell old, take it from me. The red-faced dude was old.

And also not happy to see us. "Can't you follow the rules?"

he said. "No parents on the field. Said it once, said it a hunnert times."

"I'm not a parent," Bernie said. "Well, I am, but I don't have a kid on the team."

"I cut him?"

"Nope. Something to look forward to. He's six years old."

The red-faced dude—Coach Raker, if I was following things right—got redder. "Something to look forward to, smartass? What makes you—" Coach Raker paused. He blinked a couple of times, then took a long look at Bernie.

"Bernard?" he said.

No one calls Bernie that, except for his mom, a piece of work who lives in Florida with her new husband who wears a white leather belt that led to a bit of trouble on their last visit, the belt having a very special . . . what's the expression? Mouth feel? That was it. Mouth feel: a huge and fascinating subject we have no time for now. What I'm trying to get to is that Coach Raker hadn't even said it the same way she did—BER-nurd instead of Ber-NARD. Confusing, but since we weren't working a case it didn't matter. Then I remembered the switchblade knife with the human skull on the handle, now in Bernie's pocket. I felt a bit thirsty.

"Bernard Little?" said Coach Raker.

"Hi, Coach," said Bernie. "Still doing baseball in the spring?"

"Hell, yeah. This—" He gestured toward the boys, now on the far side of the field and spread out, with a few gliding along at the front and a few barely moving at the back, with most in the middle. "This is just to keep me out of the house, save my marriage."

Bernie laughed. "Still married to Mrs. Raker?"

"Course."

"I meant the same Mrs. Raker."

"Course. Fact is she mentioned you not so long ago, crime you solved about water rights or some such. Said you work with a dog. This him?"

"Chet's the name," Bernie said.

Coach Raker gazed at me. For a moment I thought he was about to give my head a friendly pat but he did not. "Ever think about human athletic accomplishments and what certain critters in the animal world can do?"

"Yes," Bernie said.

Coach Raker gave Bernie a close look, then nodded. "Pitched for West Point after me, as I recall."

"Yes, sir," Bernie said.

"Ran into some arm trouble, was it?"

"End of junior year."

"Had you marked for going pro," said Coach Raker.

"Yeah?" Bernie said. "I wasn't good enough for that."

"Physically, just barely. But mentally you had the goods, and mentally's what does it in the end, long as you can get over the physical bar. Specially for pitchers, Bernard, specially for pitchers." He tapped the side of his head.

Around then the lead runners started arriving. Coach Raker waved them on. "Round agin! Season starts in ten days. Whatcha think they're doing at Central Tech this very minute? Round agin!"

"But Coach," called one of the boys, "it's hot."

"Round agin twice!"

The boys ran on.

"Speaking of Central Tech," Bernie said, "do you remember Rocket Saluka?"

"Course."

"On account of his speed?"

"Good speed, not great. I remember on account of I remember every roster, every year."

"They're lucky to have you," Bernie said.

"Ha!" said Coach Raker. "They hate my guts."

"Not the kids?"

"Course not the kids. I'm talkin' the powers that be." His eyes tracked the running boys, now spread out almost around the whole field. "What do you want with Rocket Saluka?"

"We're trying to find him."

"What's he done?"

"Nothing. He needs some help, that's all. Do you remember a science teacher named Mr. Kepler?"

Coach Raker did one of those dry spits, a fascinating human move, in my opinion. "Some teachers think they're too good to be teachers, know what I mean?"

"Not really."

"Too smart. Cut out for better things."

"And Mr. Kepler was that type?"

"My recollection," said Coach Raker. "But he moved on. I don't remember the teachers like I do the teams, Bernard. Only reason I remember him is we had us a little altercation."

"Oh?"

"This was at a staff Christmas party. Don't even have them anymore but things were looser then. Kepler got a little over-familiar with Eleanor."

"Your wife?"

Coach Raker nodded. "I took him aside and explained what's what."

"Overfamiliar in what way?"

"The handsy way."

"And how did he take your explanation?"

"You know how some guys'll do anything to avoid a dust-up?" said Coach Raker.

Bernie nodded. "He said all the right things, just like he meant them."

"You got it. He sobered up real quick."

"Was he drunk?"

"Maybe not, but on something for sure."

"Like what?"

"Couldn't say, but I had that impression." He glanced at me, then back to Bernie. A real quick glance but I caught something surprising. Coach Raker was a fan of me and my kind. "Never played football for me, did you?"

"Nope," Bernie said.

"How come?"

"I kind of got into boxing for a few years back then, took to hanging out at the gym after school in the off season."

"Makes sense," said Coach Raker. "Baseball's more . . . well, it's like this. You can win lots of ways in baseball. In football, if you don't have a quarterback, you're dead. Had only one QB here who was really good, only other player besides you I had marked for the pros. But like you he didn't go that route, got rich instead."

"Who was that?" Bernie said.

"Luke Kincaid," said the coach. "Maybe before your time."

"He was two years ahead of me. But I thought he was already rich."

"You knew him?"

"Not really."

Coach Raker was quiet for a bit. Then he said, "See the kind of money these athletes are makin' now?"

"They earn it," Bernie said.

The coach thought about that, and nodded. "What sort of spare time have you got, say, come spring?"

"Go on," Bernie said. "I'm listening." Although the truth was he actually didn't seem to be listening. His eyes were on the kids, specifically the kid running dead last, a chubby sort of kid falling farther and farther behind across the field, although he kept plugging along, head up, his helmet maybe a little on the snug side.

"We got almost all our starters back, talkin' baseball now," Coach Raker said. "Looks like a decent season coming up. But I could use an assistant, specially one that knows his way around the mound."

"I'll do it."

"Just like that? No questions? Don't you want to know what it pays even? It pays shit."

Which was why Bernie hadn't wanted to know! What was the point of getting paid in . . . something you could produce yourself? Wow! But there you have Bernie, always way way ahead. That was my takeaway.

We headed for home, which I can always tell from the way Bernie sits in the driver's seat, like something is softening inside him. I felt pretty relaxed myself but not quite totally, on account of the sight of the skullhead switchblade, lying on the dash. Did it have to be there? I was just asking myself that question when Bernie motioned toward it with his chin.

"An object, Chet," he said, "connecting three people. Otis, who made it. Mr. Kepler, who bought it from him for twenty-five bucks. And Rocket, who ended up with it. What's the commonality? Chisholm High. And why leave out me, since I also went there and now the knife is ours? So our path is kind of obvious, isn't it?"

Paths! Now we were in my wheelhouse, whatever that is, exactly. Wheels, yes, houses, yes, putting them together, no. But let's not go there, the point being that I know many, many paths, both in the Valley and out in the desert. I waited for Bernie to say which one we'd be on, but before he could the phone buzzed and Leda's voice came over the speaker.

Every human voice sounds different, as I'm sure you're aware. Are you like me, able to identify anyone you've ever met just by the very first sound that comes out of their mouth? If so, Leda's just about the easiest one out there. Some humans have a lot of silent air in their voices. Not her. There's power in that voice and way more available if she needs it—whoa! Kind of like the beast? Why did that have to pop into my mind? Back to Leda's voice where in the very top of the surface you can sometimes hear something almost sweet. That sweetness actually makes me a bit nervous, on account of how fast it can get swept aside when she turns things up to full blast.

"Hey," Bernie said.

"Bernie?" said Leda. "Malcolm thinks you should always answer the phone 'Little Detective Agency.'"

"You called to tell me that?"

"Of course not! But I happen to agree with him. At least think about it. I'm actually calling to ask a favor."

Bernie opened his mouth. From the expression on his face I knew something amazing was coming. But then his mouth closed and he didn't say a thing.

"Bernie? You there?"

"Yup."

"I'm in a meeting, meaning this has to be quick. The point is we're going to run past the scheduled time and Malcolm's stuck at LAX and Charlie has to be picked up from camp in twenty-five minutes."

"Want me to do it?"

"Exactly. Possibly short notice, but as I explained—"

"No problem," said Bernie. "Goodbye from the Little Detective Agency."

I heard Leda draw in a breath, but before she could say anything Bernie clicked off. He looked kind of pleased with himself. I had no idea why, but if he was pleased with himself then so was I, pleased with him and pleased with me. Is there such a thing as just plain pleased? That's what I'm trying to get across.

Saddleback Mountain is more of a hill than a mountain but it's very close to the downtown towers and from the top you can look down on them. Charlie's camp isn't at the top, but just partway up where the road ends and the hiking trails begin. They've got all kinds of fun things at camp, the most fun probably being the big swimming pool, which you can't see from the parking lot, but of course that hadn't stopped me from discovering it just from the watery smell on my very first visit, which unfortunately included an incident with Ranger Tim, head of the camp if I was understanding right, who'd been posing for a *Valley* magazine photo shoot by the pool when . . . when whatever happened happened, the worst part—although Bernie had laughed and laughed—coming later when *Valley* magazine went with the photo of me knocking . . . well, no point in going into the whole thing. What to remember—and I was thinking of nothing else as we drove into the parking lot—was that I, Chet, now remained in the car at all times on each and every camp pickup.

Kids were waiting in the shade of the big eucalyptus tree by the entrance hut. How nice was the smell of the eucalyptus mixed with the smell of the kids! Had one or two of the boys had a bit of an accident in the peeing department? Who cares? Not me, amigos.

Charlie was standing next to his pal Esmé. They're about the same height, except that Esmé—the smartest kid in his class back at school, which was on some sort of a break right now, my understanding of school not the best, probably because I'd been inside it only once, very briefly—seems taller on account of how she wears her hair in a huge topknot. Esmé was talking—she's the fastest talker I've ever met—and Charlie was listening. He looked very thoughtful, the way he does when he's picking his nose, which he was actually doing while he listened. What a fabulous kid!

"Good grief," Bernie said quietly, at the same time waving Charlie over. Esmé came with him.

"Hi, Charlie, I'm picking you up today."

If Charlie heard that, he gave no sign. "Esmé wants to give Chet a little pat."

Esmé: a fabulous kid, too. And a fine patter, as it turned out, her little hand gentle but surprisingly strong. Gentle and strong is the right petting combo, by the way, in case you're interested.

"Chet's not a purebreed, is he?" Esmé said.

"What's a purebreed?" said Charlie.

"I'll explain later." She glanced at Bernie. "Well?"

"No," said Bernie.

"You could give him a DNA test."

"And then what?"

"Then you'd know the mix."

"And then what?"

Esmé's hand, still patting me, went still. She gave Bernie a long long look, her eyes very dark, very big, and somehow deep. Then she went back to patting me.

"What are you guys talking about?" Charlie said.

I was totally with him on that. A fabulous kid and a very sharp one, no doubt about that. Bernie had started in on a long explanation when Esmé suddenly pointed to the switchblade, lying on the dash.

"What's that?" she said.

Bernie turned to look. "Just, ah, nothing really."

Esmé blinked. "It's in my imagination?"

"No, no, sorry," Bernie said. "Didn't meant it that way. It's just not important, that's all."

Whoa! The flip knife wasn't important? I'd been totally go-

ing the other way on that one. It just goes to show you that . . .
that . . .

I hadn't quite come up with whatever it was when Charlie
said, "There's a skull on it."

"True," Bernie said.

"Is there a bone inside?" said Charlie.

"Why would there be a bone?"

"Skull and bones, Dad. Pirates."

Esmé nodded like that made sense. And all at once it did to
me, too. Pirate! I had a very clear image of Pirate, could see him
standing in the dumpster, waving the toilet plunger. The skull,
the knife, Pirate! From out of nowhere I now understood the
case perfectly. If it was a case. And if not—somewhat of a possibility since I didn't recall a client being on the scene—wasn't
I still ahead of the game?

"Pirates, huh?" Bernie said.

"Like, um, that kid," said Charlie, turning to Esmé.

"Kid?" said Bernie.

"Captain Kidd," Esmé said. "No one ever found his treasure."

"That a fact?" said Bernie.

"Dad! Chet can find it. He's great at finding stuff!"

Oh, what a clever boy! And a clever girl! Two clever little
people. Treasure, was it? Of course I could find it! This very
minute!

"Chet?"

Ah. What was this? I seemed to be halfway out of the car,
on my way to wherever. But . . . but this was camp, where . . .
where Chet stays in the car. I got halfway back in.

"Or," said Esmé, "we could find the map. Pirates always
made a map so they could come back and dig up the gold."

Charlie started jumping up and down. "Dad! Look in the
skull thing!"

"For what?" said Bernie.

"The map, of course," said Esmé.

Bernie smiled. "Sorry, kids. There's no map in there."

"Did you check?" Esmé said.

"Yes. Well, no, not specifically." Bernie picked the thing up. "But this is actually a knife."

"There's no blade," said Esmé.

"It's inside."

"How do you make it come out?"

Bernie smiled. "Maybe some other time."

"Dad!" Charlie pointed. "Press that little silver thing."

Charlie and Esmé, standing by the car, leaned in closer.

"Come on, Dad," Charlie said.

"Yeah, Dad," said Esmé, *Dad* sounding almost like she was having fun about something or other.

Bernie shrugged. "Don't see the harm," he said. "This is why they call it a switchblade knife."

He pressed the little silver button. With a smooth, crisp snick, the blade shot into place, right out the front, gleaming in the sunshine. But what was this? The tip of the blade was missing—a blade with no point, the front edge straight, although it looked very sharp. Bernie looked real surprised. "Whoa!" he said, and was about to say more when someone else spoke.

"What in hell is going on?"

A tall woman had suddenly appeared. She stood behind Esmé and wore her hair in a topknot like Esmé, but she was furious about something while Esmé was not.

Seven

"I . . . I was just showing this to the kids." Bernie held up the knife. "Somewhat of a curiosity—Wyoming jade, for example, which I didn't even know ex—"

Around then was when Bernie noticed the expression on the woman's face. He pressed the little silver button. The broken blade zipped back inside the handle, and he tucked the thing away in his pocket, then dusted off his hands, kind of like nothing had just happened. Fine with me. Nothing happened. I was totally on board.

"You must be Esmé's mom." Bernie got out of the car. "I'm Bernie, Charlie's dad. Nice to meet you."

Bernie held out his hand. Esmé's mom—if that was who we were dealing with—backed away, at the same time clutching Esmé by the sleeve of her T-shirt and pulling her along.

"Mom, what are you doing?" Esmé said.

"My job," said her mom. "Which is keeping you safe."

That was when Charlie spoke up. He can surprise you sometimes. "Hey, Ez—you said it was houses."

Everyone turned to him. He closed his eyes extra tight, opened them, and said, "Like for her job? Selling houses?"

A lovely look rose up in Bernie's eyes, then quickly vanished. He turned to Esmé's mom. "We're having a bit of a misunderstanding. The kids weren't in any—"

Esmé's mom cut him off with a wave of her free hand, the other hand still grasping Esmé's T-shirt. "I don't want to hear it. As far as I'm concerned, this is strike two."

"Strike two?" said Bernie. "What are you—"

Esmé's mom jabbed her finger at Bernie. "You taught your son how to punch someone in the nose. And your son taught my daughter."

"He punched Esmé?"

"I'm not saying—" Esmé's mom began, but Esmé interrupted.

"No! He only showed me. You make a fist like this and then with a real short windup you get your legs into it and kapow!" Esmé threw a punch at the air, not a bad-looking punch at all to my way of thinking, and I've seen plenty.

"That is quite enough!" said her mom. She jabbed her finger again at Bernie. "You—" jab "are exactly—" jab "what this country doesn't need." Then she tugged Esmé away, coming close to dragging her, threw open the door of an SUV, and thrust Esmé inside.

I heard Esmé call out. "But Mom! It's how to handle bullies!"

Her mom slammed the door shut, and drove off, glaring at us through the windshield. Charlie's lip began to quiver. I hopped out of the car and stood right beside him.

"Dad? Are we still friends? Me and Ez?"

Bernie put his arm around him. "For sure. We'll get this all patched up."

On the way to High Chaparral Estates, fanciest part of the Valley, where Charlie lives with Leda and Malcolm—and also Shooter, who maybe we'll get to later although I'll be fine if we don't—we stopped at an ice cream place. Charlie was about halfway done with his—face all sticky—when he looked up and said, "How?"

"Ez's mom hates Dad," Charlie said.

"Oh?" said Leda.

She'd been pulling into the driveway when we drove up to the house in High Chaparral Estates, a big house with lots of flowery gardens and a smooth green lawn like a putting green, the kind of lawn we're not fond of, me and Bernie, on account of the aquifer issues. But no time for that now. Also no time for Shooter, raising a very loud sort of ruckus behind the front door, a ruckus that I could tell involved scratching and possibly some clawing. Eye on the ball, as Bernie says. I can also do nose on the ball, but that too will have to be a subject for later. What I'm trying to do here is get to what happened when we got out of our car and Leda got out of hers, and we met on the lawn by a bush with a gecko doing pushups on one of the branches, and Leda said, "Thanks, Bernie," and then to Charlie, "How was camp?" Which brings us to Charlie and the little problem with Esmé's mom, and Leda saying "Oh?" Oh is often said by humans and can be spoken in many ways. Leda has a way of saying it that somehow reminds me of a case we had where the door to a dark basement seemed to open all by itself.

"Uh," Bernie said, "I wouldn't go so far as hates, more like—"

"How come?" said Charlie.

"—more like we had a misunderstanding."

"Oh?" said Leda again, and this time it was clear we were headed down the basement stairs. Bernie started in on a long explanation, not easy to follow even though I'd been there at the time. All I knew for sure, just from—what would you call it? A heated expression, familiar although I hadn't seen it much recently—that rose in Leda's eyes? Good enough. The look appeared when Bernie got to the part about the flip knife. We were now fully down in the basement and the door at the top of the stairs had swung shut. The next thing that had gone down on that particular case had actually been some scuffling in the darkness followed by a bit of gunplay featuring a perp with a shotgun and Bernie with the .38 Special, and a pant leg getting grabbed, which was how our cases got closed. In the end a total win, but none of that was going to help us now.

"So, um, any suggestions?" Bernie said.

Leda gave Bernie a long look, a strange unfriendly look that somehow made her nose seem longer. "Eat crow," she said, taking Charlie by the hand and leading him into the house. Somehow she got him inside, as well as her purse, her briefcase, and a bottle of wine with a bow around the neck, without letting Shooter escape. I caught a glimpse of him, leaping and darting in the background. My, how he was growing! No way he'd grow into a hundred-plus pounder like me, of course, or be like me in any way, except . . . except there was that coat of his, all black except for one white ear, a look I'm told I sport myself. A problem, and it's led to all sorts of back-and-forth about me and a long-ago night involving she-barking across the canyon from our place on Mesquite Road, and the appearance, not too long after, of Shooter, then very small although already bothersome. Right now you might be asking, how had he come to be living here with Charlie, Leda, and Malcolm? And I know the answer, but maybe not at this very moment, on account of the door to the house slamming shut and all, with that special force you get when someone with strong legs kicks a door closed. Bernie rocked back slightly, as though struck by a powerful wind.

None of that was important. All I could think about were crows. I'd never seen Bernie eat one and hoped I never would. Chickens, like crows, are birds, unless I'm way off on this, and I'd often seen Bernie eating chicken. But there's a big difference between chickens and crows, which you must know if you've ever gazed into the eyes of a crow. Something's going on in there, big time. You don't see that in chicken eyes.

"Ms. Chen," said Coach Raker, "this here is Bernard Little, pitched for me way back when. Bernard, meet the boss, Ms. Chen."

"Principal, not boss," said Ms. Chen, a small figure sitting across from us at a big desk. We sometimes deal with no-nonsense women in our line of work. They come in all ages and shapes and sizes, but you can always tell from something in their voice, not loud or sharp or nasty in any way, just a little something that says *Don't even think about it.*

"Six o' one," Coach Raker said.

One of Ms. Chen's eyelids fluttered halfway down. A tiny movement, hardly noticeable, but it immediately made me think of Mike Tyson. Funny how the mind works.

"Nice to meet you, Ms. Chen," Bernie said.

Ms. Chen nodded. "No dog has ever been in my office."

Bernie smiled. Not very often, hardly ever really and why am I even mentioning this, he has a smile—still beautiful, of course—that goes on maybe the teensiest bit too big. That was the smile he smiled now. "Well," he said, "you know what they say—always a first time for everything."

"Damn straight," said Coach Raker.

Ms. Chen turned to him. What tiny wrists she had! Although rather nice to look at. There's all kinds of beauty in life.

"Thank you for facilitating this introduction, Coach," she said.

Coach Raker shrugged. "Didn't do a whole hell of a lot."

"And now that your part is done, I won't take any more of your time."

"Got nothin' scheduled till four," said the Coach.

Back to smiles for a quick moment, the human smile being a huge subject, by the way. In the nation within we sometimes show our teeth to say back off, bud, if you know what's good for you. Not a human look, but now, for the first time, I was seeing it in Ms. Chen's smile. She wasn't showing a whole lot of teeth the way we do, but the effect was the same.

"Coach? I'll take it from here," Ms. Chen said.

Coach Raker was already rising. "Gotcha," he said, and moments later was gone, closing the door softly behind him.

"Uh, thanks for seeing us," Bernie said. "Chet's my partner. He's used to being places where his fellows don't usually go."

"His fellows?"

"Well, members of the nation within the nation is how I think of it, the bigger nation being—"

Ms. Chen held up her hand, very small but nicely shaped. "I get it," she said. "An interesting perspective. But returning to the point, I didn't say he wasn't welcome, did I?"

"No."

"Listening skills, Mr. Little," she said. "That's something we cultivate here at Chisholm High. I understand you're a graduate."

"Yes," Bernie said, "but if we had listening skills then I never heard of it."

Ms. Chen went still for an instant, a thought clicking into place inside her head. I came oh so close to hearing the actual sound! She took a pen from a pen holder and wrote something on a pad, sat back. "In the spring, Mr. Little, we have Alumni Day, where selected graduates give a talk to the student body about how their Chisholm experience contributed to their careers." She looked up. "Any interest in being our featured speaker?"

Bernie's eyebrows have a language of their own. One of the many things they're good at showing is surprise. I'd never seen them show more of it than now. I was surprised myself. Here I'd been thinking that Ms. Chen was one of those very very few people who didn't take a shine to Bernie, when in fact she was shining all over him! Life: really just the best.

"I'm not much of a public speaker," Bernie said.

Whoa! Had Bernie somehow forgotten his keynote speech at the Great Western Private Eye Association conference? What about the laughter, and not just when all those pages got loose and fluttered over the stage, but later on, when he came to the joke about the parrot and the stripper, which maybe hadn't gone over as well as the night Bernie tried it out at Greaser's, a biker bar where I hope we're still welcome—but I remembered laughter for sure. Don't forget that some people are very quiet laughers, preferring the silently shaking approach. Would Bernie be telling the parrot and stripper joke to the kids here at Chisholm High? Something to look forward to.

"Oh, I highly doubt that," said Ms. Chen, siding with me. "How about we pencil you in for now and iron out the details later?"

"Well, I—"

"You and Chet, of course." Ms. Chen wrote on the pad, then stuck the pen neatly back in the holder. "And now let's see what I can do for you," she said. "Coach Raker tells me you're looking for a former Chisholm teacher, but he didn't say who. Or why, for that matter."

"His name is Mr. Kepler, a science teacher when I was here, although I never had him."

"Harold Kepler?" said Ms. Chen. "There's no one else of that surname in our faculty records."

"Then that should be him."

Ms. Chen leaned forward. "Is he involved in criminal activity?"

"Not that we're aware of," Bernie said. "I'm hoping he can help us fill in a few blanks on something we're working on."

"A criminal matter?"

"No."

"Do I detect some doubt in your tone?"

Bernie laughed. "Are we going to end up with you sending me to detention?" He stopped laughing and his voice got strangely small. "That's what happened the last time I was in this room."

Detention? That didn't sound good. Did Ms. Chen realize that going down that road meant dealing with me? Perhaps she did, because the next thing she said was, "We don't have detention anymore."

"Everyone's well behaved now?" Bernie said.

"It's more complicated than that," said Ms. Chen. Her phone buzzed. She glanced at it. "I have to take this," she said. "Classes start in ten days and the district suddenly wants me to admit sixty new students." Meanwhile her hands were busy, flipping through some notes, writing on her pad of paper. "I'm very much looking forward to your talk. Any connection between something you learned at Chisholm and your present work would be nice, but anecdotes are the thing. The kids love anecdotes." The phone kept buzzing. Ms. Chen tore off the top sheet from the pad and handed it to Bernie. "Here's our most recent address for Mr. Kepler." She picked up the phone.

Eight

"There were never any girls in detention," Bernie said. "And no one gave it the slightest notice. Some things that were obvious aren't so obvious anymore. I've never really thought about that, big guy."

And I hoped he'd get back to that approach, and soon. Then maybe his eyes would brighten again, and he'd be back to normal Bernie. Normal Bernie was as good as it gets, so why change a thing?

Bernie checked Ms. Chen's sheet of paper and pulled over. Bernie says condos come in waves. We've had a number of condo waves in the Valley, certainly more than two. The condos we parked in front of now looked like they came from an early wave. Bernie says you can always tell the old ones because they show signs of water damage even though it hardly ever rains. I didn't know what water damage looked like but I did smell water, specifically swimming pool water when the pool guy is way overdue. We walked to the last unit of the building and Bernie knocked on the door. A brown, stiff palm leaf from somewhere above got loose and clattered down nearby. The door opened and an old man of the roly-poly type looked out. He wore clip-on sunglasses with the clip in the up position, over his forehead, always a distraction in my opinion. A forehead, by the way, somewhat clammy looking from sweat. Don't get me started on clams, with which I've only one encounter, on our trip to San Diego. We'd surfed, me and Bernie! The clam incident happened later that same day. Bottom line: don't eat the shells.

"Ah," Bernie said, "now I remember."

"Remember what?" said the old roly-poly man.

"Seeing you in the halls at Chisholm High, Mr. Kepler. I'm Bernie Little, and this is Chet."

"Bernie Little the pitcher?"

"Well, yes, back then."

"I saw you pitch many times. Home games only."

"Yeah?" Bernie said. "Where did you sit?"

"I didn't actually go to the field. I could see perfectly well from the window of the AP chem lab on the third floor—pull up a chair and grade papers at the same time."

"I didn't know that," Bernie said.

"Of course not, teachers being somewhat of a black box to the students—which is as it should be. But science teachers love baseball, in case you didn't know. All about the math, goes without saying, the geometry most of all. Did you end up getting anywhere in baseball? But let's not broil out here. C'mon inside."

We entered a little hall with a suitcase on the floor.

"Going somewhere?" Bernie said.

"Just got back from Reno."

"You're a gambler?"

"Do I look stupid? I was there for a meeting."

"So you're still teaching?"

"Good lord, no. A business meeting." He took a bandana from his back pocket and dabbed his forehead.

"I'm guessing you don't miss the classroom," Bernie said.

"Ha! Teenagers are worse than they've ever been and that's saying something. With certain exceptions, of course, the end of the tail of the curve is always where you find the most interesting data points."

"Any of those data points have a name?" Bernie said.

"A name? Not quite following you, Bernie." He backed up a step. "What do you do for a living, if you don't mind my asking?" Bernie handed him our card. This was the somewhat bothersome card with the flowers on it, designed by Suzie Sanchez, back when Suzie and Bernie were together and she was working for the *Valley Tribune*. Then she got hired by the *Washington Post*—possibly in the end less fun than the *Valley Tribune*—who sent her to London, far away, it turned out, where Bernie said he'd be a fish out of water. Neither of us wanted that, me on account of once . . . how to put this? Once being on the scene of a goldfish out of water episode? Close enough. And Bernie must have had reasons of his own. Now Suzie was back in the Valley with the *Valley Reporter*, a start-up she owned with her partner and husband, Jacques Smallian, who like Bernie had played college baseball, but at Caltech, not West Point. "Caltech has a team?" Bernie has said more than once, and Jacques always laughs. They even seem to be buddies a little bit, kind of a surprise to some of our other buddies. A long and complicated story, when all I wanted to get to was this: Why can't we have a new card, with, for example, the .38 Special instead of flowers?

Meanwhile Mr. Kepler was taking a long time with the card. His eyes were no longer moving back and forth so perhaps the reading part was over and he was just staring at it. Finally he looked up and said, "Are you here for professional purposes?"

Bernie nodded and said nothing. Remaining silent is a big part of our MO here at the Little Detective Agency and Bernie's good at it. Would it be out of line for me to mention I'm just the teensiest bit better? Probably, so forget that part.

"You can't be working for the SEC?" Mr. Kepler said.

"Why not?" said Bernie.

"Because they're not that smart," said Mr. Kepler.

Bernie glanced beyond Mr. Kepler, toward a messy little living room with the remains of a meal or two, a saggy couch, and dust in the air.

"Not smart enough to hire us?" he said.

"That's what I said. They'd send some corporate type that would put me on guard from the word go."

"On guard about what?" Bernie said.

Mr. Kepler dabbed at his forehead again, this time knocking off the clip-ons. Bernie reached down to get them, but I was there first, hardly bears mentioning. I gave them to him very nicely. He handed them to Mr. Kepler.

"Look, Bernie, what I don't want—and what I know my associates in Reno don't want—is a lot of expensive litigation that will end by establishing the total legality of our enterprise, but leave us without the wherewithal to pursue it. What's happened to this country? We used to encourage the animal spirit. Without it what have we got? Not America, I'll tell you that."

I'd been going back and forth on Mr. Kepler. He hadn't even noticed me yet, for one thing, kind of unusual although it happens. But: encourage the animal spirit? Just like that, he was aces.

"What's this enterprise?" Bernie said.

Mr. Kepler gave Bernie a long look. "Care to guess my IQ?"

"No."

"Why not?"

"The only people who ever introduce IQ into the conversation have high ones," Bernie said.

"So?" said Mr. Kepler. "One of the biggest mistakes you can make in life is failing to blow your own horn." He moved over to a stool in the corner of the hall, swept some mail off it, and sat down, breathing heavily. "Take it from me," he said.

"What's the enterprise?" Bernie said.

"There's a doggedness about you," said Mr. Kepler.

No surprise there. We're a lot alike in some ways, me and

Bernie. The only thing I didn't understand was Mr. Kepler's tone, a tone that didn't sound enthusiastic about doggedness to my ears, ears, which I'll remind you in the nicest way, are rather different from yours, partly in how they look, but mostly by what they can do. I changed my position in the hall slightly, removing any chance of Mr. Kepler making a break for it out the front door or deeper into the house. I left him the option of diving back-ward out through the plate glass window behind him. A voice in my head whispered *Go for it, Mr. Kepler,* a not very nice voice that I ignored.

And so did Mr. Kepler. Instead of even making the first tiny back-diving move, he sat up straight and said, "Okay, Mr. Pri-vate Investigator, here goes. I've decided it's not too late to do what I should have from the very beginning—get rich. How's your understanding of algorithms, especially as they're formu-lated for blockchain design?"

"Nonexistent," Bernie said.

"Then I'll give you the metaphor. Imagine a bicycle chain, with all the links moving through the front sprocket wheel, and as they do a tiny identifier—it could even be a blob of paint—is automatically applied to every link, each paint color unique. Now, imagine running the chain backward, such that each paint blob gets scrubbed away. What have you got?"

"Money laundering," Bernie said.

Mr. Kepler's eyes opened wide. "You—you are with the SEC!" he said, and toppled off the stool and onto the floor, where he lay still.

Sometime later we were in Mr. Kepler's kitchen where we had him set up comfortably at the table with a glass of water, which he sipped while Bernie loaded the dishwasher and cleaned up the mess. Behind the fridge I found something I'd never come across behind any of the many many fridges I'd known, namely a sausage, completely intact and still quite fresh, the greenish mold hard to even see, especially in such a shadowy place. I settled down to enjoy it to the max, intending to take my time, but failed to make that part happen. Mr. Kepler's eyes, kind of dim till that moment, began to clear.

"I'm surprised the SEC lets you work with a dog," he said. "They're more buttoned up than that."

Bernie closed the dishwasher, hit the button, and turned to Mr. Kepler. "His name's Chet," he said. "And forget about the SEC. I don't care about any financial shenani—any financial plans you may have. Unless they involve this." He went over to Mr. Kepler, took the flip knife from his pocket, and set it on the table.

Mr. Kepler gazed at the knife. "What the hell? Is it really—?" He slowly reached out and felt the skull with the tip of his finger.

"Pick it up," Bernie said.

Mr. Kepler picked up the knife.

"Press the button."

Mr. Kepler pressed the button. The blade sprang out. Even though he was still holding the knife, he jerked back, as though that broken blade had a mind to come and get him. He laid the knife down on the table, as far away as he could reach.

"Where did you get this?" he said.

"First," said Bernie, "is it involved in any way with you and your friends from Reno?"

"How could it be?" said Mr. Kepler. "I haven't laid eyes on this . . . this object in over twenty years."

"Was the tip of the blade broken off then?"

"No. It was intact."

"Do you remember where you last saw the knife?"

"Certainly. I locked it in the AP chem lab hazardous materials cabinet. This was in the spring. I'd brought it in to show the class."

"Kind of a show and tell for the kids?"

"That sounds a trifle judgmental."

"Not at all." Bernie smiled that real quick and real small grin of his. "Believe me," he said.

Mr. Kepler shrugged. "Inappropriate, maybe? I don't know. Things were more relaxed back then. And they weren't really kids—they were a very small group of AP seniors a few weeks from graduation. What I would have thought more interesting to you would be the fact that the next day, when I unlocked the cabinet, the knife was gone."

"And you haven't seen it since then?"

"Haven't I already made that clear?"

"You're saying it was stolen?"

"Precisely."

"How was it done?"

"With a key, I assume. There was no damage."

"How many keys were there?"

"Just the one on my key ring. Which I kept in my pocket."

"Didn't the school have one?"

Mr. Kepler shook his head. "That was my own personal lock. I took no risk when it came to hazardous materials."

"Did you report the theft?"

"No."

"Why not?"

"Although things were more relaxed—more rational, is how I'd put it—there were still rules forbidding the possession of weapons in the building. The administration at that time— maybe all administrations at all times—wasn't good at taking context into account. I simply dropped the matter." His gaze went to the knife, then back to Bernie. "Don't tell me you stole it?"

"Me?" said Bernie.

"You were there."

Bernie shook his head. "I've already told you—I was never in your class."

"But you were in school that day."

"How do you know?"

"Because there was a game. I watched from the window. A particularly memorable game, against Central Tech. You started. Started and finished. A speedy center fielder made a game-saving catch on the very last play. I could close my eyes and see it right now."

Bernie went still and just stood there. The silence went on and on. I was almost at the point of starting to worry when he spoke, his voice quiet, in a strange way almost like it was coming from some distance. "What was his name?"

"The center fielder?" Mr. Kepler wrinkled up his forehead and seemed to be doing some deep thinking. "Rocket something or other? Might have been a nickname, now that I think about it."

Bernie gave himself a little shake, just the head getting involved, a move I understood perfectly. "You never had him as a student?" he said.

"No."

"Could he have been in the chem lab with some other teacher?"

"The big chem lab, in the basement, yes, but not the third-floor chem lab. That was AP only and I took all the AP kids. The third-floor chem lab was locked whenever not in use. I had a key and so did the custodian."

"Mr. Baca?"

"I believe that was his name. Interesting that you'd remember."

Bernie walked over to the sink, turned on the water, watched it run. Mr. Kepler picked up his glass and drank. Bernie shut off the water.

"Why did you show the kids the knife?" he said.

"Not just for entertainment purposes, if that's what you're thinking. It was actually one of those teaching moments the education industrial complex is so enthusiastic about these days. A two-part teaching moment. The knife dates way back, by the way, from my earliest years at Chisholm. The first thing you notice, if you know the slightest bit about metalwork, is the quality. Not just professional, but top-of-the-line professional. The forging of the blade, the seamless intaglio of that skull, the smoothness of the action—as good as it gets. Second, the knife was submitted as a ninth-grade science project by a kid who was failing every single subject. Do you see the point I was making?"

"You tell me."

"Isn't it obvious? School smarts aren't the only smarts. There's more than one way to skin a cat."

Have you ever thought you were paying attention when you were actually quite close to dozing off? That was me at that moment, but suddenly I was awake at my very widest. There were no cats in this condo and never had been, but . . . but what did skinning one involve exactly? I couldn't think of even one single way. My ears were up, as up as they could be.

"Meaning," Bernie said, "that this IQ fixation came later in your career?"

Mr. Kepler reddened. His mouth opened like he was about to say something, probably angry but not about cats. No sound came. His mouth closed and he turned away.

Bernie's phone buzzed.

"Hello?" he said.

The phone wasn't on speaker, but I don't need it. All sounds are on speaker to me. The voice on other end was Doug Plumtree's. A priest, perhaps? Certainly something to do with a church. But his voice for sure, although now so shaky.

"Bernie? I might have made a terrible—"

Then came a squeak, like a chair getting shifted on a hard floor, followed by a hard thump.

"Hello?" Bernie said. "Doug? Hello?"

I heard what might have been a groan, followed by the sound you get when the phone on the other end is all by itself.

"Doug? Doug?"

The droning sound went dead. Bernie tapped at the phone, put it to his ear. Now all we had was silence, except for Mr. Kepler's breathing. He turned out to be one of those heavy breathers.

Nine

The church was locked, a note taped to the door.

"'Back soon—Padre Doug,'" Bernie read. "With Padre in parenthesis." He turned to me. "Parenthesis is good for playing it both ways, big guy."

I'd have to remember that, play being one of my biggest interests. There's work of course, and play and . . . and I couldn't think what else. Work and play? That was it? Wow! Life turned out to be so simple, which had kind of been my feeling from the get-go, but now I knew. Meanwhile I was picking up a faint smell of those wafers Leda eats when she's hungry but watching her weight. I've seen many humans watch their weight. They step on scales to do it, get an unhappy look on their face, and step off. But why I am even going there? The important thing was that the wafery smell belonged to Doug. I sniffed my way after it, down the stairs to an empty parking spot on the street.

Bernie followed me. "He left the church and drove off in a car?"

Exactly right. We're a team, me and Bernie. If you're a perp we'll come after you eventually. Some lucky perps actually look pretty good in orange jumpsuits. Maybe you'll be that type.

Bernie gazed up and down the street. A small car of the kind that makes hardly any sound came around a corner and drove toward us. Hey, small car, wanna meet the beast? That was my thought, perhaps not nice. My tail drooped. I promised myself to be a nicer boy in the future. My tail rose back up. Whoa! Was I just discovering a new game, a game I could play with just my mind and my tail? Wow! I was about to give this new game a whirl when Bernie said, "Maybe that wasn't fair about the parenthesis. It's more likely Padre Doug isn't comfortable in his skin."

Oh, how horrible! I'd never heard of such a thing. I tried to remember Doug's skin, kind of pale. I had a much better picture of his big unsparkling blue eyes, but if there'd been anything uncomfortable about his skin—porcupine quills, for example, and don't even get me started on porcupines—I'd missed it. The quiet little car pulled into the empty parking space and a thin, short-haired woman got out, not seeming to notice us at all. The woman was maybe Bernie's age, thin the way women who spend a lot of time at the gym are thin, wore a sleeveless red dress and no makeup. She pressed her key fob, and the little car beeped. Then she hurried up the stairs to the church, put her hand on the knob, and saw the note on the door. She paused, read it, took a phone from her jeans pocket, tapped it, stared at it, put it away.

Bernie started to raise his hand, maybe to get her attention, but changed his mind. Meanwhile she went on not noticing us—and I'm pretty noticeable, my friends—and set off on the paved path that led around the church to the encampment in the rail yard at the back, walking very quickly. We followed, not making any attempt to hide ourselves or be especially quiet. She never once turned her head, just hurried along, leaving a scent trail of nervousness in the still air.

Out back in the rail yard the thin woman stopped at one of the first tents she came to, bigger than the others and with a canopy over the doorway. Another woman—as tall as the short-haired woman but broader, with a shoulder tattoo I'm not going to describe—stood in the shade of the canopy, stirring something in a blackened pot over an outdoor cooker. Not just something, but stew. I'm a big fan of stew, have smelled many stews, but never one like this. I moved ahead of Bernie, but only the slightest bit, really not the kind of thing anyone would spot.

"Good morning, Pepita," said the thin woman.

"Hello, ma'am," Pepita said.

"Please, Pepita. It's Francesca. How many—" She stopped herself, got rid of some of the sharpness in her tone, and said, "It's Francesca."

Pepita nodded but said nothing.

"Do you know where Doug went?" Francesca said.

Pepita shook her head.

"The church is locked."

"Si."

"Did Doug say when he'd be back?"

"Not too long."

"That's what he said?" Francesca checked her watch. "It's just that we have a meeting with the board in twenty minutes. He was supposed to swing by and get me." She raised one finger. "Moreover—"

"The padre said not too long," Pepita interrupted.

"—moreover, he's not answering his phone."

Pepita stirred the pot. Francesca turned—one of those human turns of the on-the-heel type—and headed back the way she'd come. That was when she noticed us.

"Welcome," she said. "Free hot lunch will be available in half an hour." She hurried away.

I like most of the humans I'd ever met, and even though I may have had a doubt or two about Francesca, I no longer did. A fine example of the sort of human who's cool on the outside but warm on the inside. That left only one question. How long was half an hour?

We moved a little closer to Pepita's tent. She glanced at us, went back to stirring the pot, and suddenly looked at us again, perhaps at Bernie more than me.

"Bernie?" she said.

"It's been a while, Pepita," Bernie said. "Nice to see you."

"Same," she said. "I wanted to kill you for a while, but that went away."

"Good," Bernie said.

"Don't mean I want to hug you."

"Nothing like that."

"But." Pepita raised the long spoon. "Is it true you wrote a letter to the parole board?"

Bernie nodded, just a slight nod.

"I ended up doing nine months," Pepita said. "Just enough to get myself straightened out a bit but not long enough to ruin me forever. Does that make sense?"

"I hope so," Bernie said.

Pepita laughed, and looked much younger. "A cop named Stine was on the board. You know him?"

Bernie nodded that slight nod again.

"He persuaded the others."

"Lou can be very persuasive."

"Just think if I'd actually pulled the trigger on that lil old Beretta of mine."

"Um," said Bernie. "You did."

"Oh, dear," said Pepita. "Well, then thank god I was too messed up on drugs to aim right."

"Amen," said Bernie.

Pepita laughed again, came out from behind the pot, and gave Bernie a hug. Hadn't she just finished saying that was off the table? I was finding this conversation hard to follow, but I was very close to getting my mind cracking on piecing things together—which I'm sure it could have done—when I caught sight of the drip-drip-dripping from the end of Pepita's spoon. Those drips! How to put this? Each one like a little scent bomb of pure deliciousness? Close enough. The next thing I knew I was licking little scent bombs out of the air, a first for me in this life, which just shows you that sticking around is the way to go. When the last drip had fallen I got busy on whatever I'd missed, meaning if you'd seen me you might have thought I was licking the ground. Not true, my tongue being very good at skimming what was good right off the top, and I got so involved that some time passed before I realized I was being watched.

I looked up. Bernie and Pepita were now standing side by side.

"Who's this?" Pepita said.

"Chet," Bernie said. "My partner."

"Yeah? I thought you worked alone."

"I used to."

"But?"

"But this is better."

"He's licking gravy off the ground."

"He needs to keep his strength up," Bernie said. "Chet's a hard worker."

And there you have him: my Bernie.

"Working—yeah, of course," Pepita said. She tapped the side of her head. "Duh. You must be here for a reason."

"We're looking for Doug."

"Padre Doug to me," Pepita said.

"He asked me to call him just Doug," Bernie said.

"He always says that, but why? Why doesn't he use his title from the church?"

"Maybe to be more democratic," Bernie said.

Pepita waved her hand toward the rows of tents in the rail yard. "They don't want democratic. Not from him. He's practically a saint. I have a saint for a boss, Bernie! I love him." Her jaw came forward a bit. "Not like what you're thinking."

"I wasn't thinking."

"But others do. Not about me, but about . . ." She glanced at the paved path that led around the church to the street.

"We caught the tail end of your conversation with her," Bernie said.

Oh? The tail end? The only tail possessor on the premises was me, and of one thing I was totally sure: no one had caught the end of my tail. No one ever had, which probably goes without mentioning, because if anyone had even tried I'd have whirled the rest of me around and—well, I'm sure you can imagine the rest.

"Francesca has the money," Pepita was saying. "Lots and lots of money that pays for all this. But she's ruining him."

"How?"

"How do you think? It tears him up."

"What does?"

"Do I have to spell it out?" Pepita said. "The point is now that the dam finally broke inside him he . . . he's . . . I don't want to say lost, but . . ."

"The dam broke?" Bernie said.

"You know what I mean," said Pepita. "I hate her."

"Which is why you wouldn't tell her where he is?"

Pepita's voice rose, not much, but somehow sending a message that there was plenty in reserve. "I don't know where he is."

"But you know something."

Pepita gave Bernie a long look. "You're a good man, Bernie. And also dangerous."

"He tried to reach me but we got cut off," Bernie said.

Pepita thought about that. "Is he in trouble?"

"I have no real reason to think so."

"But you have a feeling?"

Bernie didn't answer.

"Oh god," said Pepita. "But I don't know where he is."

"You said that."

Pepita took a deep breath, blew it out slowly. I smelled her breath, a combination—not that unusual when it comes to human breath—of toothpaste and onions. "He asked me about slot canyons this morning."

"What about them?"

"Whether they're safe at this time of year. From flash flooding and whatever."

"What did you tell him?"

"I had no idea."

"Was he interested in any particular slot canyon?"

"He mentioned Snakehead. Is that really the name of a canyon?"

"Yes," said Bernie. "Is Doug an experienced hiker?"

"Oh, no. In his free time—which he hardly ever has—he likes to lie in his hammock and read. But I don't think he was planning on hiking himself."

"No?"

"He said he was asking for a friend."

"What friend?"

"He didn't say."

"Does the name Martin Saluka mean anything to you?" Bernie said. "You might know him as Rocket."

"Martin Saluka is one of our guests."

"When was the last time you saw him?"

"Padre Doug asked me that. I said I hadn't seen him recently. But that's common. Our guests come and go."

"Do you think Saluka is the friend Doug was asking about?" Bernie said.

"He didn't name any name," said Pepita. "But I know he's worried about him."

"What makes you say that?"

"The look in the padre's eyes. But the comings and goings are what usually happens. I'm sure you understand."

"I understand what usually happens," Bernie said. "What's Doug's ride?"

"One of those little electric cars—I don't know the name. It's white." Pepita paused and bit her lip.

"Go on," Bernie said.

"I'm sure it was nothing but when he drove away another car sort of swung out behind. Almost like . . ."

"Like it was following him?"

Pepita nodded.

"What kind of car?" Bernie said.

"Big," said Pepita. "Red."

She scratched her shoulder, as though it had suddenly gotten itchy. I knew that one, of course, but not the point, which was that this particular shoulder was the one with the tattoo I wasn't going to describe. But it was a tattoo of a cat. Forget that immediately.

Ten

Here's something strange about the beast. The faster Bernie drove the quieter it got. We zoomed across the desert on two-lane blacktop, not a cloud in the sky and no blue either, the sky color reminding me of a furnace into which a perp name of Three Shoes Shmahovlich had tossed his .45 and then turned to us with the big grin of a winner on his face and said, "How's that grab you?" Making no sense at all, since it was me who did the grabbing, namely of his pant leg, closing the case, although the grin remained on Three Shoes's face almost the whole ride to the holding cell downtown. A confusing case—and I haven't even included the fact that he was barefoot—but the only reason I bring it up was . . . was . . . because of something to do with quiet zooming! Exactly what, I couldn't tell you. My eyelids got heavy. The beast put me to sleep.

"Dreaming, big guy?" Bernie's voice came from far away. "What about?"

I opened my eyes. There was Bernie. And what had I been dreaming about? Bernie. Who's got it luckier than me? I sat up nice and tall—a total pro—and looked around. We were all by ourselves in the middle of nowhere. It didn't get any better than that. I hopped out of the car and raised my leg beside a stunted and blackened creosote bush. We seemed to be at the end of a dirt track, the car parked before two rotting gateposts with no gate hanging between them. Behind us lay a wide stretch of rolling country with a mountain in the distance, a mountain with a rounded sort of top that I thought I remembered from a case involving a ferret, a case I wish I'd forgotten. This ferret took a liking to Bernie! Can you believe that? I love law enforcement but it's not always easy.

Ahead of us, through the gate, rose two enormous rocks, one black and round, the other red and burger-shaped, the two not quite touching. At the top, resting on both and kind of joining them together, stood the strangest rock I'd ever seen, a sort of coiled rock with a wedge-shaped head.

"The entrance to Snakehead Canyon," Bernie said. He grabbed my portable water bowl and filled it to the brim. "Drink up. It's hot."

I drank up. Bernie tilted a canteen to his lips. His throat bobbed as he drank it down and his eyes turned the furnace color of the sky. We like the heat, me and Bernie. Lots of perps do not. On a real hot day, I've seen more than one give up even before the fun gets started.

Bernie stuck two big water bottles into the backpack and was slinging it over his shoulder when a hiker came walking out from the gap between the two big boulders. This hiker was a big dude, carrying a big backpack and wearing a wide-brimmed hat and sturdy thick-soled boots, the sort of boots you'd think would make some noise, but I hadn't heard a thing. The dude, squinting in the bright light, saw us and stopped dead.

"Hey," Bernie said.

The dude had sunglasses dangling on his chest. He put them on. "Hey," he said. And on that hey floated one of those invisible clouds of mouthwash, the minty kind, mouthwash being just another one of those human things that might make sense to me one day.

"How're things in there today?" said Bernie.

"The usual," the dude said.

"See anyone else inside?"

"Nope."

The dude's face, in the shadow of the wide-brimmed hat, was hard to make out, but I could see he had one of those real strong jaws, like Bernie's but more so, a real strong jaw with a thin downward curving scar on one side of the chin. He started walking, angling away from us and headed not through the gateless gate but toward the rolling hills.

"Need a ride?" Bernie called after him.

"Nope," he called back, not turning.

We watched him walking away, me because Bernie was doing it and Bernie for reasons of his own. The hiker never once looked back. When he got quite small, Bernie said, "No car, but that's not necessarily an issue. There are hikers out here who go for weeks, just basically living wild."

Living wild? What a great idea! One more thing to look forward to. But for now we headed into the narrow gap between the two big boulders, Bernie first but then me first. On the other side we climbed an easy slope—easy for Bernie, all slopes being easy for me—that led to a cliff wall stretching as far as I could see in both directions, not quite sheer but very tall. Climbable? Certainly for me and possibly for Bernie, especially if I gave him a helpful tug or two when needed. But we didn't head right up, instead walked along beside the base, maybe searching for a place to start. We came to a narrow gap in the wall, narrower than the one between the two boulders, and extending way way up.

"As though a giant knife slashed down from the sky," Bernie said in this special voice he has for talking just to himself—and me, goes without mentioning. As for what he was talking about I had no idea but it didn't sound good. Before I figured it out—or even took the very first step—he knelt beside me, patted my head.

"Slot canyons, big guy. You've never been in one. They can be a little strange sometimes but we'll be good. Hasn't rained anywhere near here in months and there's no monsoon in the forecast." He rose. "All set?"

Whatever that was I'd missed it completely, except for the all set part. We approached the gap together, side by side. How interesting! Air came flowing out, cooler air than the air out here, and on the dampish side, quite dampish, in fact. Had there been some talk about rain? I'm pretty good at knowing when rain's on the way—the feel of the air changes in ways you can't miss—well, maybe not you, no offense—and it was not. Still, we had that dampishness, and also lots of interesting smells, including those of pennies and spiders, the big hairy-legged ones, their smell hard to describe. Think of living dirt—that's the best I can do. Anything else? Yes, perhaps just a tiny tiny whiff of something wafery.

"I'll go first," Bernie said.

Oh? Well, if Bernie says it out loud like that, what can I do? He went first, the slot so narrow he had to turn sideways to do it. I myself walked in frontwise, following along nicely, just the kind of player you'd want on your team, although it couldn't be me, my team being me and Bernie, as I'm sure you know. The light shone down from high above in lovely golden beams, glowing on the red rock floor of the slot canyon, a very smooth floor—even polished in places—that felt lovely under my paws. I enjoyed the feel and the light for a few steps and then all at once I . . . I seemed to be no longer following Bernie but more . . . more truthfully, you might say, was now in front. How had that happened? Had I actually darted straight up the sheer wall, done a sort of twisting leap, and landed somewhat beyond Bernie? I could think of no other explanation.

"Chet?"

Ah. Perhaps I'd done something—well, not wrong, more

like just not totally right. But what could I do about it? Repeat the whole bolting, twisting, leaping thing, this time backward? Only one way to find out.

"It's okay, big guy. But go slow."

Go slow? Not so easy, but what Bernie says, I do. Case closed. We moved deeper into the slot canyon. Me first. Not like that sort of thing matters. I'm cool either way.

Not far ahead the slot widened enough for Bernie to face forward. Soon we came to a turn and as we went around it everything got dark. I looked up and saw the two side walls meeting high above, shutting out all the golden light, all light of any kind. That could have made a certain type somewhat uncomfortable.

"We're good," Bernie said.

And right away, like Bernie had made it happen with his voice, a beam of light appeared up ahead, shining down all golden. I continued on in a very good mood, the comfortable type for sure, so comfortable I was hardly aware of the faintest crunch crunch from somewhere above, meaning on the roof, if that's what you'd call it, of this slot canyon, called Snakehead, I believe. The thought of snakes led me to sniff for them, but I picked up not a trace, quite unusual in our snaky part of the world, and I don't just mean outdoors.

"Something up, big guy?" said Bernie, close behind me.

No, nothing, certainly nothing snaky. Bernie's not afraid of anything but he doesn't like getting surprised by snakes, prefers a little warning. That's the most important part of my job, looking out for him. And not only with my nose, but also my ears and . . . a faint crunch crunch? Had I heard that from above? I'd almost forgotten! But not quite. Don't forget I'm a pro. I stopped and listened my hardest, now heard nothing but Bernie's steady heartbeat, thump thump thump, beating in his chest but also making tiny thumping echoes in the slot canyon.

"Chet?"

We were good to go. I trotted toward the beam of golden light up ahead, tail high. This was living! Somewhere brand-new and snake-free: What more could you ask? Would this be a good time to run around in tight circles? They'd have to be really tight considering the tightness of the canyon, but you never know what you can do until you—

"Chet? Easy there."

I stopped whatever I'd started, if I'd even started it at all, and stepped into the light, Bernie right behind me. Up ahead the floor of the canyon rose and sort of twisted from side to side, the walls also twisting and folding. Piles of red sand lay here and there, the size of parking cones, plus we had boulders to work around or even climb over, and smaller rocks lying in the shadows. From high above came a sort of click click click and a small stone, not even the size of a golf ball, bounced down from wall to wall and landed at our feet.

"That was lucky," Bernie said. He knelt to examine it. "Even a stone this small could—"

I missed whatever he said next, because at that moment I happened to look up, all the way to the top of one of the walls at Snakehead Canyon, where something strange and not good was happening. Way up there, close to the edge of one wall, stood a big boulder, bigger than any we'd passed down here on the canyon floor. That closeness to the edge was bothersome, but even more so was the fact that the boulder didn't seem to be quite steady. It wobbled a bit, and the heat haze around it wobbled more. I thought of Jell-O. Funny how the mind works, going off on its own when you actually need it for something important. For example, that boulder high above, wobbling when nothing else was wobbling, except for the heat haze, a wobbling that got wobblier and turned into what you'd have to call rocking, and then came a grunt, not loud but a grunt for sure, the grunt of a man. With one last rocking motion the boulder tipped over the edge, and at that exact moment, before the whole edge gave way and the boulder hurtled down and the landslide got going, dust balls boiling up and down and sideways—in that exact moment I caught a glimpse of a booted foot withdrawing fast from the emptiness where the edge of the wall had been and back to safer ground, the boot itself the sturdy thick-soled black hiking kind.

Things were already happening fast, but they happened faster after that. I whirled around toward Bernie. He dropped the little stone he was holding, glanced up, saw what was coming down, and dove at me, real quick, the way Bernie can move when he has to, trying to get me clear. At the same time I was diving at him, doing the exact same thing only even faster. We collided, hit the deck, rolled and rolled and rolled, and then—just when I was thinking *home free!*—got swallowed up by an enormous thunderstorm with dust instead of rain.

Eleven

Bernie!

That was my first thought.

Bernie!

I myself was perfectly fine, even though the air was full of dust. I barked, kind of to chase the dust away, if that makes any sense. Uh-oh. My bark seemed to be coming from a great distance, but how could it? I was right here! I tried a few more barks with the same muffled results. And then it hit me. The problem must be with my ears. My ears were letting me down? That had never happened. I rose—I seemed to have been lying down on my side—and gave my head a good shake. Normally when you do that, as you may or may not know, you hear a windy sound of the air going back and forth in your ears, but now I did not.

That got me angry. I hardly ever get angry and don't like the feeling at all. Well, maybe a little bit. I barked again, my anger giving that bark a lot of force and power. And presto! That did the trick. With a little pop pop my ears went right back to normal—or even better—and the first thing I heard was the thump thump thump of Bernie's heartbeat. Although not quite the same as his normal thump thump thump. More like—thump . . . thump . . . thump . . .

Bernie!

I followed that weak thumping—oh, no, not weak, just different in some way that made perfect sense—through what felt to my paws not like the smooth floor of the canyon, but more like rubble. At first I didn't notice that the dust was clearing, but I happened to glance up and see the sky, now more blue than furnacey. When I looked back down I could see everything clearly, for example, half a huge boulder blocking my way, one side round, the other flat, like it had been sliced in two. I scrambled over it, and there, all twisted in the rubble, lay Bernie.

I ran to him, got my face close to his. His eyes were closed and he was all covered in dust, even his eyelashes, his eyebrows, his hair, everything white like . . . like he was all dressed up to leave me! Could I ever let that happen? Never! I got to work, licking the dust from his hair, from his eyelashes, from his eyelids. Right away my mind tried to go back to the ending of the stolen saguaro case, a horrible ending even though the perps got what they had coming to them, horrible on account of how Bernie ended up in the hospital. That was where my mind tried to go, back to that hospital and the doc saying, "You're a lucky man, Bernie, but no more blows to the head, if it's all the same to you."

Bernie had laughed his lovely laugh and I'd been so happy! All of us—the doc, the nurses, the orderly Bernie had taught how to bob, weave, and throw the left hook, a move the orderly tried on a nasty neighbor with great success—all of us had been so happy!

And now this.

I got back to licking away the dust, finding my Bernie under that white coat. And what was this? A tiny tiny breeze? Yes, a tiny tiny breeze I felt at the end of my whiskers, a tiny tiny breeze coming from Bernie's nose. I licked some more and then Bernie moaned a moan, soft and low, maybe not the nicest sound but at this moment the very nicest sound I'd ever heard. And his heart beat went from thump . . . thump . . . thump to thump thump thump and almost to THUMP THUMP THUMP, just like he was the beast! Wow! I understood everything in a brand-new way, and if that wasn't true I at least knew it could be. Now if my beast would only open his eyes.

How do you make that happen? How do you make eyes open? Perhaps by licking them, but oh so gently? Why not try it? I tried it.

Once out at a ranch, I'd come upon a bird's nest that had fallen on the ground—through no fault of my own, by the way. My only involvement had been in chasing a perp name of Two-Ton Teddy Hindenburg up a tree, an amazing performance on Teddy's part, ending with a loud crack and the fall to earth of a large branch, Teddy, and the bird's nest I just mentioned. Unlike the branch and Teddy, the nest landed softly in a big tangle of tumbleweed, and in that nest lay a nice-sized yellow egg. I was sidling over in that direction with an idea or two in mind— actually just one—when the shell of the egg cracked open and out wriggled a tiny, glistening bird.

That's what I remembered when Bernie's eyes fluttered open, dull at first but then glistening when they saw who was up close and on watch, namely me.

"Ch—" he said. "Ch—" And then he coughed a dusty cough or two. "Chet. You all right?"

Never better! My tail started up big-time, as it does in never-better moments.

With a big grunt and a little wince on his face—almost unnoticeable, that wince—Bernie heaved himself into a sitting position.

"You look okay," he said. "I'm okay, too. Pretty lucky that—" All at once, he turned his head to the side and puked.

Uh-oh. That was a first. In all our time together I'd never seen Bernie puke, so he had every right. The problem was all about what to do next. If I'd done the puking the answer would have been obvious, just scarf the lumpy little puddle back up and get on with the day. But this wasn't my lumpy little puddle. It was Bernie's. Except didn't that make it mine, at least a bit? I was going back and forth on this issue when Bernie rose to his feet, maybe not making it look easy, but he got there. Then came that wince again, no doubt about it this time. He closed his eyes, rubbed his forehead.

"Got my bell rung a bit, big guy." He turned to me and smiled, a small smile but beautiful on his face, dusty now only in the places I'd missed. "Don't tell anybody."

He could count on me for that. And for everything. I gave myself a complete end to end shake, raising my very own dust cloud.

"You're the best," Bernie said. "Sit for a second."

I sat. He leaned down, patted his hands over me.

"Good to go," he said.

That went without saying, but of course Bernie could say whatever he liked. Meanwhile he'd gone quiet and was running his gaze up the canyon wall to the ledge. Part of the ledge was gone, carved away so the wall up there wasn't quite so steep, and down below we had all this rubble, plus the remains of the huge boulder, now in two pieces.

"Kind of odd," Bernie said. "That boulder must have been there for a long time, centuries maybe, but . . ."

He went silent. I could feel his thoughts continuing in his head. I wished he'd kept talking. I'd had the feeling he'd been going somewhere interesting, but where? I had no idea.

Bernie went over to the nearest half of the big boulder, ran his hand along the smooth flat part that had once been inside. "One thing for sure, it must have been noisy. Anyone around would have—" He raised his voice and called, "Doug! Doug!" A brief silence and then little echoes of Doug Doug came back to us.

"No reason to think he came here, if he went to any of the slot canyons at all," Bernie said. He leaned against the half-boulder, rested his head against it. Did his eyes almost close? I didn't want to see that, not one little bit. I barked, perhaps more loudly than I'd intended, and certainly more sharply, as I heard in the echo. Yes, sharper than I'd intended, but somehow thrilling at the same time, just to know I could make sounds like that. It's good to be a player in this life, and we're players for sure, me and Bernie.

He gave me a close look. "What's on your mind?"

Me? Why, nothing much. Nothing at all, in fact. My mind felt very clean, if that makes sense.

"Is there something you know that I don't?" Bernie said.

Out of the question! How could that even be, since Bernie's always the smartest human in the room? Of course, I myself am not human. An interesting thought. I, Chet, not human. There are many non-humans in the mix, as you must have noticed. But did being the smartest human necessarily mean . . . My mind tapped the brakes, refused to go any farther. It went pleasantly blank, like a TV when it gets switched off. But then came a surprise, the sudden appearance of an image in all that blankness, a very clear image of a sturdy hiking boot with thick soles. I barked again, louder and even more sharply than before.

Bernie pushed himself away from the half-boulder, stood straight and tall. "Let's take a look around."

Wow. What a great idea! And there was the proof that Bernie was the smartest anything, human or non-human, in the room. All my concerns on the subject vanished at once. We looked around, found the backpack—me actually doing the finding—then headed on through Snakehead Canyon, past the fresh rubble, over older rubble, and onto a downward-sloping earthen floor, me first.

"Some places you saw as a kid seem smaller when you go back," Bernie said, "but not this."

The sound of his voice, so like a brook burbling by, and now I was starting to pick up the smell of actual water. How perfect was that? As for what Bernie was talking about, I'll leave that to you.

We rounded a corner, a twisted sort of corner with the walls twisted now, too, mostly reddish but marked with shadowy caves here and there. Two light beams from high above shone down and met on the trail right in front of me. My paws tingled.

"I came here with my dad," Bernie said.

Whoa! His dad? This was a first.

"Not long before the stroke, so I must have been seven, maybe eight," Bernie went on. "That day was the only time he ever gave me advice. Maybe there would have been others in a different scenario, maybe not." He was silent for a bit and then went on. "I used to think it was hiking advice but lately I've wondered if he had something more general in mind."

Bernie picked up a stone and flung it high in the air, with that easy flowing motion of his. The stone passed through both light beams—shining, darkening, shining, darkening—and disappeared into a cave way up on the far wall.

"My dad said, 'Always piss downwind and downhill and you won't go wrong.'"

I was stunned. Downhill and downwind. Had I ever come across more useful advice? It was more than enough to think about forever. Bernie's dad said it? When was I going to meet him? I couldn't wait.

Meanwhile the canyon floor was sloping down steeper and steeper. At the bottom lay a dark blue pool of water that extended a long way before ending at a reddish beach where the trail started again, sloping up.

"This is where we turned back that day," Bernie said. "I don't remember so much water." He turned to me. "Feel like a swim? It's the only way across."

Feel like a swim? What a question! The next thing I knew I was in the pool. How refreshing! Bernie laughed, set the backpack down, laced his sneakers together, slung them around his neck, and glided in beside me. We swam side by side, not for the first time. As long as I didn't give into the urge to steer him back to shore we'd be good. To distract myself, I stuck the tip of my tongue in the water, just for a taste.

The best water I've ever tasted came flowing right out of a rock, on a case we'd worked involving a summer camp, kidnapping, and a mule name of Rummy with whom I'd finally come to a working arrangement. This water was nowhere near as good, a bit on the stale side, and with an odd limey edge. And . . . and something else. Something more in the line of work. I took another taste, tasted that something else again. Not a whole lot, in fact only a tiny amount. But it was there. I placed a paw on Bernie's shoulder, perhaps not as lightly as I'd intended. When he came splashing back up to the surface the sneakers, which had been hanging around his neck, were perhaps no longer there. But he didn't seem to notice and when things don't get noticed it's like . . . like they didn't even happen! Wow. What a thought! And then, amazingly, came another. If they don't get noticed maybe they didn't happen at all! My mind was on fire. The feeling, actually not pleasant, went away at once.

"Chet? Not the steering back to shore thing again? I thought we'd—"

Which was when he became aware of the possible sneakers issue. He laughed. Was there something funny about it? Good to know. I hadn't realized.

"Gonna need shoes on the other side," he said. "These ponds are never very deep. How about you just stay put while I go get 'em?"

Needing shoes, was that it? A rather strange idea, where I come from. While I was sorting that out, Bernie did what is called a duck dive and disappeared beneath the surface. I'd seen ducks do it a number of times but why humans think their duck dives are anything at all like a duck's duck dives was a mystery. I myself simply swim my way down, which is what I now did.

And there was Bernie, already practically at the bottom, reaching for his sneakers. It was a bit on the dark side down here, but the water was very clear, so I had no trouble spotting the expression on Bernie's face when he saw me, an expression of surprise, by the way. What was that all about? I had no idea.

I swam closer to him, intending to help with the sneakers in some way or other, except I got distracted by a scent—well, a scent and taste combo, which is what happens in water, maybe a subject for later—that I'd been picking up already but was now picking up way more. Once Bernie read Charlie a story about some kids following bread crumbs. How well I understood that story, although Charlie didn't like it and Bernie never read it again. Not the point, which was that what I did now was a lot like following bread crumbs, although not actual bread crumbs and also not visible. And not so nice as bread crumbs.

This invisible trail led along the pond to the far side, where we had a steep wall with a rocky slab sticking out near the bottom, making an overhang. Beneath that overhang lay a sort of underwater cave. A few roundish stones, maybe the size of basketballs—an impossible ball, really, my least favorite of all the balls—rested at the mouth of this cave, mostly blocking the view, but of course doing nothing to block scents or tastes-scents, I should mention, that now included something wafery.

By now I needed air, although not so badly I couldn't do my job. Work comes first. That's basic. I got myself right down on the pond floor, peered between those basketball-sized rocks. Just then I felt Bernie right beside me, doing what I was doing, namely peering into the underwater cave.

A man lay in the cave, facing the other way. There were no bubbles. It was very quiet. An odd thought popped up in what you might call a corner of my mind I hadn't known about: How about staying here forever?

Bernie reached in, tugged gently at the man, rolled him over so he faced us. It was Padre Doug, his eyes open but unseeing, reminding me of oysters, a Thanksgiving thing at our place. Doug came drifting slowly toward us but got stopped by those basketball rocks. One of his hands poked out, like Doug was saying, Hey, buddy, a little help here. I knew Doug wasn't saying that, even knew he'd never be saying anything again, but I pawed at one of those rocks anyway. Did Bernie start to raise his hand to make the stop sign? Maybe, but he didn't actually end up making it and besides it was too late. The rock rolled off the shelf and settled onto the floor of the pond.

We went up for air, me and Bernie, taking big big breaths. He looked at me. I looked at him.

"Good job, big guy," he said. He took a deep breath, let it out slow. "I just couldn't get him to trust us. Maybe if I'd tried—"

Before Bernie could say what he might have tried, Padre Doug rose up to join us.

Twelve

"Run that by me again," said the deputy sheriff, named Squires, if I'd heard right. We knew lots of law enforcement types in the Valley and all around, but not this one. Deputy Sheriff Squires was a big beefy-armed type, with a beefy belly and a too-tight uniform. Also, seated on a rock close to the pool on the Snake-head Canyon trail, he was feeling the heat, his round face pink and shiny with sweat. Bernie leaned against the canyon wall, his clothes drying fast, the way things do in these parts. I sat at his feet, also drying fast. Padre Doug lay on his back on the trail, just before it vanished in the water.

"What part don't you get?" Bernie said.

Some humans have a little bit of anger in them at all times. You can even feel it when they pet you, always with a quick dig or two that's the opposite of petting. One thing I've noticed is that the heat can bring that anger to the surface real quick.

"You givin' me attitude, buddy-boy?" said Squires.

Bernie didn't answer.

Squires's face got pinker. "Get this straight. I'm the deputy sheriff of this damn county." He waved our license—not our driver's license but our private detective license which Bernie had handed over earlier in our little back and forth, and maybe I should have already mentioned. "And you're some PI I never heard of. So when I say run it by me again you get to runnin' it by me and pronto."

"It'll save time if you go over your understanding of what I already told you and I fill in the blanks," Bernie said.

"Son of a bitch!" said Squires. He rose, his hand on the butt of his gun. "You lookin' to get busted for obstruction of justice?"

Bernie laughed. Things, as humans say, were going sideways and fast, and they might have gone more sideways except for the sound of footsteps coming up the trail. Moments later a tan young woman rocking the baseball cap and ponytail look—one of my favorites despite the pony part, "tail" being more important—appeared, followed by a huffing and puffing man in uniform, the same kind of uniform as the deputy's, beige shirt with green pants. This was Fritzie Bortz. I'd seen him in several uniforms, including those of Border Patrol, motorcycle unit, and mall security, although never this one.

He saw us and waved. "Hey, Bernie. What the hell's going on?"

Squires's eyes opened wide, but they were narrow to begin with so all they'd really done was up their game to normal.

"Sheriff?" he said. "You know this ass—you know this guy?"

"We go way back, me and Bernie. And Chet here. Peas in a pod, you might say, the three of us."

Fritzie is one of those types who's real good at losing you. He'd already lost me completely.

Squires looked kind of shocked, and so did Bernie. "Fritzie?" he said. "You're not the sheriff up here?"

"Oh, but yeah," said Fritzie. "As of last week. The congratulations are still pouring in so you're not too late."

"Um," Bernie said, "not too late for what?"

"Why, gettin' on the congratulations bus! Come on, Bernie—didja ever think I'd be sheriff of a whole bejeesus county?"

Bernie went over and shook Fritzie's hand and looked him in the eye. "Congratulations."

"Throw your hat in the ring and anything can happen," Fritzie said. "Isn't that what this country's all about?"

Bernie nodded. He has many nods for this and that. This was the thoughtful kind, although what the actual thought was remained hidden from me. "It's a little unexpected, that's all," Bernie said. "Last time we saw you weren't you working for—"

Fritzie interrupted. "Heh heh, Bernie. No tales out of school. How about we walk and talk a bit?" He put his hand around Bernie's shoulder and led him back up the trail.

What a lot going on! First we had Deputy Squires, staring at Bernie and Fritzie, his mouth opening and closing in a fish-like way, his face bright red. Second we had this young woman moving over to Padre Doug and gazing down at him. Her face had no red in it, no color at all. I picked up her scent, a very pleasant desert scent of sagebrush and greasewood. And beyond second, up into the numbers where I don't like to go, we had Fritzie talking to Bernie in a low voice, low voices not sounding low to me, of course.

"That was a saying of LBJ's—walk and talk."

"How do you know something like that?" said Bernie.

"Rayette told me."

"Is that Rayette?" Bernie said, gesturing slightly with his chin toward the young woman.

"Nope. That's Jane or June or something, a guide I hired—on the department's dime, nice to be sheriff, Bernie—to get me here. In all my years in the state, born and bred, I've never set foot in this county, not till day one on the job. You believe that?"

"Yes," Bernie said. "Who's Rayette?"

"Wife," said Fritzie.

"You're married?"

"In front of a JP, no guests. Otherwise you'd have gotten an invite for sure."

"Thanks," said Bernie.

"But her third and my fourth. Gotta be . . . what's the word?"

"Realistic," Bernie said. "But Fritzie?"

"Yeah?"

"Don't the voters usually want someone who knows the county, sheriff being an elected position and all?"

"Wouldn't know about that," Fritzie said. "But I didn't get elected. Sheriff before me, Gussie something or other, up and died unexpectedly and I got appointed by the governor, totally legit."

"Gussie Theffles," Bernie said. "And didn't he shoot himself while under investigation for taking bribes from the casinos?"

"Rest his soul, by the way," said Fritzie. "Gussie, not the governor."

"How do you know the governor?"

"Don't exactly know him. But Rayette grew up in West Texas with Randa Lee and they're still best buds, came out here together. Two rootin' tootin' gals from Lubbock—that's what they call themselves. And Randa Lee's married to the governor, pretty much rules the state, between you and me."

Bernie gave Fritzie a long look. "You planning on running when the term is up?"

"Just might," Fritzie said. He glanced back at the body of Padre Doug. "So I could make some hay with the voters by wrapping up whatever the hell this is nice and tidy." He thought for a moment. "What's the next step, Bernie?"

"Call in the M.E."

"Smart," said Fritzie. He called to Deputy Squires. "Dep, who we got for an M.E.?"

A muscle at the side of Squires's face jumped, like something fierce in there was trying to burst out. "Doc Rivera," Squires said.

"Get 'im in," Fritzie said.

"Doc Rivera's a her," said the deputy, his lips curling up at both ends, perhaps not the best look on him, in my opinion.

Bernie and I went back down in the pool and took pictures of the underwater cave, Bernie pointing things out, me making sure of everything, and . . . and what else? Right, the diver from State Search and Recovery taking the actual pictures. When we came back up everyone was gone except for Padre Doug and a new arrival, a small woman with watchful eyes, bitten finger-nails, and a white medical kit, who was squatting by the body— Doug's clothes now in a neat pile. Bernie and the diver took out their phones and did some tapping and then the diver packed up and went away. The woman waved us over.

"Mr. Little?" she said. "I'm Florita Rivera, chief M.E. of the county."

"Nice to meet you, Doc. It's Bernie, please. And this is Chet."

Doc Rivera gave me a look. "Ah," she said. "The one with the dog."

"Well," Bernie said. "Um. Yeah."

"What went on there?" The doc pointed to the little bump on the side of Bernie's head, perhaps seeping the tiniest bit of blood.

"Nothing," said Bernie.

"A nothing that needs to be cleaned up and iced. Did it happen in the cave-in?"

Bernie nodded.

"Deputy Squires says you knew the victim?"

"Slightly. Doug Plumtree. He's the priest at Saint Kateri."

"I've heard of him, too. Something of a public figure."

"So we'll have to be on our toes."

"I'm always on my toes, Bernie."

At the moment, squatting on the canyon floor, the doc was actually on her heels. Did she really expect to get away with that kind of thing? I decided to put Doc Rivera on close watch, and shortened the distance between us.

"Do you know Deputy Squires?" she said.

"Just met," said Bernie.

"What do you think of him?"

"Don't know him well enough to say."

"Do you share his theory?"

"What theory is that?"

"The one about the victim being killed by the same event that injured you."

"Don't have enough information to form a theory," Bernie said.

Doc Rivera gazed up at him. "Are you always this cautious?" she said.

"No," said Bernie.

The doc laughed, a quiet little laugh but very pleasant. "Want some information? Come on down to my level."

Bernie squatted down on the other side of the body.

"First, there was water in his lungs, more than enough to justify a death by drowning finding. Second, there's this." She pointed to a sort of pinkish blotch on the side of Doug's neck. "And number three."

Uh-oh. I'm locked into one and two. Three comes and goes, and after that it's a crap shoot. I've only been to one crap shoot, at a casino where a dispute broke out during a shotgun manufacturing company outing. Dice were flying everywhere, reminding me of a hailstorm that had once swept over the Valley. But the point is I was about to leave my comfort zone. I tugged one of Doug's slightly damp socks out of the clothing pile for no reason I could tell you. No one seemed to notice so it had to be the right move. I've been lucky all my life.

Doc Rivera raised one of Doug's hands, white and a bit puffy. "What am I looking for?" Bernie said.

The doc pointed to the middle finger.

"The nail's broken off?" Bernie said.

"Correct."

"How long ago did it happen?"

"Can't say yet. I may be able to when I get him back to the crime lab. Where I'll also check under all his remaining fingernails."

"For DNA?"

"Let's just call it evidence."

Bernie's gaze went to the pinkish patch on Doug's neck. He took out his phone, tapped at it, turned the screen so Doc Rivera could see. "That's where we found him," he said. "The only difference is this rock down here was up on the ledge, in line with the others."

She looked at the phone for what seemed like a long time. "Everything's different underwater."

"Meaning what?" Bernie said.

"Meaning the conclusions we'd come to on land don't necessarily apply," said Doc Rivera.

"You're saying he squeezed in there all by himself?"

"I'm not saying anything right now. I'll try to have something for you tomorrow." She held out her hand. It disappeared in Bernie's when they shook.

After that, we headed up the path toward the canyon entrance. Taking the sock, yes or no? I went with yes.

"Bernie?" the doc called from behind us.

We turned. The doc gave me a somewhat puzzled look. I considered dropping the sock and then reconsidered. It had a pleasant mouth feel. The doc seemed to force her gaze away from me and onto Bernie.

"Do you know Sheriff Bortz?" she said.

"Yes."

"The next election's in eighteenth months. Any interest?"

"In what?"

"Running for sheriff, what else?"

"Anything else," said Bernie.

Outside, the tan young ponytail woman was waiting by the beast. In addition to the baseball cap, she wore shorts with lots of pockets, a T-shirt, and hiking boots. In the faces of some humans you can still see a lot of the kid they were. She was that type.

"Hey, June," Bernie said. "Or Jane—Fritzie didn't seem quite sure."

"It's Melody," said the woman.

"Ah," said Bernie.

"I'm with EcoDesertTours."

"Haven't heard of that one."

"We're pretty new, a start-up, really. It's my dream job." She waved her hand. "I love this place."

"The desert?" Bernie said.

"Yes, but especially this canyon. When I first saw it—this was on spring break my junior year—I knew I had to move out here."

"Where are you from?"

"Wichita," said Melody. "But I didn't mean to talk about myself. Aren't you the one who solved that aquifer case?"

"Chet here did most of the solving," Bernie said.

How nice of him to say so! I took a swing at remembering the aquifer case—even one tiny thing about it—and missed. But no time to feel bad because the very next moment Melody said, "Can I pet him?"

"He rarely objects," Bernie said.

Rarely was what again? Never, perhaps? Melody knelt

down—all her motions smooth and easy—and scratched between my ears, hitting the exact same spot Bernie does, even digging in her fingers the way he did, and almost as nicely. The two best petters I've come across are Tulip and Autumn, who work in the More part in back of Livia's Friendly Coffee and More establishment in Pottsdale, although Autumn might have moved on, me and Bernie possibly helping her out with one of those no-good boyfriend types you come across in our business. Not the point, which was that Bernie came right after them, and Melody was close behind.

Melody rose. More! More! More and more rose up inside me but of course I kept that to myself.

For some reason or other Melody laughed. "He's so funny!"

"Oh, yeah," said Bernie.

She turned to him. "Bernie. Uh, may I call you Bernie?"

"Sure."

Right then I smelled a change in Melody, slight, but there. No similar change came from Bernie. Always interesting to know what's going on deep inside a human or two, although it quickly gets tiring, as you may or may not know.

"I—I want to thank you for what you did in the aquifer case," Melody said.

Bernie looked a little puzzled. "Were you involved in some way?"

"Weren't we all?" said Melody.

"Uh," said Bernie. "Um." He looked down, kicked at a small rock, perhaps forgetting that his wet sneakers still hung around his neck, meaning the kick was barefooted. The small rock didn't budge.

"The sheriff says he's going to close the canyon for a foreseeable period," Melody said.

"Foreseeable period?"

"That's what he said."

They exchanged smiles, small and quick. That special scent coming off her got a bit stronger. Still no trace of it from Bernie.

"Can I ask what happened to the man who died?" Melody said.

"That's what the M.E.'s working on," said Bernie.

"The reason I ask—and maybe it sounds stupid—is this canyon is so special. Spiritually, I mean. And now, if it's turned on us somehow, that would be devastating."

"Who's us?" Bernie said.

"Well, humanity, if that doesn't sound too pretentious." She glanced at Bernie, maybe waiting for him to say something. When he did not, she went on. "I've thought about that boulder—the one that came down off the ledge up top and caused all this, according to Sheriff Bortz." She made a little sign in the air, wriggling two fingers of each hand, a sign I'd seen before and which remained a complete mystery. "'One of them natural disasters.'"

"You thought about the boulder in what way?" Bernie said.

"Fantasized, I guess. Like sort of picturing it rolling to the edge and then toppling over. And now it's happened."

Bernie gave her a quick glance, then ran his eyes along the cliff. "What's the best way up?"

"I'll take you," Melody said. "You'll need your sneaks."

Thirteen

I've done some climbing in my career, a lot of it on the steep side. The best climber I've ever seen was Miss Princess, a goat who'd escaped from a petting zoo. What a strange case, starting with finding out there was such a thing as a petting zoo! On the one hand, as humans often say—good. On the other—bad. Once, by the way—this was on a date in the maybe less than totally happy time in his life after the divorce but before Suzie came along— Bernie had said to the woman, her name now escaping me if I'd ever known it, "Imagine if we had three hands—we'd think entirely different." "Three hands?" the date had said, excusing herself to go to the bathroom soon after, and possibly not returning. But what I'm getting at is this. Best climber: Miss Princess. Second best: Melody. She reached the top of the mesa that Snakehead Canyon cut into before we were even halfway up, we meaning Bernie. I'd planned on sticking with him the whole way, but when I saw her zooming ahead I felt it was only fair to . . . well, beat her to the top. Which I did by plenty. There's a right way and a wrong way to do everything, one of the secrets of our success at the Little Detective Agency, leaving out the finances part.

"That was awesome," Melody said as she took the final step or two, not huffing and puffing in the least. "You bounded the whole way up."

What a nice, friendly human! Together we peered over the edge and watched Bernie working his way around an outcrop still quite far down the wall.

"I wonder how old he is," Melody said, her voice soft. "Does it even matter?"

I couldn't help her with any of that. She gave me a look, as though expecting help anyway. Then came a second look.

"What's that in your mouth?"

I had something in my mouth? My goodness, she was right. I dropped whatever it was. Melody picked it up.

"A sock? Where'd you get it?"

Good question. I was still searching for an answer when Bernie came scrambling up the last little rise, not quite sticking to the route Melody and I had taken, perhaps puffing a bit more than huffing and also scraped here and there on his arms and legs, but with a smile on his face.

"By the best way, Melody, I meant easiest," he said.

Melody laughed. "You should've told me." She handed the sock—or what was left of it—to Bernie. "Chet had this in his mouth. Is it some sort of clue?"

"Hmm," said Bernie. He held the remains of the sock up to the light. "He's an expert on finding clues. But some things are just about mouth feel."

Exactly! How did he know that? But that was Bernie. Just when you think he's done amazing you he amazes you again.

Up here on top of the mesa the ground was all red and rocky, the footing hard and uneven. Melody led us to the edge of the canyon and we gazed way down to the floor, saw one of those twisty parts along the trail, the sun shining on the sand piles that looked like parking cones. Interesting, but even more interesting was the top of the canyon wall on the other side. How close it seemed! Was leaping over and landing on it a possibility? I saw no reason why not. Once I was over there I could leap back right away, not slowing down whatever we were doing at all. So why not give it a—

I felt Bernie's hand on the back of my neck, not hard or

squeezing or any of that, just there. We walked on, following Melody along the top of the ledge, total pros, me and Bernie. After a while she stopped and pointed at nothing.

"It was right there."

She went slowly to the spot, circled around. There wasn't much to see, just a darker patch on the red rocky surface. We looked over the edge and saw all the mess down below—the big hole scooped out of the canyon wall, the two pieces of the huge boulder, all the rubble. Melody turned and took careful steps from the edge to the dark patch.

"I make it eight feet, maybe a little more," she said. "I suppose some tremor in the earth could have started it rolling, but . . ." Melody looked up at Bernie, an uneasy expression on her face. "Was anyone else around when you got here?"

"A guy was leaving," Bernie said. "He passed us at the entrance."

"What kind of guy?"

"An experienced hiker, I'd say. Six two or three, two thirty, in shape. Know anyone like that?"

"Lots, actually," Melody said. "Although not many that big." She toed the dark patch, which was where the boulder had lain, if I was following things right. "But this would take someone big."

"He had a scar on the side of his chin," Bernie said.

Melody shook her head. She walked around a bit. "I don't see any footprints."

"Bad surface for footprints," Bernie said.

"What about having Chet sniff around?" said Melody.

"I'm sure he already has."

And of course Bernie was right about that. I'd sniffed out minty mouthwash first thing. No surprise. Was anyone going to mention sturdy black hiking boots with thick soles? Wasn't that important? I waited to hear.

Instead, Melody started up about something else. "You're sure it wasn't a smaller man you saw?"

"Yes," said Bernie. "Who's this smaller man?"

"I don't really know," said Melody. "But last month I had a disturbing experience with a man in the canyon. He seemed a little off."

"Off how?"

"Mentally. Emotionally. He actually looked a bit like one of those poor homeless men you see downtown in the Valley, although never up here."

I felt Bernie go still inside. Inside, yes, but the stillness seemed to leak into the air all around. "Go on," he said.

High above a big black bird was gliding around, its wings outstretched. It tilted just a little, but something was going on up there because without any effort I could see that big black bird suddenly rose and rose, turning into a speck, and then nothing.

"I was guiding a family tour," Melody said. "We take them to the pool and back. That's when this man appeared, down at the pool. He seemed agitated. There were a couple of young kids in this family and I could see he scared them, so I took him aside, or tried to."

"Tried to?"

"I said something like, sir, is there a problem? And put my hand on his shoulder, just to walk him away. Big mistake. He flat out erupted, waving his arms around and shouting."

"Shouting what?"

"Most of it was swearing at me, like I was responsible."

"For what?"

Melody nodded. "That's what I didn't get at first, but it was the water in the pond. 'Where'd all the water'—I'm cleaning it up a little, Bernie—'come from?' I tried to explain about the flash floods and all, and also possible seepage from below, but he wasn't interested. He shook his finger at me and yelled something like the fix was in and I was part of it. I guess I was kind of stupid because I made an attempt to reason with him, like what fix was he talking about. 'All this water,' he said, and called me a bad name. By then he was at the top of his lungs and I said, 'Sir, you'll have to leave. You're scaring the children.' That didn't go over well. He reached into his pocket—he was wearing cargo shorts, kind of ragged—and took out what I thought was maybe some sort of tool, like an X-Acto knife." Melody bit her lip. "Although in retrospect it had an unusual decoration for a tool, a sort of death's head. He pressed a button and this blade popped out. A switchblade knife, Bernie. I'd heard of them, but never actually seen one. That was when a very strange thing happened. I heard myself saying, 'You put that thing away right now.' It sounded so . . . so commanding, not me at all. Crazily enough it worked. He paused, looked around, maybe taking in this family for the first time, and then turned and started running out of the canyon. One more crazy thing—he was fast, really fast."

Bernie gave her a look. It reminded me of how he looks at Charlie after Charlie's come up big—saying thanks, for example. He took the skullhead flip knife from his pocket. "This it?"

Melody put both hands to her face. "Oh my god."

Bernie nodded. He pressed the button and the blade shot out. "Was the tip broken off like this when you saw it?" he said.

"I don't remember," Melody said. "I think so. But what's going on? I don't understand."

"That's how beginnings work," Bernie said. He put the knife away and handed her our card. "Anything you think we should know, just call."

Melody took the card. "I promise."

"And Melody?"

"Yes?"

"Be hard to get."

* * *

We drove. The beast was in a real good mood. "This car," Bernie said. "It just makes me want to ride forever."

So why not? What a great idea! We could drive back and forth across the desert and never stop. And whoa! What if there were other deserts? Then would we need longer than forever? The phone buzzed. Good thing, since I'd already gone past where I could take it myself.

"Bernie? Harold Kepler, ex–chem teacher, here. Got something for you."

"What's that?"

"The seating plan."

"Not following you," Bernie said.

"No? You're supposed to be a smart guy."

"Who told you that?"

"I have sources," Mr. Kepler said. "In any case you'd better be, to solve a case so cobwebby. Meaning old, Bernie."

"What case?"

"God almighty," Mr. Kepler said. "The theft of the switchblade knife. Haven't you realized that the culprit had to be one of the six AP Chem students? Isn't it one of those locked room puzzles? I thought you people salivated over that kind of thing. The point is I've been hunting around and I've found the seating plan. A clue, if you take my meaning. Want me to text it to you?"

"Yes, thanks," Bernie said.

"No charge," said Mr. Kepler.

And then he was gone. Salivating was what again? Something interesting for sure, but it wouldn't quite come to me.

You can get hungry and thirsty in our line of work. We stopped off at the Dry Gulch Steakhouse and Saloon, our favorite spot in the Valley, where they know how to take care of the hungry and thirsty. The day was cooling off by then and we sat out on the shaded patio. Pablo—he's the chef—came right over with a water bowl and a paper plate of steak tips for me.

"Anything for you, Bernie?"

"Um."

"Ha ha ha! Just pulling your leg. I've got some real nice New York strips accompanied by a new béarnaise I'm experimenting with, so for you—" He cupped a hand to one side of his mouth and whispered. "—ten percent off." Pablo clapped Bernie on the back, rumpled his hair. But he didn't quite get to pulling his leg, which was where I would have stepped in.

I believe a glass of beer came for Bernie, but my attention was elsewhere.

"Are you even tasting that?" he said after a while, perhaps a short one.

What a question! Tasting like you wouldn't believe.

Bernie laid his phone on the table. "Here we go," he said. "The seating plan."

He took out a pen, began making marks on a cocktail napkin. "Kepler's desk here, locked cabinet here, student desks in between like so, only three rows, two kids in each. At the front, Michael Pilar and Jenny Chesnut—don't remember either one. In the middle—hey—Herschel Brock and Danny Feld!"

Perhaps Bernie's voice rose during that last bit, because a waitress passing by—in fact, Tamika, who always wore a cowboy hat with sparkles on it and also had sparkles in her smile—turned and said, "Bernie? Were you talking to me?"

"Uh, no."

"Sorry. It's just that I thought I heard you mention Dr. Brock."

"I knew Herschel way back. He's a doctor?"

"A great doctor. My whole family goes to him." She picked up his empty glass and made a little gesture meaning *another?*

Bernie made a little gesture back meaning *yup*. Tamika headed for the bar.

Bernie tapped the pen on the cocktail napkin. "He was a great catcher, too. I wonder if you made a Venn diagram of all doctors who'd played baseball with a sub-Venn by position . . ." He went silent, although the pen kept tap-tapping away. Sometimes that great brain of his gets to be . . . well, not too much, I'd never put it that way, but I worry.

He stopped tapping the pen, gave himself a little shake— exactly the right move—and got back to work, if whatever was going on with the cocktail napkin was work. My worries vanished at once.

"I also knew Danny Feld," he said. "Scorekeeper for varsity baseball."

Tamika returned with the beer, glanced at my plate, now empty and properly licked. "Is he still hungry?"

"Couldn't be," Bernie said. "It was heaping."

"He's a big guy, Bernie." Some humans are good at seeing what's important. Tamika was that kind. "So," she went on, reaching into her apron pocket, "I brought a T-bone for gnawing on, just in case it's okay."

Just in case a T-bone was okay? What did that even mean? The next thing I knew it was mine.

Bernie went back to the cocktail napkin. "Last row," he said. "Evie—" He looked up. "Evie Grace? Good grief. That must be Polly's sister." He sat back, looked far far away. "Did I really . . . ?" He shook his head, then looked at me. "How would you go about disowning your younger self?"

Whatever that was, I missed it completely, probably would have missed anything at that moment. This T-bone was off the charts.

"And last," Bernie said, his gaze back on the cocktail napkin. "Luke Kincaid. Varsity QB, either rich at the time, which was my impression, or he got rich later, like Coach Raker said." Bernie put down the pen. "Michael Pilar, Jenny Chesnut, Danny Feld, Herschel Brock, Evie Grace, Luke Kincaid. We're back in high school, Chet. Where do you want to start?"

I wanted to start and finish and everything in between with my T-bone.

Tamika arrived with the check. Bernie handed her the credit card. She stuck it in her little machine.

"Uh, sorry, Bernie. There seems to be a problem."

"Oh?" said Bernie. And then, "Ah. Hmm. How about cash?"

"I love old-fashioned guys," said Tamika.

Bernie took out his wallet, fished around and . . . and had just enough, some coins in his pocket putting us over the top.

We drove home in a quiet mood. A small car I'd seen before was parked out front. The driver stepped out as we pulled into the driveway. It was Francesca, Padre Doug's friend, if I'd gotten things right. She wore black jeans and a black T-shirt, and also pearls around her neck, the pearls sunset-colored at the end of day.

Fourteen

Francesca stood by her car. Her eyes were black hollows. The sky had gone dark, too, the only light somehow still coming from those fiery pearls.

"Don't hold back," she said. "I need to know everything. Do you understand me? Everything!" Her voice rose at the end, a brief high wobble quickly choked off.

"First," Bernie said, "I'm sorry for your loss."

Francesca waved that away with the back of her hand.

"Second," Bernie said, "what have you heard?"

"What have I heard? What do you imagine I heard? That my—that this wonderful human being I woke up with this morning is gone, drowning in some godforsaken wilderness. How? Why?" She took a crumpled sheet of paper from her pocket and peered at it. "Someone purporting to be a sheriff—Bortz? Can that possibly be right?—told me you were there. So explain!"

Inside the Parsonses' house next door, Iggy started in on his yip-yip-yipping. Iggy's my best pal, although we don't hang out much anymore, on account of Mr. and Mrs. Parsons being so old and sick, and them not getting their electric fence working, meaning Iggy was mostly inside. When you get to know him you find out he actually has several kinds of yip-yip-yipping, one for when he's hungry, for example, and another for when he's not hungry but wants food anyway. The particular yip-yip-yipping he was doing now was all about being upset at the sound of Francesca's voice. I felt the same way.

"Let's go inside," Bernie said.

"No!" said Francesca. Iggy got more upset. She glanced at the Parsonses' house and lowered her voice. A very positive sign. I hardly ever write off anyone completely.

"I'd rather not. I don't want to be inside. I don't want to sit."

I'd often felt the same way, although never gotten so mad about it.

"All right," Bernie said. Iggy went quiet. "Here's are the facts. Chet and I found the body on a ledge in a pool of shallow water in Snakehead Canyon. The medical examiner determined that there was water in the lungs. A cave-in happened in the canyon and may have played a role in his death. We're waiting for the M.E.'s report. As for what Doug was doing up there, I believe it had something to do with one of the residents in the encampment."

"The name," said Francesca.

"Rocket Saluka, tent C-17. Martin's his real name."

"I want to talk to him."

"Me, too," Bernie said. "He's gone missing."

"Are you looking for him?"

"Yes."

"Why?"

"That's actually pretty complicated."

"Meaning you've signed some sort of NDA?"

"No."

"Who's paying you to look for him?"

"No one."

"You have no client?"

Here's how hopeful I can get. Even though I knew we had no client I was still hoping the answer would be yes.

"No," said Bernie.

Francesca opened the door of her little car, found a purse, fished through, produced a checkbook. I know checkbooks, amigo.

She kicked the door closed, turned to Bernie. "I'm hiring

you." She flipped open the checkbook, whipped out a pen from her pocket. "What's the retainer?"

"What are you hiring us for?" Bernie said.

Oh, Bernie. Did it really matter? I moved closer to him, pressed against his leg, sending a message. He scratched between my ears. That wasn't the message. Then it was.

"To question this Saluka person," Francesca said. "To do whatever's necessary."

"Necessary for what?"

"For finding out what happened to Doug, of course. Aren't you listening?" She wrote in the checkbook, tore out the check, handed it to Bernie. "Will five thousand do?"

"Way too much," Bernie said.

Francesca gave him a look, but on account of the night and her eyes being black hollows, I couldn't tell what kind. "That's a new one," she said.

Bernie didn't answer. He held onto the check but didn't put it in his pocket. I kept my eyes on that check. We've had problems with pockets—especially chest pockets—in the past.

"I'll expect a daily report," Francesca said.

"I'll report when there's something to say," said Bernie. "What's going to happen to the encampment?"

"I'm renaming it the Douglas Plumtree Shelter for Humanity, as of tomorrow. Other than that, not one single change."

Bernie nodded. "Two questions. One, where did Doug go to high school?"

"That's a strange thing to ask. I don't know the answer. Somewhere in northern Vermont—that's where he's from."

"How about you?"

"Me? What possible relevance could that have? I went to Exeter. It's—"

"I know what it is," Bernie said.

From above came one of those silences—maybe you don't

know them—that happen just before the sound of day turns into the sound of night.

"When will you start?" Francesca said.

"We've already started," Bernie told her. "But before you go I'd like you to search your mind for anything he might have said about Rocket Saluka."

She shook her head, then got in the car.

Bernie stood by the open window. "Or maybe he mentioned some worry he had, some thoughts he was having."

"No," Francesca said. "There was nothing like that. In any case, his worries weren't shared with me, but with that God of his. He never burdened . . ." She went quiet. Bernie said nothing. I watched the check, still in his hand. "He did mention a new sermon he was working on. I remember thinking the topic was odd for a sermon."

"What was it?"

"Male jealousy," she said.

"What did say about it?"

"Nothing. Male jealousy, that's all I know."

"Do you think he wrote it up? Or at least jotted down some notes?"

"I'll look around."

The window slid up. Francesca drove off. It was one of those real quiet cars. Just before the taillights blinked off at the curve down the street, I thought I picked up, very faintly, the sound of her sobbing. Iggy started in on his yip-yip-yipping. He'd heard it, too.

"How's this for a plan?" said Bernie the next morning. "We're going to squeeze time from both ends until it spits out the answer."

That sounded messy and incomprehensible all at once. I

waited for some sort of understanding. Bernie waited for a traffic light to change. The traffic light changed first. Good enough.
My mind cleared.

"Meaning," Bernie went on some time later as the hospital appeared on my side, "we'll work backward from now and
forward from high school." I knew the hospital pretty well on
account of how that's where Bernie ended up after the stolen
saguaro case, and got uneasy whenever it was in sight. We didn't
even slow down, and the uneasiness melted away, leaving nothing but ease in my mind. As for what Bernie had just said, here's
hoping you caught it, because I did not.

There are lots of office parks near the hospital. We turned
into one of them, entered a building like all the others, and
went into an office on the first floor. Ah, a waiting room. What
you do in waiting rooms is sit and keep a lid on it, as Bernie has
mentioned more than once. This time he did not, instead shooting me a quick look that said the same thing. I shot him a quick
look back that possibly could be seen in various ways.

He went to reception. I sat by the magazine table. What interesting magazines, giving off the scents of many, many humans,
a surprising number of them perhaps not feeling their best. And
what did we have here? Doughnut crumbs? They smelled like
doughnut crumbs and looked like doughnut crumbs but in our
business you have to make sure of things. I made sure. Yes,
doughnut crumbs. Were we done in this place?

"Good morning," Bernie was saying to the woman behind
the glass. "Is Dr. Brock in?"

"Do you have an appointment?" said the woman.

"No."

"Are you a patient of his?"

"No. Please tell him that Bernie Little would like a few minutes of his time. We're happy to wait."

He came over and sat beside me. The receptionist spoke

to a woman working at a desk behind her. That woman rose and disappeared through a door at the back. Bernie glanced around at the other people in the waiting room, none of them perp-like, and was reaching for a magazine when a door on the other side of the waiting room burst open and a big guy in a white coat came striding over to us, a huge smile spreading across his face.

"The Cucumber Kid!" he said.

Excuse me? I was confused and so was Bernie, which hardly ever happens. One or the other but not both, when it comes to confusion. That's always been our MO. The big guy in the white coat saw the look on Bernie's face and said, "Oh, for god's sake! Don't tell me you didn't know that's what we called you?"

"I had no idea," Bernie said.

The big guy took in the folks watching in reception and the waiting room, all with their mouths opening. "Youngest player on varsity and cool as a cucumber, our stopper on the mound. Meet Bernie Little, best high school pitcher ever to come out of the Valley." There was a bit of clapping, soft and sort of puzzled. Bernie rose and shook hands with the big guy.

"You were our best player and it wasn't even close, Brocky," Bernie said.

"BS," said Brocky. He pulled Bernie in. They pounded each other on the back very hard. Everyone was watching, all mouths now fully open. Did they want me to squeeze in between and break it up? That was my take, but before I could make my move Bernie and Brocky parted.

"Looking good, Bernie," Brocky said. "Filled out some."

"That's one way of putting it," said Bernie. He gestured to me. "This is Chet."

"Oh, I know all about him," said Brocky, quickly on his way to being a primo dude in my estimation. "I followed that aquifer case very closely."

"Hey, doc," said an old guy in a wheelchair, "you were a ball-player? You never mentioned that."

"A long time ago," said Brocky. "Please give us a minute or two, everybody." He put his hand on Bernie's shoulder, led him to the door on the far side of the waiting room. I followed, actually squeezing through the doorway first. Brocky laughed. Why, I didn't know, but he had a very pleasant laugh, deep and soft at the same time.

We ended up in a small room that reminded me of a similar one Amy the vet has in her setup. Brocky sat on a stool. Bernie leaned on the long and narrow kind of table they have in rooms like this, a table I planned not to get on no matter what. But we didn't seem to be moving in that direction.

"Great to see you, Bernie," Brock said. "What brings you here? Last week at the supermarket a guy stopped his cart and asked if I had a quick moment to dig some wax out of his ears."

Bernie laughed, so there must have been something funny about that story. Maybe you can figure it out. "It's nothing like that." He took the flip knife from his pocket and laid it on the table. "Ever seen this before?"

Brocky picked up the knife, turned it in his hand, pressed the button. The broken-ended blade sprang out. "I had an ER fellowship for a couple of years after med school so I've seen a number of these, although not many of the out the front kind like this." Brocky pressed the button and the blade snapped back out of sight. He handed the flip knife to Bernie. "But this, with the skull decoration, is the first switchblade knife I ever saw. An example of fine workmanship, executed by some long-ago Chisholm student, and shown to the class by Mr. Kepler, the chem teacher, ostensibly for some edifying purpose but most likely to demonstrate his coolness."

There was a pause and then Bernie said, "I was hoping you'd do a little better than that."

Then came another pause, very brief, and Brocky laughed. "Had me there for a minute. You haven't changed."

"That's alarming," Bernie said. "Did you ever see the knife again?"

"Not that I recall."

"Was the point broken off when you saw it?"

"No. How did that happen?"

"Excellent question," Bernie said.

"You don't know?" said Brocky.

"Nope."

"What's this all about, Bernie? Or do I have to figure it out?"

"You probably could. I always thought you were the smartest kid in the school."

"Skipping past the issue of definition, you were wrong. Danny Feld was the smartest kid in the school. He was also in that same chem lab, by the way."

"Do you remember the others?"

"Let's see. Mike Pilar was one. He was a patient of an oncologist friend of mine, died of a rare form of liver cancer years ago. It was pretty bad. Then there was Jenny Chesnut. I think she's a chef, maybe owns a restaurant. Who else? Luke Kincaid. He must be in the family business."

"What kind of business?" Bernie said.

"I don't know, exactly. They own a lot of land south of the Valley, or did back then. As for the class, I'm remembering just one more kid—Evie Grace. Not easy to forget—prettiest girl in the school, Prom Queen, and also a top student. Didn't you date her little sister?"

"Polly," Bernie said in his normal sort of voice, although his face was maybe a bit on the pinkish side. "We went out a few times. It wasn't serious. Any idea what became of Evie?"

"I think she went to college back east somewhere. Yale? Princeton? Like that." Brocky's phone beeped. He took it from the pocket of his white coat, checked the screen. "Have to cut this short, Bernie. Meet for a drink sometime?"

"For sure. One last thing—do you remember Rocket Saluka?"

Brocky, on his way to the door, looked back. "Of course."

"Did you keep up with him at all?"

"No. Why do you ask?"

"He's been having a tough time of it and now he's disappeared. We're looking for him."

"Does it have something to do with the knife?"

Bernie nodded.

"I'm not surprised he's having a tough time. He had a tough time back then, too."

"He did?"

"His father was in prison, and didn't something bad happen to his mom? I believe he was on his own at Chisholm until he dropped out."

"I had no idea," Bernie said.

"This shouldn't be too hard," Bernie said, doing things on his phone. "Jenny Chesnut, restaurants, the Valley." He glanced over at me. "The Cucumber Kid? I never felt that way inside. But is putting up a good outward show all it takes? Maybe it changes you inside and becomes the real thing." He checked the screen. "Bingo." He stepped on the gas. We shot forward, the beast rumbling in that contented way it had.

Pretty soon after that, we were walking into a small restaurant not far from Valley College, a restaurant of what I believe is called the vegetarian kind. I'd been in a couple before, and this one smelled exactly the same. I just didn't get it.

There was no one around except a woman in an apron, standing by the bar and paging through a sheaf of papers. She didn't like what she saw, two deep up-and-down grooves appearing on her forehead, just between her eyebrows.

"We don't open till eleven," she said. "I could do you a coffee if you like."

"That'd be nice," Bernie said. "And some water for Chet, here, if you don't mind."

"It'll be a pleasure," the woman said. "He's the coolest customer we've had in ages."

Well, well, what a fine restaurant, even if there was nothing to eat. We sat at a table. The woman poured coffee from a pot behind the bar, squirted water from one of those squirters you find in bars into a bowl, and came over. She was about Bernie's age, but not happy like him, and also tired, with dark pockets under her eyes.

"Thanks," Bernie said, handing her some money. "Keep the change."

"You're actually a little short," the woman said.

Bernie laughed this quiet laugh he has for laughing at himself—not my favorite of his laughs—and gave her more money. "We're looking for Jenny Chesnut."

She backed up a step. "If you're from the collection agency this is outrageous. My lawyer said you have no right to dun me in person."

Bernie held up his hand. "We're not here for anything like that. I just want to show you something." He took out the flip knife and laid it on the table. "Have you ever seen this before?"

"What is it?" she said.

"A switchblade knife," said Bernie.

"I've never seen it."

"You're sure?"

"I've got no memory of seeing it. But you must have a reason to think otherwise or you wouldn't be here."

Bernie smiled. "So far all Mr. Kepler's kids turn out to be real smart."

"Mr. Kepler from Chisholm High?"

"Specifically the AP chem lab." Bernie pressed the silver button and the broken-ended blade snapped out.

Jenny pointed. "What happened there?"

"I'd like to know." Bernie handed her our card. "We're working a missing persons case. The knife turned up. It may be a clue. We follow up on clues."

Whoa! We follow up on clues? I hadn't realized that. But now that I did, heads up.

"Who's the missing person?" Jenny said.

"You're not letting me do this in my own way, are you?" said Bernie.

"I'm pig-headed," she said.

How could that make any sense at all? Before I took the first step in deciding if I was even going to take a swing at this one, Bernie said, "The missing person is Martin Saluka. Back in the Chisholm days he was known as Rocket."

Not too steadily, Jenny reached for one of the chairs at our table and sat down.

"You knew him?" Bernie said.

She nodded.

"Was he in the AP Chem class?"

"Oh, no."

"You say that like it was out of the question."

"He wasn't AP material, to put it harshly. Neither was I by then, but I had a feel for the subject."

"Chemistry?"

"Yes."

"It's probably not unrelated to what you do now."

She gave him a look. "That's very acute of you."

Bernie sipped his coffee. "This is very good," he said.

Jenny shrugged.

He put down his mug. "What did you mean by not being AP material by then?"

"I was running on fumes. Or make that my academic reputation. But looking back I'd already entered my wasted years, although my therapist says not to think of them like that."

"Wasted how?" Bernie said.

"In the usual, tedious way—I got into drugs. Weed at first, then this, then that. I dulled down all the sharp parts in my mind, never even applied to college, got to know some truly disgusting men. It went on for years. Then one day—I was working as a dishwasher in a restaurant in San Antonio—one of the line cooks didn't show up and I got pressed into service. That was the beginning—not of the road back, but at least a better one."

"Sounds like you got those dull parts sharpened back up again," Bernie said.

"Don't kid yourself," said Jenny.

The door opened and a man with lots of ink showing came in, carrying a bicycle wheel.

"Morning, boss," he said. "Cool pooch."

"Morning," Jenny said.

The man disappeared through a door at the back.

"Anything else?" Jenny said. "We've got a busy day ahead of us." She glanced at the sheaf of papers. "Thank god."

Bernie picked up the flip knife, put it in his pocket. "Any idea where we should be looking for Rocket?"

Jenny shook her head. "I haven't seen him since high school."

"What was your relationship with him?"

Jenny looked Bernie in the eye. "He was my dealer," she said.

"Rocket dealt weed?" Bernie said.

"And other things." Jenny rose.

"Who was his supplier?"

"His dad, or associates of his dad."

"I thought his father was in prison back then."

"That didn't stop him." Jenny's eyes got an inward look. "What's the AP chem lab got to do with all this?"

"Maybe nothing," Bernie said. "But Kepler says he showed the knife to the class, ostensibly demonstrating the quality of the workmanship."

"And non-ostensibly?" said Jenny.

Bernie smiled, that very nice smile he has for when he's starting to like someone. "Maybe to show the kids how cool he was."

"That was him," Jenny said. "So you're trying to find out if he was telling the truth?"

"Yes," Bernie said.

"Meaning you're going to check out all the kids from the class?"

"That's right."

"Have you tried Luke Kincaid?"

"No," Bernie said. "Why him specifically?"

"Just that he's my landlord. Not him, personally, but a company of his. They own the whole block. He'll be easy to find." She looked down at her hands, strong hands, bearing a scar or two, and ringless. "I've actually been working up the nerve to call him myself."

"Why?"

"It's embarrassing."

"Go on."

"They're doubling the rent. That'll put me out of business. I thought, pathetically, of calling upon this long-ago and almost nonexistent connection to . . ." Her voice trailed away.

Bernie patted the back of her hand. "It's a good thought," he said.

Jenny looked up. Their eyes met. "I don't want to leave you with the wrong impression."

"About what?"

"Rocket. What I said about him not being AP material maybe sounded mean. He wasn't dumb, not at all—just not interested in academics. And he was the sweetest guy."

"He was?"

"Oh, yes. All the girls liked him. It didn't hurt that he was so good looking."

"He was?" Bernie said again.

Fifteen

"Bernie Little? Florita Rivera here. The autopsy is complete, with an inconclusive finding. Father Plumtree died of drowning but I couldn't determine whether the drowning was accidental."

"But Doc," Bernie said, "what about those marks around his neck?"

"Not around his neck, but near it, closer to the collarbone. I could not determine the cause."

"Did you run the fingernail check you mentioned?"

"Yes. No foreign DNA was found, but the body had been underwater for at least two hours before its discovery, which may or may not be a contributing factor to the non-finding."

Bernie thought about that. Up ahead traffic was coming to one of those sudden stops. His gaze was faraway but somehow his feet knew what to do, handling things on their own, nice and smooth.

"Two hours?" Bernie said. "Does that mean the drowning and the cave-in were unrelated?"

"I wondered about that," said the doc, "even though it's not in my remit, strictly speaking."

There was a pause. I could feel them both thinking, Bernie right here and Doc Rivera wherever she was.

"Good luck," she said.

Traffic started up. Bernie's feet got to work. His mind was already working. I could feel it. Unlike the beast, for example, it made no sound but . . . but was Bernie's mind like the beast in some way? What a thought!

✿   ✿   ✿

At the hot time of year the sky often turns brassy, the same color as the downtown towers. We sat parked in front of one of those brassy towers under a brassy sky, Bernie's eyes taking in the tower, and me taking in Bernie. His eyes, too, seemed on the brassy side, a somewhat troubling sight.

"Kincaid Tower," he said. "One of those building names you hear, but I never made the connection."

We went inside, came to one of those security setups they have in the downtown towers.

"Here to see Luke Kincaid," Bernie said.

There were two security dudes, both with unfriendly faces and those tiny white sticks in their ears, never a good look in my opinion.

"That would be Mr. Kincaid?" one said.

"Correct."

"Got an appointment?" said other.

"No," Bernie said. He handed our card to the dude with the slightly less unfriendly face, although it was hard to tell. The dude stuck it into a machine, pressed a button. Time passed. The white sticks in one of the dudes' ears were playing music, although you yourself might not have known that. The other dude's ear sticks were silent, so cheer up, you'd have gotten that right. After a while a woman broke that silence.

"Send him up."

The first dude gave back our card. The second one said, "Last elevator on the left."

We deal with a lot of problems in this business, elevators being the worst.

"You've done it before, big guy. It'll be over in a flash. You can do it."

And more of that kind of thing from Bernie. Meanwhile I stood just outside the open elevator door doing the back and forth at the same time move I have for this situation. My move for the inside of elevators is shaking and sometimes puking.

"Come on, Chet. Otherwise you'll have to wait in the car."

We rode the elevator to the top of Kincaid Tower, Bernie's hand resting on the back of my neck. I shook a bit but did not puke. We're tough customers at the Little Detective Agency, just one of the reasons for our success, leaving out the finances part.

"Right this way," said a woman in a black suit and red leather high-heel shoes, maybe the best shoe leather I've ever smelled. She had a small red leather purse on her hip, held by a gold chain over her shoulder. I was just realizing she had a gun in that purse, although not recently fired, when we came to a door that appeared to be made of beaten gold.

"Visitors," said the woman, not raising her voice.

"Send 'em in," said a man, also in an unraised voice although it seemed to come not through the door but from somewhere above. The woman tapped the face of her watch and the door opened. We went in, just me and Bernie. The door closed behind us.

Was this an office room? If so it was the biggest I'd ever seen, with a high ceiling that looked like a blue sky with some puffy white clouds, floor-to-ceiling windows with that same sky outside—hey! Were we above all the brassiness?—and a cool polished stone floor that my paws loved. At the far end of the room stood a large but worn and battered-looking wooden desk. A man behind that desk was just hanging up a phone.

He rose. A man of about Bernie's age and size, although possibly slightly taller and broader, but very very slightly, if at all. He wore a silk shirt and a silk tie—the smell of silk impossible to

miss, reminding me oddly of certain insects I'd come across—
the top shirt button undone and the sleeves rolled up. Whoa!
Bigger wrists than Bernie's? I refused to believe it.

He came forward, a strong man with a strong walk, on the
fair side with some freckles and sandy hair, thinning on top.
Some humans, Rocket, for example, have eyes that try to hide
from you. This man's were the opposite, out there and confident.

"Bernie!" he said. "Lookin' good." Then after a bit of a pause:
"Alive and well."

"You, too." They shook hands, maybe the most powerful
handshaking I'd ever seen. "It's been a while."

What a brilliant thing to say! You can always count on Bernie
at times like this.

"Sure has," said Luke. "I've been trying to think of the last
time I saw you."

"Probably somewhere in the halls of Chisholm, your senior
year."

Luke shook his head. "Nope. Pretty sure it was at the ball
field. I was in the stands and you were on the mound. I was jealous of that live right arm of yours."

"Huh?" said Bernie. "Weren't you all-state QB two years in
a row?"

"That was all about the strength of the program," Luke said.
"And we hardly ever threw the damn ball. Raker loved to run
the wishbone, like he was living in 1952."

"Didn't you play in college?"

"Couple years," Luke said. "I got bored with all the yakety-
yak and came home to get started in all this." He made a motion
taking in the room, the floor-to-ceiling windows, the blue sky
with the puffy clouds.

"Was this building, um, tower here when we were at
Chisholm?" Bernie said.

"Oh, no. We were operating out of a dump in South Pedroia

back then. This is practically brand-new. We broke ground three years ago come September."

"I never really got a handle on what you do," Bernie said.

Luke laughed. "There's what we did and what we do, big difference. But before we get into that—" He turned to me. "—this must be the famous Chet."

My tail started wagging. I didn't stop it, stopping it not so easy even if I didn't want it to wag, which for some strange reason I wasn't sure about at the moment.

"Truth is I'd lost track of you completely until that case made the news, the one about vineyards and the aquifer. I'd actually been toying with a vineyard idea or two, but I backed off after that. But c'mere and let me explain."

He got a hand on Bernie's shoulder, turned him toward one of the glass walls, at the same time doing something with his phone. A section of the wall became a screen and on that screen we seemed to be flying over rough, empty country. Interesting, but usually when folks say the famous Chet they want to pet the famous Chet the very next thing, and that didn't seem to be happening. No biggie, of course. One other small thing: there were no treats in that old wooden desk. Also no biggie. But was it possible two no-biggies made—? That was as far as I could take it on my own.

"I'm the luckiest guy in the Valley, Bernie," Luke said. "What you're looking at is our spread, sixty thousand acres southeast of the Valley that's been in the family for decades. For years and years, we tried all kinds of shit—cotton, beets, sheep, for god's sake, copper, tourism, you name it, but revenue was iffy and we were mortgaged up to here."

"Was this while you were at Chisholm?" Bernie said.

"Before, during, and after. Then, about ten years ago—this was after my dad retired—I got this hunch. What do you know about rare earths?"

"Nothing."

Luke held up his phone and shook it. "No rare earths, no this."

"Maybe we'd be better off."

Luke smiled. He had big teeth, very white and even. "I know you're joking, Bernie. You're way too smart to be a Luddite."

That had to be right, whatever Luddites were, Bernie always being the smartest person in the room. As for whether he was joking he hadn't sounded especially jokey but Bernie's quite the jokester so you never knew.

Meanwhile Luke had gone to his desk and taken a sort of silvery cube from a drawer. He tossed it to Bernie, not a soft underhand toss but hard and over the top. Bernie caught it the way he catches things, his hand folding softly around it, the thrown object always silently disappearing.

Bernie opened his hand. The silvery cube sat there, not shiny, not particularly hard looking.

"Erbium," Luke said. "One of seventeen known rare earths, more properly called rare metals, and never found as free elements, although they're not that rare. Finding deposits worth working is what's rare. I'd done a little reading, was pretty sure we had monazite sand ores on our east parcel. One day I took a Geiger counter out there and bingo. Turns out we've got three more deposits, two already in production. China has eighty-five percent of the world's rare earth supply, which is why we've got fans in DC and on Wall Street."

"Congrats," Bernie said.

"Real lucky," said Luke. "But luck is the residue of design. Isn't that a baseball expression?"

"Branch Rickey," said Bernie.

Luke nodded. "How come you didn't play football?"

"I don't know." Oh? Wasn't the reason something about taking up boxing in the fall? I was a bit confused. "How come you didn't play baseball?"

"I prefer contact sports," Luke said.

They gazed at each other, a real quick gaze, here and gone, kind of blank on both sides, but for some reason the hair on my neck stood straight up. Then Luke held up his hand. Bernie tossed back the silvery cube, a real soft toss. Luke shut the cube back in the drawer. "But you're probably not here to listen to me run my mouth. What can I do for you?"

We walked over to the desk, side by side, me a little in front. Bernie took the flip knife from his pocket and laid it on the desk. "Ever seen this before?" he said.

There was a pause, and in that pause I thought I heard Luke's heartbeat, strong and slow like Bernie's, speed up. But almost at once it slowed back down. Meanwhile I was noticing that Luke had green eyes, just like the skull. You run into all kinds of interesting sights in my line of work.

Luke leaned closer. "What is it?"

Bernie pressed the silver button. The broken-ended blade flashed out.

"A switchblade knife?" Luke said. "Nasty. I don't—oh, for god's sake. Kepler, that weirdo." He turned to Bernie. "Did you ever have Mr. Kepler, the chemistry teacher?"

"No," Bernie said. "Why do you call him a weirdo?"

"Probably the wrong word. Egomaniac's more like it. He was always trying to impress us. Like with this knife. He showed it to us one day, supposedly because of the workmanship but really as a demonstration of how cool he was. I suppose I remember because of the skull, kind of distinctive." He extended his hand, almost touching the knife but not quite. "Where'd you get it?" he said, his eyes still on the knife.

"A long story," Bernie said. "What else do you remember about that day?"

"Nothing, really. By then I was just counting the hours till graduation."

"Do you remember what Kepler did with the knife after showing it to you?"

"Nope. Why is it important?"

"Did you know Rocket Saluka?" Bernie said.

Luke half closed his eyes, wrinkled his forehead, seemed to be thinking hard. "Rings a faint bell."

"He was a year behind you, played baseball."

Luke shook his head. "Can't picture him."

"He's gone missing," Bernie said. "The knife may be a clue."

Luke's gaze went to the knife again. "How so?"

"At some point it ended up being his, but he left it behind when he disappeared."

"That makes it a clue?"

Bernie smiled a small smile. "It's all we've got. Any chance you knew Doug Plumtree? He was the priest at Saint Kateri."

Luke shook his head.

"That's the church with the big homeless camp in back," Bernie said.

"Hmm," said Luke. "It's possible we gave them some money. I'd have to check—we do a lot of charitable work these days."

"Padre Doug died a couple of days ago," Bernie said.

"Sorry to hear it," said Luke. He glanced down at his hands— big hands, resting quiet and still on the desk. "What from?"

"He drowned in Snakehead Canyon, possibly by accident, possibly not."

Luke nodded to himself and then said, "Is that one of those slot canyons?"

"Yes."

"I've never been in one. Too damn dangerous. Just the idea creeps me out."

"But you've got no problem with mines?" Bernie said.

Luke laughed. "With the kind of mines you're thinking, yeah, I do. But we're strictly open-pit."

Bernie picked up the knife, put it in his pocket. Luke's eyes followed it until it was tucked away.

"So this is a missing persons case?" he said.

"Yes."

"And Rocket—what was the last name?"

"Saluka."

"Rocket Saluka's the missing person?"

"Correct."

"I assume you have a client."

"That's right."

"Because if you don't, or if you need extra funding, I'm here."

"There is one thing you could do. Jenny Chesnut would like a break on her rent."

"Jenny Chesnut from Chisholm?"

Bernie nodded.

"You spoke to her, too? About this knife thing?"

"We did."

"What did she say?"

"She said she'd never seen it before."

Luke turned to the big wall screen, where we were still flying high over land that went on and on. He was silent for what seemed like ages. Finally he said, "What's that Japanese movie?"

"*Rashomon*."

"This is like that."

"I hope not," Bernie said. "You're a fan of Japanese movies?"

"Uh-uh," Luke said. His eyes shifted. "But my first wife was the artistic type, kept trying to educate me." He laughed a little laugh and shook his head. Then he rubbed his hands together, like he was warming them up. "Am I Jenny's landlord?"

Bernie nodded. "She owns a restaurant near the college and she's struggling right now."

"That would be Kincaid Urban Development," said Luke.

"Consider it done—just give the details to one of my assistants out there." He gestured toward the door.

"Thanks, Luke."

"No thanks necessary. Us aging jocks need to stick together. Don't be a stranger."

Luke smiled and kept smiling the whole time Bernie and I were crossing the huge room to the door. I couldn't see the smile, of course, since it was at our backs, but I felt it.

Sixteen

After a nice sleep curled up on the shotgun seat—really one of the best ways of sleeping there is, especially with Bernie's voice in the background, talking quietly on the phone—I awoke to find we were driving into the parking lot at Central State Correctional. A dude in an orange jumpsuit, his face all about tattoos, was sweeping up outside the visitor's entrance as we walked up. He grinned a big grin at the sight of us.

No tattoos on his teeth. My own teeth felt good about that, a bit odd, and perhaps the kind of thing I should be leaving out.

"Chet!" he said. "Bernie! Hey!"

We stopped in front of him.

"Um," said Bernie.

"What the heck?" he said. "Don't recognize me?"

The truth was I did, but only through his scent, which included a strange mix of M&Ms and whatever they put in those red ant traps.

"It's me," he said. "Dak Duckworth."

Yes, Dak Quacky Duckworth, a safecracker we'd brought in when we'd actually been working another case. Some details you forget, but I remembered the Quacky case very well, especially how he'd blown up the whole bank although the safe remained undamaged. We'd been inside at the time—something about insufficient funds, whatever those happened to be—which was how we'd gotten involved.

"You've, uh, changed," Bernie said.

"Oh?" said Quacky.

"The tats."

"You don't like?" he tilted his head this way and that, giving us views from different angles.

"It makes a statement," Bernie said.

"Exactly. You're so smart. That's what I told my wife. Not that you're so smart. The statement thing. Well, I did tell her you were smart, but not recently. She's divorcing me."

"Sorry to hear that."

"No biggie," said Quacky. "I've still got my girlfriend on the side. I'll just have to move her to the center, that's all. She understands."

"About the tattoos?"

Quacky nodded. "Gotta develop some interests of the intellectual kind, you wanna survive in this place."

"When are you getting out?" Bernie said.

"Officially none too soon, but I'm hopeful on account of the overcrowding thing. They've been lettin' guys go by the shitload. So why not me? This is America, right?"

Bernie nodded. He has many nods. This one I couldn't read.

"What're you guys here for?" Quacky said.

"Interviewing an inmate. Maybe you know him—Martin Saluka, Senior."

Quacky's eyes shifted. He lowered his voice. "Not well," he said, "which suits me just fine."

"Why is that?" Bernie said.

"I guess I'm fussy." He opened the door for us. "Have a nice visit."

We visit inmates in our business. Sometimes we meet them outside in fenced-in yards with picnic tables where they even have swings for the kids who come to see their dads. That's my favorite type of inmate visit. Then there's an indoor kind in a room with chairs and tables bolted to the floor and a guard at the door. Finally there's the kind where the inmate is on one side of the glass and you're on the other, and all the talk is on phones even though everyone's right there! And of course I can hear the whole thing anyway without phones. That's my least favorite, and the kind we had going down today.

A guard let us into the room with the glass and the phones, a guard we knew, in fact, name of Zenia Murillo.

"Who just keeps on getting better looking?" she said.

"Well, I—" Bernie began.

"Chet, I'm talking about." Zenia slipped me a treat and closed the door.

Bernie sat in front of the window. I sat beside him. On the other side lay a small room that was all unpainted cement—walls, ceiling, floor. A door opened back there and two dudes in orange jumpsuits entered, one pushing a wheelchair, the other sitting in it. The wheelchair had a little tank strapped to the side, with a thin see-through hose leading from it right to the nostrils of the dude in the wheelchair. The pushing dude pushed the wheelchair up to the glass, turned, and left the room. Bernie picked up the phone.

The dude in the wheelchair stared at us. We stared right back. Some men—but not as many as you might think, even among the perps—are hard men. No matter what, they never do right by you. I can smell that wrongness and I smelled it now—you really didn't think a little glass slab could get the better of my nose, did you?—not just the anger inside, but also a sourness, plus darkness. Put them all together—anger, sourness, darkness—and what you get is the lash, if I can put it that way. As for what he looked like: old, bony, clumps of white hair sticking out here and there, real thin colorless lips.

Bernie made a gesture for him to pick up the phone. The

old dude didn't move for the longest time. I waited for Bernie to make the gesture again. He did not. Finally the old dude said something short and nasty that Bernie didn't seem to hear although I sure did, and picked up on his end.

"Martin Saluka, Senior?" Bernie said.

"Naw," said the old dude. "The king of France."

I missed that one completely, even though I was hearing him twice, once through the phone Bernie was using and once through the glass. All I knew was that we were off to a bad start.

"I'm Bernie Lit—"

"I know who you are. What do you want? Ain't got a lot of time."

"Warden Reese didn't tell me you were funny."

Martin Saluka, Senior—if that was who we were dealing with—didn't like that one little bit. Hot pink patches rose on his pale and wrinkled face.

"I'm here for one reason, you son of a bitch," he said. "On account of Reese's gonna do me a solid."

"She is?" Bernie said. "Or did she say she'd try?"

Martin Saluka, Senior, clutched the arms of his wheelchair real hard. His hands were huge for a man his size, which wasn't big at all, huge and veiny. "You deliberately wanna mess this up?"

"Just don't want you looking at the world through rose-colored glasses," Bernie said.

One of Martin Saluka, Senior's eyelids trembled. A tiny movement but for some reason it reminded me of a way bigger one, namely the cave-in at Snakehead Canyon.

"What's the favor you want from her?" Bernie went on.

"It's not obvious? You're suppose to be smart." He grabbed the nose end of his tube and waved it at us, almost like it was a weapon. "Compassionate release, man, that's what I want. Cancer fourth stage or fifth, whatever's the most. What the hell's the point of keeping me here?"

Bernie didn't answer, instead took out his phone—not the big one he was using for this back and forth in the visiting room—and did some of what I believe is called scrolling. He looked up. "Says here, Martin, that you murdered your wife. That would be one reason."

Martin shook his finger at us. Was springing right through the glass and biting that finger clean off a possibility? Something to look forward to, perhaps.

"There's a big difference between what a jury—nine women and three men, one of them gay, if you can believe it—says and what happens in real life," he said.

"You're saying you didn't hit—" Bernie checked the screen of his phone and continued, "—Dorothy Saluka repeatedly over the head with a hammer, resulting in her death?"

"If I did it was self-defense. She attacked me."

"With what?"

"Words. Words is weapons, case you don't know."

"Don't tell me your lawyer tried that one in open court?"

Martin shook his head. "He turned out to be stupid. Plus a thief."

"I don't care about that," Bernie said.

"You don't care about a sick old innocent man rotting out his life in this hellhole? Innocent as the driven whatever the hell it is?"

Bernie shook his head. "Also I don't care about your refusal to accept guilt—although any board looking into a compassionate release petition will."

Martin flinched slightly, almost like . . . like he'd been on the receiving end of the lash. I came close to understanding what they'd just been talking about. How can you beat a job like this?

Martin got the nose end of the tube back in its place, fumbling on account of those big hands of his going a bit shaky on him. Bernie watched that happen the way he watches some non-living thing, like, say, a hubcap by the side of the road. That non-look, if that's what to call it, came close to scaring me, but of course nothing Bernie could do would ever scare me.

"What I do care about is your son," Bernie said.

"My son?"

"How many have you got?"

"Only the one." Martin smiled a quick smile with just one side of his mouth. Most smiles have at least a little bit of beauty in them, but not this one, which was ugly and nothing but.

"Martin Junior, sometimes known as Rocket?" Bernie said.

"Huh?" said Martin. "Rocket? New one on me."

"You didn't know he was called that in high school?"

"Nope. Rocket? What's up with that?"

"Did you ever see him play any sports?"

"How do you mean?"

"Like taking him to games or practices."

"The bi—that was Dorothy's job. She did the housework. I made the money."

"Selling drugs."

Martin shrugged. "Hell, half of what I did would be perfectly legal now. I'd be sittin' in the Chamber of Commerce."

"So you never knew your son was fast?" Bernie said.

"Fast how?"

"On his feet. Running."

Martin shook his head. "But it makes sense. I was a real good athlete as a kid, coulda gone pro."

"In what sport?"

"You name it, bud."

"I'm not your bud," Bernie said. "I was—I am a friend of your son."

"Yeah? I thought you were a private detective."

"That, too," Bernie said. "When was the last time you saw him?"

"Who you talkin' about?"

"Rocket Saluka. Your son."

"Rocket, jeez." Martin's voice got a bit wheezy. He just sat there for a bit. I listened to the air hissing into his nose. After a while he straightened up and said, "That's so weird, him getting a cool nickname like that."

"What's weird about it?"

Martin shrugged his bony shoulders. "Nothin' cool about him. He was a mama's boy."

I felt a surge of something very violent in Bernie, all of it kept inside, a real lucky break for Martin Saluka, Senior. "I asked you a question," Bernie said, his voice as quiet as I'd ever heard it.

"Run it by me one more time."

"When was the last time you saw your son?"

"Have to think." Martin closed his eyes, rubbed his forehead. "Maybe in here, long time ago."

"In this room?"

"Sure. Kid comes to see his pa."

"When was that?"

"Told you—long time ago."

"How long? How old was he?"

"Dunno. Teenager, maybe? Sixteen, seventeen?"

"So a year or two after the murder?"

"You don't listen too good," Martin said.

Bernie gave him a long look, the kind that ends up with most folks turning away. But not Martin Senior. "What did the two of you talk about that day?" Bernie said.

"Well, we had to be careful on account of—" Martin clamped his mouth shut.

"What did you have to be careful about?" Bernie said.

"In this cesspool? You're joking, right? Every single goddamn step, gotta be careful, or else—" He drew the edge of one hand sharply across his neck.

"Let's move on to something else," Bernie said.

That surprised me. We don't move on to something else easily, me and Bernie. Suppose you get hold of a sock in the laundry room, for example. Do you let go of it easily, say if someone's trying to snatch it away from you? If you're like us, you do not let go. Also Martin seemed to relax a bit. How could that be good? But I trusted Bernie, goes without mentioning.

"Sure thing," Martin said.

"In fact," Bernie said, "let's go to the present. Any idea where your son is now?"

"Not a clue."

"Did you ever hear from him after that last visit?"

"Not that I recall."

"Any idea how he's doing these days?"

"Couldn't tell ya."

"Because he was his mama's boy and so you wrote him off?"

"Wouldn't put it that way," Martin said.

Bernie nodded. "I've been over the police reports, the trial transcript, everything. Interested in my take?"

"Not specially."

"I don't think they got it right."

Martin perked up. "No?"

"There's nothing in it about Rocket, not a single word. Where was he, for example, on the night of the murder?"

"Hey! You're saying he mighta done it?"

"Not quite. I'm saying he might have been a witness to the murder of his mom."

"No goddamn way. He was at church camp for the weekend

when I finally—finally!—grabbed that ham—" Those thin lips clamped shut again. He gave Bernie a look like he wanted to do real bad things to him.

Bernie put down the phone and we were out of there. It felt great to be outside.

Warden Reese was waiting for us in the parking lot, standing by the beast. There are all kinds of ways humans wear their hair, really one of the most interesting things about them, if you stop and think, which I almost never do, not both at the same time. But my favorite human hair look is dreads, and Warden Reese had them big-time.

"God above," she said. "He couldn't still be growing."

"I know," said Bernie. "It doesn't make sense."

That back-and-forth whizzed right by me, but then Warden Reese gave my neck a nice pat pat and took my mind off any worries I wasn't going to have anyway. She gave the beast a little pat pat, too.

"New ride?"

"Yeah."

"Must be fun to be you."

Bernie has a look when something new comes along and surprises him. I saw it now. "I'll hang onto that."

"Word is you're going out with Weatherly Wauneka."

Bernie nodded.

"Want some advice?"

He nodded again.

"Don't screw it up."

He nodded once more.

She gestured toward the prison wall. "Fun interview?"

"Not for me."

"Dark humor, Bernie." Warden Reese handed him an envelope. "Fifteen, twenty years ago Saluka ran a drug operation out of his cell, long before my time. There was an investigation that went nowhere, the way investigations did in here back then. This is all I could find."

"Thanks," Bernie said. "Is there any chance he's getting out of here?"

"Not if I can help it," she said. "But times are changing. Maybe they've already changed and I didn't get the memo."

"I know that one," Bernie said.

They shook hands.

Seventeen

Weatherly called as we were pulling out of the Central State visitor parking lot.

"How's your day going?" she said.

"I feel like I need a shower," said Bernie.

Which made no sense to me since Bernie had already taken a shower after his morning coffee, and although it was warm-ish outside they keep it cool inside Central State—and all the prisons I'd ever been in, by the way. An inmate buddy of ours name of Clarence "Upside" Downing, who'd once made a lot of money selling fish that hadn't been born yet, the trouble coming when they ended up not getting born, had even explained why: "Folks get tetchy in the heat," he'd said.

Bernie started in on some explanation, but at that moment I happened to spot a big red SUV parked at the side of the road, engine running. If you're on the road a lot, like we are, you see plenty of big red SUVs, so many you kind of stop noticing them. But noticing is part of the job here at the Little Detective Agency, and so I watched the driver of this particular big red SUV as we went by. And what do you know? He was watching us. I don't always take kindly to being watched, so I amped up my watching of him, as I'm sure you would have done in my place—something that will never happen, this shotgun seat being mine forever—and in this state of amped-up watching I saw his face clearly: dark-eyed with thick dark eyebrows. Had I seen him before? At first I didn't think so but then I noticed how strong his jaw was, and that brought back a memory of a broad-brimmed hat and a face mostly in shadow. But not the whole face, not completely. And on one side of his big chin there'd been a thin, downward curving scar. This dude, his big strong arm resting on the door, seemed to be growing a beard, but I could still make out a trace of that scar, like a tiny road in a tiny forest. Plus I caught—not as we passed by but very soon after, the way these things work—a faint scent of minty mouthwash.

That did it. I barked in no uncertain terms.

"Whoa!" said Weatherly over the phone. "What's with the big guy?"

Bernie glanced at me, then checked the rearview mirror. At the sound of Weatherly's voice I'd taken my eyes off the big red SUV, and now when I looked back, it was on the move, sliding into traffic and immediately slipping in behind a huge RV and out of sight. Out of sight but almost right on our tail! A very bothersome situation. I barked again, really letting that big red SUV have it.

Bernie gave me another look. "I don't know. Is Trixie there with you?"

"On my foot."

"I think Chet senses that."

"So he's sending her a message over the phone?"

"I believe so."

No! That wasn't it at all! It was all about the big red SUV, and that big hiking dude—yes, the hiking part came back to me, that's how on fire I was—with the scar on his chin. At that moment, with her timing, always the worst, Trixie barked. Barked at me, no doubt about it, and although not as loud a bark as mine—probably no need for me to even include that—there was something high-pitched and extremely penetrating at the top of it that my ears hated. What could I do but bark back? I barked. She barked. I barked. She—

"For god's sake!" Bernie said.

I believe, through all that—not noise, let's just call it sound—I believe through all that sound I caught something about exercise, and me and Trixie needing it bad. Soon we were outdoors—I had no idea where, although the tops of the downtown towers were in sight, up there with a cloud or two—and I was showing Trixie what charging back and forth and up and down and sideways in rough country was all about. The problem I have with Trixie is that I sometimes get the feeling that she thinks she's showing me. Have you ever heard of such a thing? What could be more bothersome? It makes me want to charge back and forth and up and down and sideways all the harder and in even rougher country at speeds no one could possibly—

But there she was! I won't say ahead of me, but beside? I'm okay with that although—what? I am certainly not okay with that. What was my mind thinking? A mind has to be on your side or what's the point? I surged ahead by a nose. Then Trixie surged ahead by her nose. Then I, then she, then—and suddenly, right in front of us was coiled a largish green and black snake. Did we take care of that snake or what? Actually I can't tell you. All I remember is hissing and dust, followed by me and Trixie prancing side by side down some mountain we seemed to have climbed, and joining Bernie and Weatherly at a picnic table in the shade of a big cottonwood tree.

They glanced at us and went back to whatever they were talking about. No good job, or look at you guys, or any of that. That was disappointing but sometimes, like after a real good bout of rompin' and stompin', you're too tired to care about much at all. I lay down in the shade. Trixie did the same, both of us on our sides, keeping an eye on each other through half-closed lids.

"How do you know the warden?" Bernie was saying.

"She's sort of a cousin on my dad's side," said Weatherly.

"She's got a high opinion of you."

"It's mutual."

Bernie opened the envelope, took out some papers, leafed through.

"What's that?" Weatherly said.

"Evidence."

"Of what?"

Bernie looked up. "Of me going through high school in a state of oblivion."

"This is about that Rocket guy?"

Bernie nodded. "Seems he was dealing drugs. The supplier, indirectly, was his father, a wife-killer still locked up."

"He murdered Rocket's mother?"

Bernie nodded.

"Did Rocket witness the crime?"

"He was away at church camp, according to his father."

"But you'll verify that."

"Yes, sir," said Bernie.

They looked at each other. Under the picnic table—perhaps I should have mentioned that they were sitting on opposite sides and that she was wearing her Valley PD uniform—Weatherly slipped off her polished black shoe and ran her foot up Bernie's leg.

"Folks on my mom's side are pretty buttoned up, but on my dad's side not so much," she said.

"No?" said Bernie.

"For example, take my Aunt Melba, an old friend of the

warden, by the way. There's disagreement in the family about the number of husbands she's had, but all the exes are miserable without her. Last Fourth of July, at the fireworks show over in Rio Bonito—that's where she lives—she made what she called an observation but I think she was giving me advice."

"Which was?"

"Quote, the fire you light in the bedroom heats the whole house."

Bernie thought that over. "I look forward to meeting her."

"That won't be happening," said Weatherly. She slid her foot back down his leg and straight into her shoe. "Meanwhile," she went on, "are you saying Rocket's father has some sort of underling on the outside?"

"Maybe not anymore, but yes." Bernie handed the papers to Weatherly. She started scanning the first page. "Dickie Incognito? I know him."

"Is that his real name?" said Bernie.

"Everyone calls him Ickie."

"I meant—"

"I know what you meant. Ickie runs a stolen goods ring out of a self-storage unit. Want to meet him?"

"Yeah."

"Do you know El Fundo Street in South Pedroia, the one with all those self-storages?"

"Um," said Bernie.

"You do? You don't?"

"Oh, I do," said Bernie.

Weatherly gave him a curious look. "His is the green one on the corner, next to the gun shop. Meet you there."

Weatherly and Trixie rode ahead in her squad car, Bernie and I following in the beast. Once Trixie stuck her head out the window and gazed back at us, a long, lazy gaze that would have infuriated anyone.

"Easy there," Bernie said. "I'm not thrilled about this either."

Then lean on the horn, Bernie. Lean on the horn till Trixie gets the message.

But Bernie did not lean on the horn. And maybe his problem wasn't even with Trixie, because the next thing he said was, "I haven't told her about the Hawaiian pants."

Uh-oh. The Hawaiian pants. Have I mentioned them already? What about the tin futures disaster? Well, not disaster, let's just leave it at thing, almost always the way to go. Once we got into a throwdown with a couple of roided-up musclehead twins that almost didn't end well. The Hawaiian pants and the tin futures were also like twins, perhaps not roided up or armed with tire irons as the muscleheads had been, at least at the beginning of all the to and fro, but there was one big difference. The muscleheads lost. The Hawaiian pants and tin futures won.

There. I've admitted it. The plain truth about the Hawaiian pants and the tin futures. The Hawaiian pants had come first. One night after a bourbon or two, or possibly after a visit to those strange places beyond two, Bernie smacked his hand on the table and said, "Hawaiian pants! People love Hawaiian shirts but no one's thought of Hawaiian pants! We're going to be rich." Pretty soon Bernie found just the guy we needed in some faraway place, borrowed a boatload of money from the bank—not the bank we're at now—and not long after that our boatload of money turned into a boatload of the most beautiful—and only—Hawaiian pants you'll ever see. A real actual boatload! I've seen pictures. Then, for reasons unknown to me and Bernie, no one bought a single pair, the whole boatload stacked to the ceiling in our self-storage on El Fundo Street in South Pedroia, reason number one for the state of our finances, reason number two being the tin futures play, which we have no time for now.

Bernie was silent for the whole ride. As we drove down El Fundo Street and passed our unit—black with black trim—Bernie's eyes were drawn to it like they were getting pulled by a powerful force. We parked behind the squad car at the end of the block, joined Weatherly and Trixie in front of a self-storage unit like ours, only green. A scrap of cardboard with writing on it was taped to the door.

"'Gone for munchies,'" read Weatherly. "'Back at 2.'" She checked her watch. "Leaves us half an hour to kill." She glanced around. "And nowhere to go in this godforsaken whatever it is, certainly not neighborhood."

"Well," Bernie said, "there is something you might be interested in."

"Oh?" said Weatherly.

Bernie didn't answer, just turned and headed back down the block to the black self-storage with the black trim. We followed, me from in front. Weatherly was silent. So was Trixie, her paws absolutely soundless on the pavement. My own paws were also soundless, although not absolutely. Nothing was easy with Trixie around.

Bernie unlocked the door. We all went in. It was dark in the self-storage, except for narrow dust-filled yellow light beams entering from tiny holes in the siding here and there. The smells, as usual, were of cotton, dust, and pineapple, the pineapple part a puzzle I've never solved. Bernie switched on the light, a single bulb hanging from the ceiling.

Weatherly gazed around, took in the sights: Hawaiian pants in tall stacks, Hawaiian pants hanging from hooks and beams, Hawaiian pants overflowing from boxes and spilling across the floor.

"This is amazing." Weatherly put a hand to her chest. "Like . . . like art." She turned to Bernie. "Is it an exhibit of some kind?"

Bernie laughed. "All it needs is a title."

"I don't get it."

"A long story," Bernie said.

Weatherly checked her watch. "We've got twenty-six minutes and three seconds."

Bernie started in on the story of the Hawaiian pants. Trixie lay down on a pile of them and fell asleep. That didn't seem right to me so I stayed awake for what seemed like the longest time, and maybe wasn't totally asleep when Bernie came to the end.

"The women's section is over there." He pointed. "Pick yourself out a pair if you like."

"I intend to," Weatherly said. "And I'll be wearing them frequently."

"You will?"

She nodded. "Also I've got a title for the exhibit."

"What's that?" Bernie said.

"Mahalo," said Weatherly, losing me completely, but I could tell from the look on his face that Bernie loved it.

Back at the green self-storage unit, the cardboard sign was no longer taped to the door. Weatherly knocked. "Yo," called a man inside. Weatherly said nothing. "Yo," called the man again.

"Ickie," said Weatherly. "Just open the damn door."

"That you, Sergeant Wauneka? And it's Dickie, please."

Weatherly was silent. I heard footsteps inside, the footsteps of someone who wasn't good at trying to be quiet. The door opened and a man rocking that more-than-one-chin look peered out. He also had a cigar sticking out the side of his mouth, so the lower half of his face had a lot going on. The top half was very much the other way.

"Hey, Sarge," he said. "What's with all the dogs?"

"Your lucky day," said Weatherly. "Ickie Incognito, say hi to my associate Bernie Little."

"Associate meaning he's a cop, too?" said Ickie. "And it's Dickie, please."

"No, he's not a cop," said Weatherly.

"And what about the Dickie part?" Ickie said.

"Good question." Weatherly pushed past him.

"Hey!" said Ickie. "You got a warrant? There's nothing to see here."

"Then why would I need a warrant?"

Ickie's mouth opened and closed. While that was happening I looked around and saw that the nothing to see part was absolutely true. Ickie's self-storage unit was completely empty except for a single lawn chair with a beer in the cup holder.

"Like I told Judge Finn," Ickie said, "you're looking at a reformed human being. Just give me a chance and you'll never see me in this court again. I saw the light, your honor."

"Judge Finn?" said Weatherly. "I thought she retired."

"It was her last day," said Ickie. "She put me on probation. And as you can see"—he gestured to the emptiness—"I'm entirely out of business. I'm just in here trying to figure out what kind of nonprofit charity could best use the place."

"A happy ending," Weatherly said. "But we're not here about the thievery, the fencing, the hijacking, your whole CV."

"No?" said Ickie.

Weatherly turned to Bernie. "Bernie?"

"Just a couple of questions, Ickie."

"Sure thing."

"First, when was the last time you saw Rocket Saluka?"

"Hmm. Name doesn't ring a bell."

"His real name's Martin Saluka, Junior."

Ickie screwed his eyes shut tight, wrinkled up his forehead, not a pretty sight. "Nope," he said. "Got nothing. Total blank."

"How about Martin Saluka, Senior?"

"Same," Ickie said. "Total blank."

"I have reason to believe you're not being totally candid," Bernie said. "So try again. Take your time."

"Time won't help," Ickie said. "And I'm being as candid as candid can be."

He seemed to like the sound of that, and said it again. While that was going on I heard a quick, very high-pitched sort of beep. So did Trixie—I could tell from how she cocked her head—but all the humans appeared to miss it. The next thing that happened was unexpected, namely the entire back wall of the self-storage proving to be one of those garage doors of the roll-up kind. It rolled up, revealing the presence of an 18-wheeler parked right outside and the driver climbing down from the cab.

"Hey, Ickie. Ta-da! Got all them routers plus ten boxes of the M1 chips and some A14s. Also—" At this point Ickie was making go away motions that the driver thought were hi-good-to-see-you motions so he made some as he went on. "—coupla cases of dynamite fell into my hands, which you can have for low low green, but if that don't grab, no biggie."

At that moment the driver seemed to notice the rest of us. His eyebrows rose in a questioning way.

Bernie turned to Ickie and said, "Let's start over."

Eighteen

"I woulda preferred having our confab back at the self-storage," Ickie said. He glanced around, took in the surroundings, namely the grassy strip beside the Burger Heaven parking lot, the only picnic table there occupied by us, us being me, Bernie, Weatherly, Trixie, and Ickie.

"Not your kind of food?" Weatherly said.

"It's not that," said Ickie. "The fries are nice and crispy, just the way I like them." He dipped one in a big ketchup pool and popped it in his mouth. "But Sarge, you're in uniform. What if someone sees me?"

"They'll think you kept your word to Judge Finn," Weatherly said.

"Hey!" said Ickie. "It could work to my advantage."

"Now you're thinking," Weatherly said.

"And while you're in that mode," Bernie said, "take us back to how you got together with Martin Saluka, Senior."

"What's mode again?" said Ickie.

"It means when you're on a roll," Weatherly said.

Bernie's eyebrows, with that language all their own, rose in surprise, specifically the good kind.

"Okey-doke," said Ickie. "Me and Marty—that's what I called him—met in the pen. He was in for something not too good, and I was in on some bogus frame-up."

"What was the something not good?" said Bernie.

"We never talked about that," Ickie said. "Some sort of homicide, wife homicide, if I recall. The point is he's in like forever and I'm gettin' out in a month."

He scooped up some fries, plunged them into the ketchup pool, and stuffed them into his mouth, but a few got loose and fell toward the ground. I'm real good at snagging falling food right out of midair and . . . and in this case I found that Trixie had already done so. The team was me and Bernie, end of story. Not everyone seemed to be understanding that.

"Out in a month," Ickie went on, speaking around all those fries, "but without any what you might call prospects." He waved a fry at Bernie. "That's the drawback of our whole incarceration system, my friend. Marty was aware of that. No one better at understanding the incarceration system than Marty. So he did me a solid, namely setting me up with a decent-paying marketing job on the outside."

"Marketing what?" Weatherly said.

"Nothing much in the grand scheme of whatever," said Ickie. "Weed, mostly. Coke from time to time. Odds and ends like that."

"How did it work?" Weatherly said.

"Like, um," said Ickie but before he could get beyond that, Weatherly's phone beeped. She glanced at it and rose.

"Got to run," she said. "Enjoy your lunch, Ickie." She fistbumped Bernie, a fist bump that looked like any other, except it wasn't, in ways I can't describe but felt for sure. Then Weatherly whistled a single low whistle and Trixie jumped up from under the picnic table, bounded across the parking lot, and leaped through the open passenger side window of the black-and-white. Weatherly hopped into the driver's seat, hit the siren, and they sped out of the lot, fishtailing slightly onto the street.

Ickie watched her the whole way. "Explain me something. Where do women like that come from?"

Bernie didn't answer right away, and when he did it was in

the voice he has for talking to himself—and to me, hardly needs mentioning. "There aren't any others," he said. He cleared his throat and turned to Ickie. "She asked how your drug business worked. Let's hear it."

Ickie raised his burger bun, squirted in more ketchup. "I wouldn't call it a business," he said. "That makes it more real that it was."

"More real?" said Bernie. "Didn't real money change hands?"

"If you put it that way, yeah, I guess. But if anyone was getting rich, it sure as hell wasn't yours truly. Marty had a guy on the border and my job was to drive down there once a month or so, pick up a shipment, and wholesale it out to other guys up here on the retail level. Kind of like the grocery business except not with strawberries." Ickie took a big bite of his burger. A bright red ketchup blob shot out of his mouth and splatted on the table. That reminded me of one or two real bad things I'd seen in the course of my work. Ickie dabbed at his lips with a paper napkin, then placed the napkin on the splatter mark, not cleaning it up, which had been my intention, but hiding it from view.

"What was the name of the guy on the border?" Bernie said.

"Little Al," said Ickie. "No longer with us."

"What happened to him?"

Ickie rubbed his forehead. "Something not good, down in Sonora. Garroting, maybe? I only heard third-hand, so it wouldn't be admissible. Course with Mexican courts, who knows? Heh heh." His hand, kind of like the scoop on a backhoe, shifted over to the plate of fries.

"Was Rocket Saluka one of your retailers?" Bernie said.

"Yup," said Ickie. He wagged a greasy finger at Bernie. "I know what you're thinking. He was just a high school kid. But let me tell you, he wasn't the only one. Made perfect sense when you think about it. Got to factor in the customer base—other high school kids, right?"

"Except Rocket was different from all the others," Bernie said.

"Yeah? How so?"

"Figure it out."

Ickie thought for a bit and then said, "He had trophies. Sports trophies. Pothead kids don't have sports trophies. Although, come to think of it, some of the cokeheads do. Never thought about that before. Wonder if it means anything."

"Where did you see those trophies?" Bernie said.

"At his place. He had a little studio thingy in one of them old stucco apartment buildings they used to have down Chisholm Road, past the high school. All gone now, of course, with the gentrification and such."

"Is that where you made the deliveries?" Bernie said. "At Rocket's studio apartment?"

"Nope. The sales force came to me. That's how I had it organized. I even wrote out a whole—what's it called?"

"Flowchart," Bernie said.

"Yeah, that's it. You're a smart guy, huh? Any money in the private detective game?"

"It comes and goes," Bernie said.

Wow! Money comes and goes. I'd have to remember that.

"What I don't get," Bernie was saying, "is how come, given the flowchart, you saw his trophies?"

"That's easy. I went there one time to have a little talk with the kid."

"About what?"

"It was what you'd call a mentoring session. I just wanted to give him some friendly advice."

"What kind of advice?"

"Good question. You ask good questions, uh, what was your name again?"

"Bernie. And this is Chet."

Ickie glanced over at me. I was busy with a bite or two of burger that had come my way, where from I couldn't tell you.

"His teeth are huge," Ickie said.

"Nothing to worry about," Bernie said. "As long as you stick to the truth. His tolerance for untruthfulness isn't the greatest."

"But he's a dog."

"You lost me there," Bernie said. "Back to the mentoring session."

"Sure thing," he said, noticing that Weatherly had barely touched her onion rings and scooping up a few. "In business you're only as good as your intel, and intel in that business is off the charts. I got intel that Rocket had a particular customer—for coke, as I recall—we didn't want him to have."

"Why not?"

"Risk benefit, Barn—Bernie. If word had gotten out, leading to the customer getting busted, for example, there coulda been problems. We stayed under the radar. Anything that took us over the radar was a no-no. That's exactly how I explained it to Rocket, the radar thing. He got it."

"Who was the customer?" Bernie said.

"Can't recall his name, if I ever knew it. But he was a chem teacher at the high school, and was even sub-dealing to some of the other teachers."

Sometimes a sort of wave of stillness—which maybe makes no sense—passes though Bernie. Makes no sense yet it was happening now. Ickie saw it, too.

"See, Bernie, in business there's a right way and a wrong way of doing everything. Have you read any management books?"

"No," Bernie said.

"I've read hundreds," said Ickie. "Figuratively hundreds. But if I had to recommend just one, know what it would be?"

"I'm ready," Bernie said.

"*Where Your Heart Is: How Jesus Would Have Made a Killing in Sales.*"

Bernie had an odd expression on his face, like he hadn't actually been ready—which wasn't him at all.

"I could send you a copy," Ickie said. "Just need an address."

Bernie handed him our card.

Ickie took a good look at it. "Hey! Flowers! Cool! Sends a message."

"What message is that?"

"Whatchamacallit. Nonviolence." He caught an expression in Bernie's eyes. "Or violence only if nothing else works." The expression was still there. "Or at least not first thing right out of the gate." The expression faded away. Ickie checked his watch. "Anything else? I'm a little pressed for time."

"What's on your agenda?"

Ickie's eyes shifted, then shifted back. "Just one straight and narrow thing after another. I'm on your team now, you and the sergeant's."

"Then let's get back to the question of what made Rocket different from all the other dealers."

"Dint I already do that one?"

"Try again."

Ickie tried again. That involved screwing up his face and biting his lip. At last he shook his head and said, "Got nada."

"Rocket was the son of the boss," Bernie said.

"Oh yeah. So, um . . ."

"Why would he want his boy dealing drugs for him?"

"Ah," said Ickie. "I see where you're coming from. First, he made sure I gave Rocket a real good deal. Twenty percent off, as I recall. No one else got any discount at all. Second, I think Marty was tryna make up for things."

"What things?"

"Things like what happened to Rocket's mom."

"Meaning Marty killed her."

"That's what the jury said."

"What do you think?"

Ickie shrugged, reached for another handful of fries. Bernie grabbed Ickie's wrist in midair.

"Ouch," said Ickie.

Bernie didn't let go, in fact pulled Ickie closer, so their faces weren't far apart.

"Yeah, I think he killed her," Ickie said. "You know the worst part? Rocket was in the house when it happened."

"How do you know?" Bernie said.

"Where else would he be?"

"Church camp."

"Church camp? Where'd you get an idea like that? The mom was a stripper. They weren't church camp types."

"Strippers can be church camp types."

"Have it your way. Meantime you're hurting my wrist."

"Take comfort in the card," Bernie told him. Whatever that meant caused a change in Ickie. For the first time I smelled real fear coming off him. Bernie leaned in a little closer. "Whatever you're not telling us, now's the time."

"Okay, okay," said Ickie, "but it doesn't prove nothing. We were cellies over at Central State for about six months. Marty was a real good sleeper, but one night—Christmas night, after turkey and all the fixins—he had a nightmare. Rollin' around, strugglin', all that. And in the middle of it he yelled out, "'What you doin' up? Go back to bed, you little fool.'" Ickie went silent, maybe waiting for Bernie to say something. When Bernie did not, Ickie went on. "Doesn't prove anything, like I said. But it's the best I can do."

Bernie let go of Ickie's wrist. Ickie made no play for the fries. Maybe he'd had enough.

Nineteen

We stopped at a convenience store we sometimes stopped at, although Bernie never actually went in. Instead he dealt with a dude who hung around outside, selling loosies. The dude hustled right over.

"Hey, Bernie, it's been a while."

"I've quit," Bernie said. "Basically."

"Congrats, man!"

"I'll take three."

"Three it is."

"Make it five."

"Can do. That'll be two fifty."

Bernie handed over some money. The dude handed over the loosies, glancing my way at the same time. "See that look in Chet's eyes right now, kind of sparkling? What do you think it means?"

"I don't know," Bernie said.

"Me neither," said the loosie dude. "But whatever it is I'd like some."

"We've got choices," Bernie said, releasing a little smoke ball from his mouth. This was a kind of play. As someone with a lot of experience with all sorts of balls—tennis balls, baseballs, volleyballs, for example, and not leaving out lacrosse balls, my favorite, with that wonderful mouth feel—I know ball playing when I see it. There's lots to like about humans, but the fact that they can make balls out of smoke is probably numero uno.

"The most obvious," he went on, "being another chitchat with Mr. Kepler. But I'm feeling a kind of pull from Snakehead Canyon. We could nose around a bit, maybe do a little digging on that hiker we saw coming out—"

The phone buzzed, not a good moment for that, interrupting a very promising idea featuring nosing around and digging.

"Bernie?"

"Yes."

"This is Danny Feld. Herschel Brock gave me a heads up that you might be getting in touch about old times at Chisholm. I just wanted you to know I'm ready whenever."

"How's now?" said Bernie.

"Now is good. Do you know the old Cottonwood Speedway?"

"Sure," Bernie said. "Why there?"

"Nixon Panero tells me you've got a new ride you might want to stretch out a little on the track."

"You know Nixon?"

"I'm a longtime customer. I own the speedway now, maybe you didn't know."

"It's back on the racing circuit?"

"Oh, no," said Danny Feld. "It's just my little hobby. My immature, wasteful, environmentally incorrect little hobby, to give it the full family name."

"God in heaven, Bernie," said Danny Feld, pulling off his racing helmet. "Where'd you learn to drive like that?"

Come again? My ears weren't quite themselves, in fact had never been in this state, a state where a sort of muffled roaring kept washing back and forth, although it was practically not roaring at all compared to the amazing roaring that had just been going down with the beast whirling round and round the old Cottonwood Speedway, Danny in a long, low one-seater silver car sometimes behind us, sometimes alongside, never in front. Oh, the thrill! Why couldn't it have gone on forever?

"Um," said Bernie, unbuckling and unstrapping me from the shotgun seat, but not removing his racing helmet because he hadn't worn one despite Danny having come pretty close to insisting. "It's not me, it's the car. Nixon seems to have souped it up."

Danny laughed and patted the hood of the silver car. "He souped this up, too, to the tune of five hundred K. And I've taken private lessons from Richard Petty. So if it's not you, what is it?"

"You met Richard Petty?" Bernie said.

"The King himself," said Danny. "I did get the feeling he thought I was hopeless but was too nice to say so."

Some humans—not a whole lot, in my experience, especially if you don't count the kids—are just plain happy. Danny—a little guy with young-looking skin although his hair was going gray—was in that group. You can always tell because they smile at just about anything. Right now, as we walked off the track and headed toward a garage on the other side, he was smiling at me.

"Brocky says Chet's a natural athlete if there ever was one," Danny said.

"So's he," said Bernie.

"And you."

"Nope."

"You were always too modest, Bernie. That was one of the things I liked about you. I'm not surprised by your success. Which I wasn't aware of at all, until I read about that case with the country music singer. I sometimes play that song she wrote about Chet for the kids."

"You play an instrument?"

"Several."

"Were you in the band at Chisholm?"

Danny shook his head. "I came to music late. But it's just math. Like so many things."

Bernie shot Danny a quick glance as we entered the garage, a glance Danny missed. This was the cleanest garage I'd ever been in, and all the cars inside, some up on lifts, were spotless. A guy with a wrench peeked out from behind an open hood and said, "Hey, boss, grab you a coffee?"

"That'd be nice." Danny turned to Bernie. "Or something stronger?"

"Coffee's fine," Bernie said.

We sat on camp chairs beside a long low car that looked a lot like the silver one, except for being white, Bernie and Danny on the chairs with coffee mugs, me on the floor with water, plus a tasty little rawhide chewy the wrench guy happened to have on him.

"All these cars are yours?" Bernie said.

"I'm afraid so," said Danny. "It's really getting out of hand. My wife says it's a personality disorder." Whatever that was couldn't have been very bad, Danny looking kind of pleased about it.

"What's her name?" Bernie said.

"Greer. Greer Ansonia, actually."

"The actress?"

"For now," said Danny. "What a terrible business! Makes mine seem like a garden party."

"What is your business, exactly?" Bernie said.

"I'll keep it short because Greer says it's the most boring subject on god's green earth—that's the way she talks, Bernie, don't you just love it? She plays all these walk on the wild side types but she's the most wholesome person imaginable. I still can't believe my luck."

"Congratulations."

"Thanks, Bernie."

"How did you meet?"

"One day eight years ago I saw an interview with her and got intrigued. Some people I know in the entertainment business gave me her number. Fast forward—two kids and another on the way. How about you?"

"Not so good on the marriage front," Bernie said, "but I do have a son."

"Is he a jock like his dad?" Danny held up his hand. "No offense. You weren't just a jock, Bernie, which was why you were popular across the whole spectrum of kids at Chisholm."

"I was?"

"Come on," Danny said. "Not even a teenage boy can be that unselfaware."

Bernie got a faraway look in his eyes. Danny caught it and got a look in his eyes, too, like maybe he'd slipped up somehow.

"In answer to your question," Danny went on, "I just kept doing what I'd always done, play around with numbers. After I dropped out of MIT—"

"I didn't know you went there."

"On a full ride. My mom and dad were both kindergarten teachers and the day the acceptance came they burst into tears at the same time, so dropping out was traumatic for them. But I wanted so bad to get started."

"On what?"

"On what?" Danny gestured to everything around him. "But I don't mean it in a materialistic way."

"What else can it be, Danny?"

Danny nodded. "That's what Greer says. But just because I can't articulate it doesn't mean it's not true."

"She lets you get away with that?"

Danny laughed, but for the first time his eyes weren't part

of it. "All right then. It's all about the fun of competition, with numbers as weapons. Specifically what I do is identify wrong-headed hedge funds and bet against them. Sorry you asked?"

"The opposite," Bernie said. "It was fun just listening." He took out the switchblade knife. "Ever seen this before?" He handed it to Danny.

Danny turned it in his hands. "What is it?"

Bernie didn't answer.

"Could it be—?" Danny pressed the button. The blade sprang out. "Whoa!" Danny said. He looked up, his forehead wrinkling, the happiness that had been on his face now hard to see. "No, Bernie," he said. "I've never seen this, or any other switchblade knife, except onscreen. You push again to make it go away?"

Bernie nodded.

Danny pressed the button. The big blade snapped back into the handle and out of sight. "What's going on?" He gave the knife back to Bernie.

Bernie reached in his pocket, took out a sheet of paper, unfolded it, and handed to Danny.

"What's this?" Danny said.

"Mr. Kepler's seating plan for the AP chem lab."

Danny gazed at the seating plan. "I remember that lab, of course, but where are you headed with this?"

"Any thoughts on Mr. Kepler?" Bernie said.

"A bit eccentric, maybe, but don't longtime high school teachers get pushed off-center? Imagine going over the same stuff, day after day, year after year. But he wasn't a bad teacher, as I recall." Danny raised his open hands. "Other than that, I've got nothing."

"Eccentric how?" said Bernie.

"I guess he was quick to leave the beaten path, bring up things that had nothing to do with chemistry."

"Such as?"

"The difference between Ponzi schemes and pyramid schemes. He loved to talk about all that. There's lots of math in pyramid schemes so I was pretty interested whenever it came up."

"Anything else?"

"Not that I recall."

"So you have no memory of him showing this knife to the class?"

"If I did I'd tell you, Bernie. Geez. What's this all about?"

"Kepler claims he showed it to that class." Bernie pointed to the sheet of paper, still in Danny's hand. "Brocky remembers the occasion very well."

"Yeah? He's a real smart guy but there's no way he has a better memory than mine."

"Oh?"

"Photographic, and I'm not saying that to brag. It's just a fact—like you being a war hero."

"Whoa," said Bernie. "Where'd you get that?"

"It's not a secret," Danny said.

"It's also not true."

"Exactly what I'd expect you to say. But reputations take on a life of their own, beyond your control. So you might as well accept it."

"Nope."

Danny laughed. "Still the same old Bernie."

"That's not true either. But how come Brocky remembers Kepler's knife show and tell and you don't?"

"Do you know the date it happened?"

"No." Bernie thought. "But later that day we played Central Tech for a slot in the state championship."

"Home or away?"

"Home."

"Was that the game that ended with Rocket Saluka's diving catch?"

"Yeah."

"Then we can establish the date." He took out his phone, tapped a few times. "Here we go—May fifteenth of my senior year."

"How do you know that?"

"I keep a diary."

"Going that far back?"

"Going back to when I learned to read and write, meaning age three. Some of those early entries are pretty funny. This one just says, 'Admitted to Caltech today, but only on partial. Still waiting on MIT. We beat Central one zip, Little going the whole way and Rocket making a game saving catch. Dad offered me a glass of wine at dinner.'"

Danny tucked the phone away. "But I wouldn't need the exact date. Chem lab was last class and I had permission to skip all last classes on game day so I'd have time to get the lineups to the booth and give Coach Raker my scouting report on the opponents."

"You scouted the other teams?"

"Sometimes live, but mostly through stats."

"Did Raker listen to you?"

"Sometimes."

"Yeah?"

"Well, hardly ever. It always came as a surprise when he did. For example, whenever he decided to make a pitching change he made this little tsk tsk sound before he even stood up. In that particular game he did it just before you faced that last batter. I heard it and looked over at him. He tried not to sit near me, but the dugout was mostly empty, with us in the field. So he saw me looking. And I just shook my head, meaning don't do it. He kind of gave this little nod and sat back. So Rocket saved my ass with that ridiculous catch. Any idea how he's doing these days?"

"Not good," Bernie said. "That's why we're here."

"What's wrong with him? Women trouble?"

"Why would you say that?"

Danny shrugged. "Not that I knew him well—wasn't he a year or two behind me?—but didn't the girls like him? Especially the older ones? He had that little lost boy look, with the big eyes and that lock of hair drooping down. Like one of those old movie stars, James Dean, maybe."

"I don't know about that," Bernie said. "Or about women trouble being part of the problem. But he's homeless, begging on the streets, real mixed up, and now missing."

"My god. That's terrible. Are you looking for him?"

Bernie nodded.

"I'd like to fund that."

"Thanks," Bernie said. "We already have a client. Can you think of any specific girls who liked Rocket?"

Danny started to shake his head, then stopped. "Ha! I remember this one time—it's sort of funny in a way, except for what you're telling me now. It was a Saturday night, senior year but before baseball season, and I was out bowling with my parents. So there's a picture for you! And it gets worse—I even sometimes bowled with them on school breaks from MIT."

"Were you good at it?"

"Terrible. We all were. Anyway, this one night I saw Rocket a few lanes over—this was at Mama's Bowlerama. You know that place?"

Bernie nodded.

"I recall two things, just from glancing over there from time to time. First, Rocket was a great bowler, real smooth, but the ball just zoomed and the crack of it hitting the pins was like an ack-ack gun. Second, the girl he was with—it looked like a double date situation—was a lot older, like a college student. She sat on his lap when he marked up the scores."

"Did you know the other couple?"

"Just the girl, Polly Grace. Her big sister was Evie Grace, the prom queen. A prom queen with a head on her shoulders, as no one says anymore. Went to Princeton, I think, and here she is in AP Chem." Danny held up the seating plan and pointed. "Back row, next to Luke Kincaid. Did you know him?"

"Just to see around. He was two years ahead, didn't play baseball and I didn't play football."

"But you knew Polly," Danny said. "Didn't you date her?"

"Sort of. It wasn't serious."

"What was she like?"

"Very nice."

"Smart like her sister?"

"I really couldn't say."

"Why am I doubting that?"

Bernie smiled. "Danny? This works better if I ask the questions."

Danny thought about that, but not for long. "Explain the importance of the knife."

"That's pretty close to a question," Bernie said.

"But on the surface a simple imperative sentence," said Danny.

I could see that Bernie wasn't in a smiling mood at the moment, but he smiled anyway, a smile that faded quickly as he started to speak. "Rocket's out there somewhere and the knife is really our only clue. According to Kepler, someone stole it from the locked cupboard where he kept dangerous chemicals either later that day or that night. He thinks the thief had to be one of the six chem lab kids."

"Ah," said Danny. "You came to rule me out. Or in."

Bernie nodded.

Danny sat back. "I was wrong," he said. "You have changed, Bernie. You were never scary."

Bernie's face showed nothing, but I felt things going on inside him.

"As for Kepler's theory," Danny said, "he seems to have left out one obvious suspect, namely Mr. Baca, the custodian. He'd have had a key."

"Apparently not," Bernie said. "Kepler installed his own lock."

"That would never have flown with Mr. Baca," said Danny. "He wasn't just a crusty old guy. He was delusional, thought he ran the whole place from that dark little basement office of his."

"You knew him?" Bernie said.

"The equipment managers get to know the custodians," said Danny.

"Even so, he wouldn't have known about the knife," Bernie said.

Danny swirled his coffee around, gazed into the mug, finally nodded.

"Did you know Rocket was selling drugs at Chisholm?" Bernie said.

Danny looked up in surprise. "I did not. What kind of drugs? Oops. I withdraw the question."

"Weed and coke."

"Geez. I had no idea. Coach Raker would have gone ballistic."

"That might have been a good thing. What do you know about Rocket's family situation at the time?"

"Nothing."

Bernie went into Rocket's family situation. Then they sat

quietly for a bit. The wrench guy strolled past, slipping me another rawhide chewy on the way, behind his back. Would we be seeing more of him from now on? That was my hope.

At last Danny spoke. "Do you think we go through high school in a kind of intense fog?" There was a long pause and then he said, "Oops."

Twenty

Bernie had a hard expression on his face. Mr. Kepler, opening the door to his condo, noticed it first thing, and closed the door on us. Not on both of us, as it turned out, what with me being already inside by the time the latch made its little click. Right then we had an unusual situation, namely me and Mr. Kepler on the inside and Bernie on the outside. Mr. Kepler, roly-poly, wearing only a bathrobe with a few holes in it, his bare ankles swollen and purple, looked at me. I looked at him. He opened the door.

"Hi, there, Chet," Bernie said. "Thanks for letting me in."

That had to be one of his jokes, Bernie being quite the jokester, although he never looks so fierce when he's in a joking mood. No need to thank me, of course. I would always let Bernie in, now and forever. He stepped inside, closed the door with his heel, just one of those cool Bernie moves that could happen at any time.

"I hope we're not disturbing you," he said.

"The fact is," said Mr. Kepler, taking his clip-on sunglasses from the pocket of his robe—a robe of what I believe is called the ratty type, although there wasn't a trace of rat scent in the air, mouse scent, however, being an entirely different story—and putting them on. The clip-on part was down. He flipped it up but it broke loose and fell to the floor. I picked it up. My first instinct was to give it right back, but then I thought again and held onto it. Wow! Thinking twice. You don't see that every day.

"The fact is," Mr. Kepler went on, "I'm pressed for time at the moment."

"That's too bad," Bernie said, "because I can't get that little observation of yours out of my mind."

"Oh? What observation was that?"

"The one about teachers being black boxes to their students."

"Thank you—Bernie, was it?—but it's not particularly original."

"You're too modest. Is the black box rule universal, or are there exceptions?"

"Not quite following you, I'm afraid," said Mr. Kepler.

"The last part is reasonable," Bernie said.

"Last part?"

"About being afraid."

Mr. Kepler shrank back, although not very far, since I'd already changed position slightly, crimping any room for shrinkage, especially the kind that might turn into some sort of making a break for it.

"How about we get specific?" Bernie said. "Don't you think folks learn better that way? For example, you might say chemistry can be dangerous. Or you could simply take a little blob of white phosphorus from its water jar and plop it on the desk."

Mr. Kepler flinched. Whatever white phosphorus happened to be, I wanted no part of it.

"Instead of white phosphorus," Bernie said, "let's substitute Rocket Saluka. Were you a black box to him?"

Sweat beads popped out on Mr. Kepler's face and it went all grayish.

"Do you want to sit down?" Bernie said.

"I want you to leave," said Mr. Kepler, his voice a little weak.

Bernie took him by the arm, led him to a mail-strewn padded bench, swept the mail aside, sat Mr. Kepler down. That was when I bit down on the clip-on thing for no particular reason. That made a satisfying crunching sound, the reason coming after the doing, which is often the way I roll. I tongued out all the pieces.

"Better?" Bernie said to Mr. Kepler.

"No."

"Rocket's not doing so well either," Bernie said. "We're going to find him and you're going to help."

Mr. Kepler licked his lips, his tongue turning out to be as grayish as his face. "How?" he said.

"By answering this simple question. Did you trade him the switchblade knife for drugs?"

Mr. Kepler's mouth opened and closed.

"Whatever calculations you're making," Bernie said, "take into account that we know you were buying and selling and using coke and weed while teaching schoolchildren at Chisholm High."

A small light went on in Mr. Kepler's eyes. "We're long past the statute of limitations."

"I know some very creative people in the DA's office," Bernie said. "No matter what, it's a good story. Veteran chemistry teacher ran a drug ring from inside one of the Valley's most historic high schools. TV trucks will be up and down your street."

Mr. Kepler stared at his bare feet. I've seen lots of thick yellow toenails in my career, but never like these.

"There's also your pension," Bernie said. "But in fairness I don't know the regulations on that."

Mr. Kepler kept staring at his feet, like . . . like he was noticing those toenails for the first time. How could that possibly be?

"One other thing," Bernie went on. "Those associates of yours in Reno, and that backward bicycle chain start-up. I wonder whether . . ."

Mr. Kepler's head came up. "I did not trade the knife to Rocket Saluka or anyone else for drugs or for any other reason. It was stolen from the chem lab cupboard just as I told you."

"Then how did Rocket get hold of it?"

"I have no idea."

"How did he know about it?"

"I have no idea about that either. How did you get hold of it?"

"This works better if I ask the questions," Bernie said, "and you'll be wanting it to work well, if only for your own sake. Did Rocket have any friends in your chem lab?"

"I couldn't tell you. I never paid much attention to all the adolescent ferment."

"Was he selling drugs to any of them?"

"Not that I know."

"Were you?"

"No."

"I'm going to name them. Michael Pilar. Jenny Chesnut. Danny Feld. Herschel Brock. Evie Grace. Luke Kincaid."

Mr. Kepler shook his head after every name. "I only dealt with faculty," he said. "I knew where to draw the line."

Bernie gave him a look I'd never want to see directed at me, and never would, not with Bernie loving me the way he did. I've had a lot of luck in my life and I also have a very strong feeling that there's plenty more to come.

"Did you and Rocket do your deals in the chem lab?"

"Certainly not. And these were not regular events, which you seem to be implying."

"How often is not regular?" Bernie said.

Mr. Kepler had something close to hatred in his eyes at that moment. Hatred for Bernie? I knew then that there was something wrong with Mr. Kepler, poor guy.

"Once every month or two, over the course of maybe a year and a half. Those were unusual times and I was still young in many ways. I've long since forgiven myself."

"That's nice," Bernie said. "If not the chem lab, where?"

Mr. Kepler shrugged. "Various parking lots, that kind of thing." His eyes shifted, just the tiniest movement.

"Go on," Bernie said.

"A trivial detail," Mr. Kepler said, "but in the interest of accuracy there was one time when we didn't meet in a parking lot. It had to have been a weekend because he told me he was at his weekend place."

"Rocket had a weekend place?" Bernie said.

"That's what he called it, but somewhat ironically—at least that was my impression. I never actually saw it. We met at a gas station."

"In what town?"

"It was just a miserable little desert crossroads like so many others. It didn't even have a name. And don't look at me like that. I'd tell you if I knew. Now that you've . . ." Mr. Kepler had a thought that made a tiny smile cross his face, like he was pleased with what was coming. "—unearthed the secrets of my past, I have nothing to hide and I want this case solved."

"Why?" said Bernie.

Mr. Kepler's eyebrows—maybe the thinnest I'd ever seen on a man—rose. "How else am I going to get my knife back?"

"I don't understand," said Bernie.

"What's so difficult? It's mine."

Bernie backed away a bit. I thought we were out of there, but then he said, "Where was the miserable little crossroads?"

"Up north. I can't say exactly, but on the way to one of those slot canyons."

"Snakehead Canyon?" said Bernie.

"Sounds right," Mr. Kepler said.

Back home we went into our closet, where Bernie keeps his clothes and where I sometimes hang out for quiet time with a sock or two, especially if they haven't been washed. Bernie picked out a suit, easy peasy since there's just the one. He brushed off a cobweb, got dressed, examined the ties, of which there were . . . three. Three! My goodness! I'd stumbled on three. Didn't that have to mean I'd gotten past two? No telling where this could end. But back to the ties: the gold number with the dice, won at a card game south of the border just before the shooting started; the new one he'd gotten last Christmas, red with flashing lights; and plain blue. He chose the Christmas tie and was tying the knot when he saw himself in the mirror and changed his mind, switching to plain blue.

I keep one personal item in the closet, my black leather dress-up collar. My everyday collar is the gator skin one, a long story and somewhat scary in parts that we have no time for now. Bernie took the black collar off the hook, and I helped him with the switching of the collars, tossing my head this way and that while Bernie took care of the unfastening and fastening.

We parked as close as we could get to Padre Plumtree's church, the little brick one with no bell tower, not close at all, what with all the cars already there. Bernie slowed down as we walked toward the church. Bouquets of flowers were scattered all over the lawn. So many flowers! Their aromas swirled up and down and around, a sort of invisible flower dance that came close to making me dizzy.

"Change of plan," Bernie said. "Let's stay here and see who comes out."

Fine with me. In fact, sitting seemed like a good idea at the moment. We moved into the shade of the only tree on the property, a small eucalyptus with many dead leaves on the branches. The dead leaf smell mixed with the flower smells in a way that made me sad. Bernie leaned against the tree. I sat beside him, possibly leaning on him just a bit.

He glanced down. "You okay, big guy?"

Sure! Never better! I should have pranced around to prove it to him, but I just didn't feel like it.

Bernie felt in his pocket and found a loosie, much to his surprise although not to mine. Soon he was smoking happily away, and we had the aroma of smoke mixed in with the flowers and the dead leaves. Right away the whole smell experience turned cheerful. I could have pranced around to my heart's content, and very well might have, but that was when the door to the church opened and some men and women came out, carrying a long wooden box. You get familiar with boxes like that in my line of work. They carried that box out to a long black car that's always on the scene at these events and loaded it in the back. Some other people, not many, came out of the church and headed for other black cars waiting in line. One of those people was Francesca, dressed all in black, her eyes black circles and a tear on her cheek that somehow looked black in the sunshine. She glanced our way, maybe not recognizing us at first, but then she did, and it was possible she didn't find us a pleasant sight. Hard to believe, with Bernie looking so beautiful in his suit, and me with my dress collar. Francesca stopped, turned, and came toward us. The tear on her cheek melted away but I could still smell it. Bernie ground the cigarette under his heel.

"I've been very patient," Francesca said.

"Much appreciated," said Bernie. "When we have something solid to report I'll let you know right away."

Her lip quivered. "It doesn't have to be solid."

Bernie didn't answer, just reached out and touched the back of her hand. Francesca quickly withdrew it and hurried down to the street, almost stumbling. She got into one the black cars and they all drove slowly away.

We stayed where we were, Bernie giving me a scratch or two between the ears. The end of my tail was touching the trunk of the eucalyptus. I got the feeling the tree was on our side, as if we weren't already the toughest team in the Valley. And now trees on our side? Look out below.

More people came out of the church, some in little groups, some alone. Hardly any of them noticed us but we noticed each and every one, of course. We're real good at noticing, me and Bernie. Finally we recognized someone, just about the very last to leave, a small woman of the no-nonsense type: Ms. Chen, boss of Chisholm High, according to Coach Raker. Bernie picked up the remains of the ground-out cigarette and stuffed them in his pocket. He waved to Ms. Chen. She came over, her sunglasses way too big for her face, a slightly troubling sight.

"Ah, Bernie, nice to see you. The whole school's looking forward to hear what you have to say."

"Excuse me?"

"On Alumni Day! Surely you haven't forgotten."

"Um," said Bernie.

Ms. Chen picked up a bouquet. "I don't see any harm in taking these, do you? A memento of a very fine man."

"Did you know him well?" Bernie said.

"We served on several committees together. Doug was a rarity in that world. He made things happen. It's a terrible loss for the whole Valley." She took off her sunglasses. She had the kind of eyes that can suddenly look inside you with no warning. I tried to think of some way to get her to put the sunglasses back on and came up empty. "I understand you found the body," she said.

"It was mostly Chet."

"Were you actually looking for him or was it incidental to something else?

This was where Bernie would normally say things worked better when we asked the questions, but here with Ms. Chen, among all the flowers, he did not. "Both," he said. "Padre Doug knew someone we're interested in."

"Mr. Kepler?"

"No. But we did find Mr. Kepler, thanks to you."

"Is Mr. Kepler somehow related to . . . ?" Ms. Chen made a gesture with the bouquet.

"I don't know," Bernie said.

"Word is the medical examiner's report was inconclusive."

"Correct."

"What's your opinion?"

Bernie gazed down at her. Was he finally getting annoyed that she kept asking the questions? I waited for him to put her straight in no uncertain terms. Instead, very quietly, he said, "He was murdered."

"Why do you think that?"

"I don't think it," Bernie said. "I only feel it at this stage. The thoughts haven't lined up yet."

Ms. Chen nodded. "The human condition," she said.

"Emotion runs the show?" Bernie said.

"And the rational mind is sort of the legal adviser," said Ms. Chen.

Bernie smiled down at her. "I wish I'd had you as a teacher."

Ms. Chen shook her head. "I taught calculus," she said. "Emotions played no part." She checked her watch. "Is there anything I can do to help?"

Bernie nodded. "The case we're working on has roots at Chisholm, back when I was a student, although I was oblivious back then. The custodian has been mentioned a few times. His name was Mr. Baca. He was pretty old at the time. If he's still alive I'd like to talk to him."

"Fernando Baca?" said Ms. Chen. "He's still the custodian,

and only looked old through your callow eyes. He's actually younger than me and I'm sixty-seven."

"I'll never believe another word you say," Bernie said.

Most people don't like hearing that from us, but Ms. Chen laughed happily. Some humans you just like more and more.

"School's not in session," she said, "but Mr. Baca is there eight to five, Monday to Friday. The delivery door around back's your best bet. The combination is pi to six digits."

Twenty-one

It's not that pie is something I can take or leave. Food of any kind is only for the taking, in my opinion. Let's just say that pie is low on my list, with the exception of a dish called chicken pot pie that I once found on a countertop, just out of the oven, and made short work . . . and sampled. Sampled is how to put it, and only the tiniest little sample. At first. Right now, behind Chisholm High, the practice field empty, I smelled no pie of any kind, but I had faith in Ms. Chen.

Meanwhile Bernie was busy with the lock, clicking, tugging, and muttering, the muttering usually not a good sign. "Ignoring the decimal point, is it three one four one five six? Three one four one five seven?" Click, tug, mutter. He glanced at me. "I was too embarrassed to ask, like I was really back in high school." Bernie turned back to the lock. "Or am I supposed to factor in the decimal point in some way, the one actually having a fractional value of one tenth, meaning . . ." Bernie gave another tug, this one very forceful. You might have called it violent, but I won't. The lock made a strange metallic squeak and sprang open.

"Ha!" said Bernie. "Something to think about, Euclid my man."

Euclid? A new one on me, but just from the tone of Bernie's voice I knew he was a perp of some sort. I hope you look good in orange, Mr. Euclid, but the truth is not many do.

A big silent building with no one in it: this was our kind of thing. We moved very quietly, me because that was how Bernie was doing it and Bernie for reasons of his own. We went down a hall lined with lockers. Through the little vents of one drifted the smell of a fish sandwich with mayo and pickles that had been in there for a long, long time. Soon we entered a gym, with basketball nets at both ends and empty stands along the sides. Bernie walked slowly to center court, then looked all around.

"This is where they had the junior prom, big guy. I took Polly Grace—even though she was a junior and I was a sophomore which seemed huge at the time. Probably the most daring thing I'd done in my life up till then." He breathed deep, let the breath out slow. "I remember her hand on my back, kind of sizing me up, although I didn't think of it that way then." He closed his eyes. "I didn't think at all." Whatever this was I didn't like the way it was going, and maybe Bernie didn't either, opening his eyes and giving himself a good shake, so often the right move. "Not long after that I stepped on her foot, and pretty hard, and that wasn't the worst of it." He laughed. "Soon she was dancing with others and there was no good night kiss when I drove her home. Served me right, in retrospect, but why does comprehension have to take so long?"

I had no answer, and also no clue what he was talking about. He went over to a rack of basketballs and just gazed at them.

"The whole place was so electric back then," he said. "Where did that go?"

He picked up a basketball and started dribbling. Dribbling is a basketball thing that gets me going, I won't deny it. I tried my hardest not to race round and round while he dribbled toward the nearest basket but there was nothing I could do. Bernie went up for what I believe is called an easy layup. The ball clanged off the rim, bounced a somewhat surprising distance away, and then was caught in midair by me, Chet the Jet. Caught, but not for long, basketballs being what they are, namely the most impossible balls around. The ball got loose and bounced away, like it had a mind of its own, which I was pretty sure it did, and I sprang after it, clamped on, or at least partly on, and sent a message, maybe a slightly stronger message than I'd had in mind. The basketball sighed and got very small.

"Hmm," Bernie said, and was about to pick up this flattened—you might almost say sleeping—version of the basketball, when a voice, not friendly, called from the far end of the court.

"Hey! Fella!"

We turned and saw a man watching us, not young, with long stringy white hair and a stringy white mustache, but tall and lean. Lean's not the same as skinny, one of those facts of Bernie's that can come in handy in our line of work. What else? This lean old guy had a vacuum cleaner strapped to his back. I'm no fan of vacuums. We were off to a bad start. He pointed the nozzle at us, actually sort of jabbing with it.

"Hey! You deaf?"

What a strange question! Bernie hears quite well for a human, and as for me—well, for example, I could hear this old guy's heart beating from across the court. First impressions are important, as humans often say. Maybe this guy hadn't gotten the news.

We walked toward him. He jabbed the nozzle at us again. "We're closed. What the hell are you doin' here anyways?" His eyes, narrow to begin with, narrowed some more. "And howja get inside in the first place?"

"Geometry, Mr. Baca," said Bernie.

"Huh? Do I know you?"

"We've met. I'm Bernie Little and this is Chet."

His angry gaze went to me. "A dog? A dog is in the school? What's a dog doing in the school?"

"Working," Bernie said. "We're looking for the answer to a question."

"I got no time for questions. You take off now or I call the cops."

"That's a thought," Bernie said.

Mr. Baca, if that was who were we dealing with—and of course we were, since Bernie had just said so!—lowered the nozzle. "What's that sposta mean?"

"Whatever you want it to," Bernie said. "But no need to make this into a big production. All we want to know is if you've ever seen this before." He reached in his pocket and took out the flip knife.

"Nope," Mr. Baca said. "Never."

Bernie pressed the button and the blade did what it did. That caught Mr. Baca's attention. He shrank back. Then the sight reeled him back in. The knife had some sort of power over Mr. Baca. He couldn't take his eyes off it. Bernie pressed the button again and the blade slid back to its hideout.

"Here," he said, "take a good look."

He tossed the knife to Mr. Baca. A real accurate toss, like all Bernie's throws, but it slipped through Mr. Baca's fingers, Mr. Baca turning out to be the butterfingered human type, of whom I've encountered many, although none smelling at all of butter, one of the easiest smells out there. I snatched up the knife before it hit the ground—probably goes without mentioning—and held it for Mr. Baca to take.

"Go on," Bernie told him. "He won't bite."

True. How would I even do that with this knife in my mouth? But after? Things happen, amigos, things you sometimes can't control, and here's a surprise: they're often the best things in life. But forget all that. What matters is that Mr. Baca took the knife in a hesitant way, and I didn't bite him even though my teeth really wanted to, very very badly. But we were on the job and on the job there's a time to bite and a time not to bite. I knew right away this was non-biting time. I'm a pro. The biting could come later and it often did. Life takes care of you if you let it.

Mr. Baca gazed at the knife in his hand. One of his fingers curled in and felt the skull ornament. He looked up. "What's this about?"

"That's what we're trying to find out," Bernie said. "When was the last time you saw it?"

Mr. Baca got one of those—I don't like even thinking the thought—fox-like expressions on his face. In fact, there'd been something fox-faced about Mr. Baca from the get-go. Here's what you need to know about foxes. They're a snap to chase away, but they always come sneaking back for whatever it is they want. It's all about wearing you down, which never happens in my case, as several foxes have learned in a way they'll never forget. I'm afraid a surprising number of humans have foxish faces, maybe not twenty-four seven, but sometimes, for example, when they're up against something they think they understand and don't.

"When did I say I ever saw it?" Mr. Baca said.

Bernie smiled. "We're way past that. Is the AP chem lab still up on the third floor, overlooking the diamond?"

"How do you know a thing like that? You taught here or somethin'?"

"You're close."

"A student, huh? What's your name again?"

"Bernie Little."

Mr. Baca squinted at Bernie. "You played ball?"

"You've got a good memory," Bernie said. "That'll be very helpful. Let's go on up to the chem lab."

"Why?" said Mr. Baca.

"In case there's any connection between the chem lab and what you've got in your hand."

Mr. Baca gave the knife back to Bernie real quick, like it was too hot to hold onto. "Are you a cop?"

"What do you think?"

Mr. Baca looked my way. "Canine, huh?"

"That's for sure," said Bernie. "But private." He gave Mr. Baca our card.

Mr. Baca peered at it and looked a bit more relaxed. "Well, Mr. Private Cop who I don't need to talk to for one more second, I ain't done nothin' wrong."

"Good to hear. Who did?"

Mr. Baca licked his lips, thought about it, licked his lips again. "You're lookin' for information?"

"That's right."

Mr. Baca nodded. "These days information's one of those—what's the word?"

"Commodities," Bernie said.

"Yeah. Commodities. Commodities get bought and sold."

"No question."

"So are you buying?"

"Depends on what's for sale in the chem lab," said Bernie.

My very first chem lab experience. Mr. Baca stood by the desk at the front. Bernie and I walked around the room. What amazing smells, most already known to me, but not all, and even the ones I knew were much more powerful. I had a very strange thought. This was HQ, not HQ of just Chisholm High, but HQ of the whole human shebang.

Bernie paused at the window, perfect reason for me to do the same. Down below lay a baseball diamond, the grass so green—green grass never bothering Bernie in the case of baseball diamonds—and the basepaths a lovely sort of desert red. Basepaths have a wonderful paw feel, if I can put it that way, as I've proved to myself on more than one occasion, the last time at a big league park where we'd watched a big league game, or at least part of it. A lovely evening, which was what I was thinking about at that moment. Bernie, also gazing out, was having thoughts of his own. They must have been powerful thoughts because they made him go still as a statue. Finally he said, "Hmmf," and turned to Mr. Baca.

"Remember Mr. Kepler?" he said.

"Sure," said Mr. Baca.

"He kept the dangerous chemicals in a locked cupboard."

"If you say so."

Bernie pointed. "Was that the cupboard?"

"Nope. Everything got changed out in the remodel."

"But it's where the cupboard was," Bernie said.

"Now we're talking commodities," said Mr. Baca.

"What's the price?"

"Twenty bucks. But just for the cupboard thing. Kind of like an installment plan, if you get me."

"I get you," Bernie said. He signaled for Mr. Baca to come. I know that one. Mr. Baca pushed himself away from the desk and came. Bernie took out his wallet, handed over a bill, the one with the picture of the narrow-faced dude.

"Yeah," said Mr. Baca. "That's where Kepler had the chemicals."

"Locked with his personal lock."

"Uh-huh."

"What kind of lock?"

"Padlock. Home Depot cheapo."

"Did he lock up anything else in there?"

"Maybe yes, maybe no."

"You're a hard bargainer," Bernie said.

Mr. Baca shrugged.

"I never realized that when I was here," Bernie said.

"Nobody knows nothin' about the custodian," said Mr. Baca.

"That can work in your favor."

Mr. Baca shrugged again.

"Financially, for example," Bernie said. He gave Mr. Baca another one of those bills with the narrow-faced dude. Some humans, like Danny Feld, have faces made for smiling. The narrow-faced dude did not. Neither did Mr. Baca. He tucked both notes away in his chest pocket, a chest pocket with a zipper that he zipped closed. Bernie's chest pockets did not have zippers, which had led to problems in the past. I had the feeling we were getting somewhere.

"Yeah," Mr. Baca said. "He locked up other shit in there, turns out, asides from the chemicals."

"Turns out?" said Bernie.

"Which I only found out after I opened up and—"

Mr. Baca hit the brakes, but a little too late. Hitting the brakes a little too late was a perp move you see a lot in our business. Was Mr. Baca a perp? If so we might have some action in our future and very soon. Knowing there's action on the way is one of the best feelings there is. I admit I got a bit excited inside, which maybe explains my mouth suddenly filling with drool, a drooly string or two getting loose and settling on the floor. What's that human expression? You can't make an omelet without breaking eggs? On second thought, perhaps the drool issue had nothing to do with omelets. Right there's the problem with second thoughts, which I usually stay as far away from as possible.

"How did you do it?" Bernie said.

"Do what?" said Mr. Baca.

"What you just told us—open the cupboard."

"I didn't say that."

"Sure you did. Don't tell me you stole the key from Mr. Kepler?"

"I ain't no thief."

"How about borrowing it from him, then?"

"What's the sense in that? Specially when down in my office I got master keys for practically—"

Mr. Baca hit the brakes again, and again too late. He gave Bernie a real nasty look, like somehow it was Bernie's fault.

Bernie didn't seem to notice. "That leaves us with why," Bernie said.

"Why what?" said Mr. Baca.

"Why you broke into the cupboard and stole Mr. Kepler's knife."

Mr. Baca's voice rose. "I told you, I ain't no thief."

"You've got a moral code," Bernie said.

"Damn straight. I opened up the cupboard is all. You gonna shoot me for that?"

Bernie glanced at Mr. Baca, a quick hard glance that made Mr. Baca give off the first faint scent of fear. Did he really think we were just going to up and shoot him? We weren't even fighting yet! And Mr. Baca, strong and lean for his age, had a sort of pointy chin that would not do well on the receiving end of Bernie's uppercut. Plus we weren't carrying, but of course with his human nose how could Mr. Baca know that, poor guy?

"No shooting, I promise," Bernie said. "I believe you—you opened the lock with a master key and that was the end of it."

"Plain and simple," said Mr. Baca.

"So that just leaves the question of motive."

"Motive?" The lines on Mr. Baca's forehead deepened.

"The reason you went to all that trouble. Why did you do it?"

"Ah, got ya," said Mr. Baca. "But come on, man, why does anybody do anything?"

"Someone paid you?"

"Now you're talkin,'" said Mr. Baca. He laughed for the first time, a creaky sound, like something needed oil. "We's like the tortoise and the hare."

Bernie laughed, too, no oil or anything else required, his laugh always perfection. "You being the hare and me the tortoise?" he said.

"Heh, heh," said Mr. Baca.

Had I ever been more lost? But why? I knew all the pieces—tortoises, hares, Mr. Baca, and Bernie, of course—but they wouldn't come together.

"Thanks for waiting up for me, Mr. Baca," Bernie said. "Who paid you?"

Mr. Baca smiled and rubbed his hands together, veiny hands with all the fingernails bitten close. "Now we're back in the commodity market."

"What's the asking price?" Bernie said.

"Make me an offer," said Mr. Baca.

"One hundred dollars."

"That don't even get you in the room."

"The thing is," Bernie said, "most of the work is done. We're down to six candidates—Michael Pilar, Jenny Chesnut, Herschel Brock, Danny Feld, Evie Grace, Luke Kincaid." Bernie's voice sounded casual as he went through all that, but inside he was on high alert, like he was waiting for something, and he was watching Mr. Baca real close. Did whatever it was happen? If so I missed it.

"So what?" Mr. Baca said.

"So with most of the work done, the final piece isn't worth as much," Bernie said. "Let's make it two fifty."

"Funny," Mr. Baca said, "that's exactly ten times what I got to open it up in the first place."

"Then it's meant to be."

Bernie started counting out the money. Mr. Baca raised his hand.

"Two fifty won't cut it."

Bernie's hands went still. Their hands, his and Mr. Baca's, weren't far apart, a strange sight. I came close to understanding all sorts of things, what with human hands being a lot like tiny humans in some ways.

"What will?" Bernie said.

"Way more."

"How much more?"

Mr. Baca's eyes shifted, like some thought in his head was pulling them sideways. "Have to think about that."

"We won't stop you."

Mr. Baca shook his head. "Think on my own." He checked his watch. "Gimme an hour or so. I got your card. I'll call you with the magic number. But you may be adding a zero to that two fifty, my friend. Be prepared."

Bernie's the best wheelman in the Valley. He can do things with a car that make you puke if you're not ready, or even if you are. But why did I have to go there instead of, for example, the time some cartel boys showed up offering big green for Bernie to drive for them? "En otra vida," he'd told them, a complete puzzler to me but the cartel boys nodded silently, shook hands, and split. Or what about how Bernie can follow without being seen, from way back or up close or many lanes over and even from in front. Following in front, can you imagine? But that's Bernie.

Right now we followed an old but clean and dentless pickup away from Chisholm High, a city bus between us, and Mr. Baca at the wheel of the pickup. We entered one of those many flat neighborhoods in the Valley with not much in the way of shade, small houses on small lots, but everything neat and tidy. The bus took a freeway ramp and we dropped back. The pickup kept going straight ahead and turned into a driveway on the other side of the street, a driveway with an empty trash can out-side. Bernie pulled over and parked behind a van with a sagging tailpipe. Up the street, the garage door rolled open. Mr. Baca drove in, got out of the pickup and hauled the empty trash can inside garage. The garage door rolled down. Not long after that the curtains closed in the front room of the house.

We sat.

Twenty-two

Sitting on a dude in this business doesn't mean you're actually sitting on him. It took me some time to get that straight but now I'm an expert. For example, sitting on Mr. Baca meant staying right where we were, parked down the street from his house and on the other side. Nothing much was going on except for a kid wearing earphones and chewing on a big wad of gum who zipped by on a skateboard without noticing us, and a long-tailed chipmunk who popped out from behind a spiky bush on somebody's lawn and hurried across the street with something on his mind. For some reason I got curious about exactly what that something might be, and therefore—

"Ch—et?"

And therefore I stayed put in the shotgun seat, the most comfortable shotgun seat of my whole career, so soft and yet so firm. My eyelids started getting heavy. When it comes to falling asleep any old time, we in the nation within are a lot different from you in the . . . in the . . . in the nation without. The nation without! What a thought! But perhaps a little on the uncomfortable side. It vanished at once, replaced by the lovely scent of sausages on the grill, in a dream that was on its way.

Sometime later things turned a dark orange color. I opened my eyes. The day seemed to have moved on without me, and now the sun was going down, the houses on our side of the street in soft shadows, the houses on the other side deep reds and oranges, except for their windows, which all seemed to be on fire.

Bernie's face—so near me, how lovely was that—seemed to

be on fire, too, and so did the screen of his phone, resting on the dash, but then the soft shadows found us and things went back to normal.

"Nice nap?" Bernie said.

Why yes, and so thoughtful of him to ask. I wriggled around a bit, got more comfortable. I'd been totally comfortable during my nap, but sleeping comfort and waking comfort are very different—you don't need me to tell you that! Meanwhile here we still were, sitting on Mr. Baca. That meant nothing had changed. Sitting could sometimes go on and on, meaning you had to be patient. What's harder than being patient? I thought for a while and came up with zilch.

Bernie glanced at his phone, then gazed down the street at Mr. Baca's house, where the shadows were taking over. "He said he'd get back soon. I should have pinned him down on that. What's he doing in there? How much time does he need to think it over?"

I had no idea. In my experience you came up with whatever it was right away or not at all. I tasted—but did not gnaw on— the wonderfully fine leather of my seatback.

"Or," Bernie said. He sat up straight. "Or . . . or could it be? Is he trying to bid up the price? Meaning—" Bernie was already opening the door, and I was in midair, hopping out. "—he's got another interested party?"

All of that zipped right by me. All I knew was that we were done sitting.

And just when I'd had enough! How patient I'd been! Was it one of those learning experiences? If so, I'd learned that I was a pretty good boy.

We crossed the street, two shadows in a world of them, and approached Mr. Baca's house. It was silent inside and the curtains were still drawn. We passed the house itself, then walked to the garage, Bernie cocking his ear, meaning he was trying his hardest to hear. Totally unnecessary, of course, since if there'd been anything to hear I'd have let him know, but you had to admire him for trying, and no one admires Bernie more than me. I was hit by a very strange thought: who was second when it came to admiring Bernie? The answer came at once: Weatherly. Why her? I had no clue, but it felt right.

We moved along the side of the garage, came to a small door. Bernie tried the handle. Locked, but there were two windowpanes in the door, both very dusty. Dust is blowing in from the desert all the time, which is why we almost bought a car wash. This was around the time of the Hawaiian pants, where our money went instead. Later on we met a carwash couple who own a bunch of them and live on the same street as Leda, Malcolm, and Charlie in High Chaparral Estates, the fanciest part of the whole Valley.

Bernie brushed the dust off both windowpanes, one for him and one for me. We peered inside. Mr. Baca's garage was one of the tidiest I'd seen, with all the stuff we keep in piles on our garage floor up on wall hooks instead. The only odd sight was the driver's side door of Mr. Baca's pickup, hanging open. The problem with that, as Bernie and I have learned several times, is that if you leave the door open the car might not start the next time you head out for a spin.

That was my take. It's possible Bernie's was very different because he smashed out the glass in one window, stuck his hand through, and opened the door from the inside. We entered the garage, circled the pickup, Bernie stooping to look underneath. I have a way of sort of stooping myself, which I did only because Bernie was doing it. I already knew nothing was under Mr. Baca's pickup, nothing smellable. But in the garage in general I was picking up a minty scent of mouthwash, a scent already in what you might call my scent memory, which is actually maybe clearer than my other memory, if that makes any sense. The hair on the back of my neck rose. Then came a low growl. That had to be me.

"Chet?"

Bernie's hand moved toward his pocket and stopped, realizing we weren't carrying. That might sound strange, but I know Bernie's hands, which have little thoughts of their own. We walked out of the garage, not making a sound, and leaving the pickup door unclosed. That bothered me, although I didn't know why.

We walked around to the back of the house, found ourselves in a small fenced-in yard, mostly dirt with brown grassy tufts here and there and a rusted out lawnmower standing in one corner. Bernie went to the back door while I quickly marked that lawnmower. It seemed like the right move, and moving right is how we do things at the Little Detective Agency.

I joined him at the door. He was doing that cocked ear thing again. There was nothing to hear in this house except the soft humming of a fridge. Bernie glanced at me and then knocked on the door. It swung open, and the knock hadn't been that forceful, meaning the door had mostly opened on its own. We'd had other cases where this very same thing had gone down, the end results never good.

First came the kitchen with that humming fridge. No lights were on but there was still a bit of daylight around, like it was taking its time to hit the road. Everything was tidy: no dishes in the sink, nothing on the counters except a toaster, coffee maker, and salt and pepper shakers, all neatly lined up. Tidy and also clean. The only non-clean things I'd seen so far were those two dusty windowpanes in the side door of the garage. What was a custodian, again? You hear about custodians once in a while, and I was pretty sure Mr. Baca was one of them, but as for what they did I was lost.

We moved out of the kitchen and down a hall, the house

growing darker with every step, like we were bringing the night, me and Bernie. Hey! Wasn't that a big part of what we did? We brought the night to perps, often to their surprise. And what about everybody else? What were we trying to bring to them? Daylight? Something like that. I thought I was just about to understand Bernie a little better, but how could that be when I knew him perfectly already? I nudged my way to the front, just in case we had some sort of silent trouble waiting ahead.

There are many small houses like Mr. Baca's in the Valley, all of them much the same, so we already sort of knew our way around. We checked the living room, bedroom—which had an empty fish tank on the bureau, no fish, no water, just some gravel at the bottom, and also not the slightest fishy scent, meaning there'd been no fish for a long time—and entered the bathroom.

We stopped, both of us just inside the bathroom, me slightly in the lead: a large bathroom for this sort of house, big enough for a two-sink setup, a separate stall shower, and a full-size tub, where a human could stretch out and just lie there in the water, which Bernie never did. Mr. Baca's tub was full of water, almost to the top, but he wasn't in it. Instead he lay naked and face down in front of the toilet, not moving.

Bernie spoke to him. "Mr. Baca?" he said, but I could tell from a deep little something in his voice that he already knew. I also knew, of course, probably goes without mentioning. The smell of a human—or any creature, now that we're on the subject—starts to change when whatever it is inside that lights them up goes out, and that was where we were with Mr. Baca.

Bernie knelt over Mr. Baca, pressed his finger to Mr. Baca's neck, waited a bit, then took a deep breath and gently turned Mr. Baca sideways. His body ended up sideways but his head flopped around a little more, revealing a deep bruised dent in his forehead. There was also some blood in that dent, more blood around it, a small pool on the floor, and a splash of it on the rim of the toilet bowl, all the blood thick and close to being dry. The water in the toilet bowl itself was pinkish. Was there anything else I should mention? The aroma of minty mouthwash, perhaps?

Bernie rose. Mr. Baca's head kind of eased its way back sideways, in line with the rest of him. One of his hands was sort of wedged underneath him but the other rested on the floor, fingers stretched out like he was reaching for something.

Bernie took surgical gloves from his back pocket and snapped them on. We searched the whole house, checking under Mr. Baca's bed and every other piece of furniture, looking through every cupboard and drawer, even tapping on the walls. What were we searching for? I had no idea, but whatever it was we didn't find it. Bernie got out his phone and made a call.

"Valley PD," said a woman.

"Captain Stine," said Bernie, Lou Stine being one of our best buddies downtown, possibly making captain on account of us in some way, the details not available right now.

"One moment," said the woman.

Then came a click and a beep, and the voice of a man. "Yo," he said.

Bernie looked puzzled. "Lou?" he said.

"Nope," said the man, a high-voiced type who sounded a bit familiar. "On vacation."

"Who's this?" Bernie said.

"You first," said the man.

"Bernie Little."

"Hey, thought I knew that voice. Del Spratt here."

"What are you doing in Lou's office?"

"Minding the store," said Spratt.

"I don't get it."

"Nothing to get. I'm in charge here until the return of Sweet

Lou. Gone to Disneyland with wife and babe. But no worries, Bern. I got your back."

Bern. We hated that, me and Bernie.

Somewhat later it was fully night, but Mr. Baca's house was brightly lit inside and out. We had uniform guys and gals, crime scene guys and gals, and EMT guys and gals. It was the first night that wasn't real hot in a long time, and everyone was in a pretty good mood, except maybe Bernie. We stood in the back-yard, Bernie explaining things about a car door left open and an ambush to Del Spratt, a pudgy, moon-faced type in a too-tight tan suit. The actual moon was low in the night sky, pulling off the whole thing more pleasingly than Spratt, in my opinion. After a while he held up his hand, a big hand, but soft.

"Whoa right there, Bern," he said, his high voice somehow matching up nicely with his moon face. "Why make complications where they don't exist?"

"What are you talking about?" Bernie said. Bernie's patient and likes just about everyone, but he sounded—I didn't even want to have the thought—a little on the impatient side now.

"Just the facts, Bern," Spratt said. "Elderly guy taking a bath. Suddenly needs to piss, like elderly guys do, but he's . . . what's the word?"

"I have no idea," said Bernie.

Spratt snapped his fingers. He was one of those very loud finger snappers, actually hurting my ears. "Fastidious! That's it. An elderly guy who needs to piss but he's fastidious, won't piss in the tub, so he hoists himself out, not so easy for elderly guys, and heads for the toilet. Only his feet are wet and he's splashed around some and his balance ain't so good to begin with and the next thing you know—swoosh!" Spratt shot up his pudgy arms like he was diving into a swimming pool. "Oingo boingo—he cracks his skull on the edge of the toilet bowl and we've got lights out. Classic slip and fall, seen it a billion times, case closed."

Case closed? Was closing cases Spratt's job? How would that make sense? Closing cases was my job, and that meant grabbing perps by the pant leg. I eyed the pant leg of Spratt's too-tight tan suit.

"Maybe," Bernie said. "But the timing is too convenient."

"Yeah?" said Spratt. "Who for?"

"That's a real good question. Right now all I can tell you is it's inconvenient for us. Mr. Baca had information on a job we're working."

Spratt tilted his head to one side, like the moon going down. "Any chance it's the same job you were working up Snakehead Canyon way?"

"How would you know about that?" Bernie said.

"Come on, Bern. I've been a detective on the Valley force for twenty years. You accumulate knowledge in this business."

Spratt tapped the side of his moony head. Once Bernie told Charlie we never see the back side of the moon, and made a drawing in the sandbox, Charlie being a little younger then. The whole thing had whizzed by me but now, without any fuss, I circled Spratt and took in the back of his head. Hey! He had one of those boils on the back of his neck. It looked kind of painful. I began to understand a little better. He was right. You accumulate knowledge in this business.

"But because we're pals, you and me," Spratt went on, "I'll let you in on a secret. I grew up with Herm Squires. Fact is we're cousins, the removed kind, once or twice, never got it straight. But the point is we're in touch."

"You're talking about Deputy Sheriff Squires?" Bernie said.

"Ding! Give the man a prize. Deputy Sheriff Herm Squires,

who thought he was next in line for the big job up there until something squirrelly went down, involving a doofus name of Bortz. Herm's in a mighty pissy mood these days. But what I'm conveying here is that Herm's in the know up Snakehead Canyon way, and he tells me your attitude up there was a lot like the attitude you got going here."

So much to get my head around, as humans say. My head doesn't really like doing that, preferring action that's more like soft butting, hard to explain. But my goodness! Squirrels! Pissy moods! And not just pissy moods but mighty pissy ones. Mighty pissy. I stalled out right there.

"So therefore?" Bernie said.

Oh, what a strange conversation! First all that piss, and now Bernie was handing off a so-therefore, when his own so-therefores were one of the best things we had going for us?

"Pretty simple," Spratt said. "Up at Snakehead Canyon you were pushing to turn an accidental death into a homicide and now you're doing the same thing here. I ask myself, why? The other way around, that's easy. Selling homicide as an accident, I can see you having a motive for that."

"Like what?"

Spratt smiled a big smile, a bit of an odd one, straight, with no upward lip curl at the ends. "Supposing you yourself was the perp, for example."

I might regret what happened next, if it hadn't gone by in such a rapid blur, not easy to remember. A bit of action involving the torn pant leg of a too-tight suit, and possibly the tiniest taste of blood, much less than a drop? That sounds right. The next thing I knew we were driving away in the beast and the beast was blasting a message for everyone on Mr. Baca's street to hear.

"Who's a good boy?" Bernie said.

Twenty-three

"Are they going to charge me with non-murder?" Bernie said. "That would be a first."

I tried to give that some thought, but got distracted by something caught between my teeth. I put my tongue to work and after not too long was able to get rid of a stringy little ball of suit material. Bernie was silent for a long time, not speaking until we turned onto Mesquite Road, dark tonight, Mesquite Road being an early to bed early to rise sort of street.

"Here's a problem," he said. "No water on the floor. He gets out of a full tub and goes over to the toilet, but there's no water on the floor. How's that possible? The bath mat was dry and hanging on a rail, alongside a dry towel, by the way." Wow! Hadn't we just been in that bathroom? But hearing all this from Bernie was like he'd been somewhere else. For the tiniest moment I came close to a horrible thought, namely that he was a mystery to me. But I didn't quite get there. You've got to watch your own back sometimes in this life.

"Hey! What's that all about?"

What was what all about? A possible licking of the side of Bernie's face, but very quick, over and done with before you'd even notice, and in no way messing with the driving of the car, especially given how slowly we were going, just rolling along our quiet street on a quiet night.

"How about this instead?" Bernie said. "Mr. Baca was not alone. Maybe he went into the bathroom alone, maybe he even started to fill the tub, but before he got in, someone else entered the room. That someone else cracked Mr. Baca's skull on the edge of the toilet bowl, maybe not intending to kill him, maybe just trying to get him to cough up something or other. After that, to make it look like what Spratt thinks he saw, he—or she, no reason to rule that out on the basis of what we saw—got the tub filled to the top and cleared out." Bernie glanced my way. "Not buying it? What if we delete the part about not intending to kill him, and add that the he or she involved wore gloves. That better?"

It was all good, from my point of view, the coughing up something or other being my favorite part. I even had a guess about what got coughed up, namely a thready ball of suit pants cotton! We're a team, don't forget, and right now the Chet side was on fire.

Bernie raised a finger. "But not making sure to splash around some water at the end? That was a big mistake. A real pro doesn't make a mistake like that." His fingers tap-tapped on the wheel, like other players in a band taking over for a while. "And," Bernie said, "neither does a woman, pro or not. After all, who cleans up the bathrooms, coast to coast?"

Not me. That was all I knew. Was there actually anything I cleaned? I worried a moment or two and then it hit me. Plates. I've cleaned a lot of plates in my time. I wriggled around on the shotgun seat and felt pretty good about myself.

Meanwhile we seemed to be passing our own house but not turning into the driveway or even slowing down. Bernie gave our place a very close look as we went by. From inside the darkness of the Parsonses' house next door came Iggy's yip-yip-yipping. I felt like doing some yip-yip-yipping myself.

We drove around the block, which you can only do one way, Mesquite Canyon lying on the other side, meaning right behind our place, just another reason to be pretty pleased about . . . well, everything.

"As for who this guy is," Bernie said, "we know that someone got Mr. Baca to unlock the cupboard door in the AP chem
lab. Did it make much of an impression on him at the time? If
so it faded long ago. But when we came along he realized he
could make some money out of this, especially if he could drum
up another customer. And did he have someone in mind? Just
speculating now, but if he did one choice would be Person X,
who got him to open the cabinet in the first place, meaning
the knife thief. But Mr. Baca wouldn't have been out for a
whole lot of cash. He'd be assuming X just wouldn't want this
minor theft known, this youthful slipup in the past. Therefore
Mr. Baca didn't understand the knife, didn't realize its true
worth, didn't know the risk he was taking. Otherwise he'd never
have reached out. He'd have dickered a bit with us and taken
our money." Bernie glanced my way. "How's that sound to you?"

Beautiful. I can listen to Bernie go on and on forever, but
tonight he was especially good, his voice reminding me of a
gentle breeze with maybe some nice cool weather on the way.
As for what he was talking about, you tell me.

We turned into our driveway and walked to the front door.
Then we just stood there, which was kind of unusual, like we
weren't home.

"We good, big guy?"

Yes, but we'd be even better once we were inside. This was
home. I could smell my kibble, just waiting for me. My own
kibble, mine personally, just for me and only me. That would be
Chet the Jet, if you're keeping track.

Bernie opened up. We went inside.

Bernie went from room to room, switching on lights. I stood
over my bowl, planning on getting through the first few
mouthfuls—which I absolutely had to have—very quickly and

then tapping the brakes, taking my time, enjoying every little taste. The first part of my plan went perfectly. You have to give me credit for that.

Not long after that all the lights were off, except in the kitchen, where Bernie sat at the table with a glass of bourbon, paper, and a pencil, and I lay beside my empty bowl. Sleep, which Bernie says knits up the raveled sleeve, was on the way. I don't wear shirts of any kind, sleeveless or not, but I love sleep, especially the kind that comes after a long working day. Clink clink went the ice cubes, my eyelids got heavier, and then the phone buzzed.

"Bernie?"

It was Suzie. Have I mentioned her already? Those dark eyes that shone like our black kitchen countertops? There was a time Bernie thought about her eyes a lot. I know because some of that thinking was aloud, when it was just the two of us. This was back in the days when Bernie and Suzie were still together. Then her career took off—like a meteor, Bernie said, whatever that happened to be—and they were together at long distance and later not at all. But now she was back running the *Valley Reporter* with her husband, Jacques Smallian, and at the wedding those eyes of hers, from way up front, happened to meet Bernie's way at the back. And a look rose in Bernie's eyes, there and gone in a flash, but the kind of look a human gets when they have a sudden pain deep inside. I never wanted to see that again.

"Hey, Suzie," he said, his eyes brightening but . . . but not in an over-the-top sort of way. I came to an amazing understanding, not my kind of thing at all. It wasn't that Bernie was done with Suzie—maybe he even still sort of loved her—but we were done with the sudden deep inside pain look. It wouldn't come again. Why? How? I had no idea, but it was good news. And on top of that, right in front of my nose on the floor, lay two plump kibble bits. Good news on top of good news. Who was first in line when the luck got handed out?

"We're working on a story about Father Doug Plumtree and your name came up," Suzie was saying.

"All on its own?" Bernie said.

"Of course not! And do you think I wouldn't tell you? There were two sources, actually. One was Florita Rivera, the M.E. up there where it happened. I've known her for a long time. She thinks you're not buying her finding and suggested I talk to you."

"Never heard of an M.E. doing something like that," Bernie said.

"She's special," said Suzie. "The other source is Fritzie Bortz. First, how can he possibly be the sheriff of anything?"

"There's your story."

Suzie laughed. "You should be in my business."

"Ha!" said Bernie.

"Fritzie also doesn't buy Floritas's finding," Suzie said, "but he's not buying your theory either. Fritzie thinks it was suicide."

Bernie mouth opened and stayed open for as few moments. I'd never seen that before, not from him. "How did he come up with that?"

"He heard that Father Doug was having an affair and from there concluded that breaking his vows resulted in a suicidal depression."

"He said that?"

"Not in those words. As for his source on the affair part, a friend of a friend of one of his past wives knows someone who works in the kitchen at the homeless encampment."

"Pepita Frias?"

"Maybe. Fritzie couldn't remember the name. But that's the source. Do you think there's anything to it?"

"Not to the suicide part," Bernie said.

"But the affair?"

Bernie didn't answer. He glanced at me, almost like he was looking for help. But with what? I had no idea. Also I was almost asleep. But the next thing I knew I was at the kitchen table, sitting beside him.

"I withdraw the question," Suzie said.

There was a long silence. Then Bernie said, "Um."

"Out with it," said Suzie.

"It's not related to Father Doug."

"Go on."

"More like unrelated, period. Actually on the personal side."

"Oh?"

"It's, uh, the aging jock thing."

"You're losing me."

Bernie cleared his throat. "Is that how you'd sum me up? As an aging jock?"

"Where'd you get that idea?"

"Someone threw it out there the other day."

"Yeah?" said Suzie. "Whoever that was is no friend of yours."

This was hard to follow. I knew jock straps, of course, knew them well, but I just couldn't take the next step. I returned to my empty kibble bowl and curled up around it.

Sometimes you dream about things that have actually happened to you. Once, working a case involving muscleheads that I never got straight in my mind, I found myself locked up all on my lonesome in a very messy locker room, like a brawl had gone down in there, things all over the place. For example, a hamper of dirty laundry had gotten knocked over, spilling a sort of river of jock straps across the floor. I've dreamed of that little scene many times—one of my favorite dreams and very hard to come out of until it's over, the real life situation ending with Bernie, somewhere outside the locker room, saying, "Anybody seen Chet?" Curled up in my dream, I hadn't heard him yet, but I heard something. My eyes opened.

I was in the kitchen, still by the kibble bowl. The kitchen was dark and no light seeped in from the rest of the house. Bernie was asleep. I could hear him breathing sleep-type breaths in his bedroom down the hall. What else could I hear? From old man Heydrich's place on one side came a TV voice talking about pillows. Old man Heydrich sometimes watched TV all night. On the other side Mrs. Parsons was coughing her horrible cough. Mr. Parsons said something to her. I picked out "sweetie" but nothing else. Out front, the street was almost silent, except for water running in the big pipe way underneath. We have a smaller pipe that goes into the big one and very expensive problems can sometimes arise where they connect, which is how I know about all this underground stuff.

Our most interesting night sounds—the hiss of a diamondback, for one example—usually come from Mesquite Canyon, out back, but tonight the canyon was quiet. I was picking up no sound at all from that direction, kind of unusual, and I was all set to slide back into dreamland when I heard a soft crunch, and then another. Was there also a very low machine-type hum? I thought so, and then I didn't. I closed my eyes.

They popped right open on their own. Taking over the wheel would be one way to put it. Different body parts can sometimes be the boss for a while.

I rose, crossed the kitchen, and went to the back door. On the other side is the patio with the swan fountain and a bit of lawn, although not the green grassy type. We don't do that anymore, me and Bernie. It's all about the aquifer, which I'd happened upon once at the bottom of a construction site. Just a little muddy dribble. You see that once and it's goodbye to green grassy lawns, although thinking back I don't recall Bernie at the construction site. Not everything in life makes sense. Remember that and . . . and I'm not sure what happens next.

If you're ever on our patio—maybe something to look forward to one day—for sure you'll notice the high wooden fence on both sides and the high gate at the back. Beyond the gate lies the canyon. No human seeing our gate would ever think, *Hey, maybe I'll just hop right over it!* That doesn't mean it can't be hopped over. It can be and has been. Shooter—no longer a puppy, now grown so strangely big, and still growing according to Malcolm, who'd turned into Shooter's biggest fan—was the proof.

Crunch.

A very soft crunch from somewhere in the canyon, somewhere close by. As for a low machine hum, I now heard none. I'm in charge of security—not just here in the house but all along Mesquite Road, by the way, and points beyond. One thing you learn after a while is that not every crunch in the canyon is a security matter.

Crunch.

But you want to do your job right, and that means making sure. We'd done so much work on doorknobs, me and Bernie, that I came close to getting sick of treats! Well, no. I just thought it would be fun to think that for a moment, the moment now over, and over for good. Back to doorknobs, the back kitchen door having the easiest kind of all, not even a knob but one of those levers a human presses on with a thumb while we in the nation within use a paw. The only problem comes at night, when Bernie slides the bolt into place. Unsliding it is not so easy. But not impossible, especially if someone has a big supply of biscuits from Rover and Company, the best biscuits in the Valley. Once I'd spent time in their test kitchen! Just a fact. Don't be jealous.

Crunch crunch.

There's a kind of little metal ball at the end of the bolt. You get your paw under, push it up like so and . . . You get your paw under and push it up like so and . . . You get your paw under and push it up like so and . . . and up it goes, easy peasy. Next— and my other paw is actually better at this part—you do this sideways thing—not like that, the other way, and . . . not like that the other way, and . . . presto! The bolt did its job and I did mine, pressing down on the lever. Then I gave the door a little shoulder lean and stepped outside and onto the patio, suddenly wide-awake and feeling tip-top.

Why is it that being outdoors is so fine? I had no idea, would never even ask the question. I only bring it up because it's something Bernie once said around a campfire with bourbon, me, and a handcuffed perp we were bringing in. A perp we both liked, me and Bernie. He said, "If I give you the answer will you let me go?" That made Bernie laugh and laugh. We smothered the fire with sand and brought him in.

Crunch.

I went still, ears up, tail up, hair on the back of my neck up. This crunch came from outside the gate—a high metal gate, not of the see-through kind—and very near.

Thump. A quiet thump against the gate itself, near the top. I barked a low, rumbly bark, not for Bernie, more like just warming up. From the other side of the gate came a deep silence. There's a kind of deep silence you get when no one's there, and another kind, even deeper if that makes any sense, when someone is, which was the kind of silence we had going down now.

I moved slightly closer to the gate. At the same time there was a tiny whoosh of air and a small dark airborne something came over the top of the gate and plopped down on the patio. I knew what it was already but went over to inspect it anyway. Yes, a nice juicy steak, the smell, one of the best there is, unmissable.

I took a close-up sniff or two, kind of like the way guys and gals in fancy restaurants stick their noses in a wine glass, a very amusing sight, and . . . and whoa! What was this? Another smell, definitely unsteaky, wrapped inside the steaky smells? Are you familiar with pill poppers, where a human, Bernie, for example, hides some little pill from Amy the vet in a special tasty treat with a special empty space inside? This was like that, only whatever was in there didn't smell like Amy's pills. The smell actually reminded me of a case we'd worked involving an unhappy lost teenager and some drug—not the smoking, sniffing, or swallowing kind, but the one Bernie never likes to see, namely the needle kind. The unsteaky smell reminded me of that poor kid's needle drug. In fact the smell was exactly the same.

One rather obvious fact around pill poppers. You can eat around the pill or simply spit it out when you get to it. I finally realized that pill poppers had to be some sort of simple game, but never mind that now. I began to nibble at the steak, so nice, juicy, bloody, fatty, working my way closer to whatever was in there. Ah, there it was, or at least one end of it, a plump purple pill-like thing, although much larger than your normal pill. Was there any reason not to give this big baby a quick, tiny lick, just by way of exploration? I was going back and forth on that when I got the feeling I was being watched. I turned toward the gate, and yes, someone was watching, perhaps someone very tall, the tallest human I'd ever come across, because he was peering at me over the top of the gate, meaning he was still on the other side, if you see what I mean. And I should add that I knew he was male from the smell, not the sight, on account of the fact that he wore a mask, covering his whole face excepting the eyes and mouth.

Our eyes met.

"Eat the damn thing," he said, his voice a low whisper.

I backed away from the steak, lowered my head.

"What the hell?" His voice rose a little. He glanced past me to the house, still dark, then amped things down. "Eat. I haven't got all night."

Eat the steak? If this dude was pushing for that it was out of the question. At that moment I caught a whiff of his breath, a whiff of minty mouthwash. My nose took over the thinking. I moved closer to the gate in this low, powerful walk I have, and gathered myself.

This masked dude gazed down at me. From the look in his eyes I saw that like other humans he did not believe. I got set. His expression changed. He began to believe. It made him angry and frustrated, although not scared, which is what you might expect.

"Am I supposed to have a cannon for an arm?"

Cannon for an arm—that was baseball lingo known to everyone who watches games on TV, which includes me. The masked dude was doing something with his hands, blocked by the gate from my sight. Then he raised one hand into view. I expected that hand would hold a baseball, but it did not. Instead it held a dull metal tube—maybe the length of a bicycle pump—with a sort of string dangling from one end.

He raised his other hand. In this one he held a cigarette lighter. By now I wasn't expecting a baseball, had forgotten all about baseball, but for some reason the lighter bothered me. Couldn't it have been something else, almost anything? He flicked open the top and thumbed whatever it was in the lighter that gets thumbed. A flame sprang up, very bright in the night, a moonless night which I was just noticing now.

The masked dude was no longer looking at me. Instead he was concentrating on what he was doing close up, namely holding the lighter under the end of the string that dangled from the end of the metal tube, just so. Pzzz. The end of the string caught fire. The dude brought it close to his mouth and blew on it. The flame began to run up the string, like the mask dude had chased it with his breath. He glanced beyond me and beyond the patio to our house, took that tube with the dangling, fiery string, reared back, and—

And I sprang.

Twenty-four

The look in the masked dude's eyes as he started to realize what was what! You see something like that and you know you're in the right business.

I soared up and over the gate, and as I cleared it I hit the masked dude good and hard, knocking him off a ladder he seemed to have been standing on, and therefore not by far the tallest human I'd ever seen, although he was certainly on the biggish side. Meanwhile we had a lot of action going on, starting with the masked dude's mask slipping a bit and revealing a curved silvery scar on one side of his chin.

Oops. That might not be the place to start. Probably more important was the fact that as he fell he was still in the act of throwing the metal tube with the burning string at the end, although now he was twisted around so when he did let go the tube went spinning not toward our house, which had possibly been his plan, but out into the canyon, spinning and sizzling like something you'd see on the Fourth of July, my least favorite holiday for exactly this reason. Then we were all in downward motion, the masked dude landing hard, not far from the gate, me soaring much farther and touching down on all fours—fours! Wow! Was I past two or what? But let's not leave out the metal tube tumbling and tumbling through the night, finally landing on a stumpy rock, bouncing up and KA-BOOM!

Oh, what a tremendous ka-boom! It took charge of everything, making all kinds of broken things—rocks, bushes, tree branches—take flight, raising an enormous dust cloud, and lighting up the darkness in one way-too-bright flash. In that too-bright light I spotted an ATV parked not far away at the top of a trail that led down into the canyon and across to the other side. And what was this? The masked dude already up and running, and not only that but running toward the ATV, and not even only that but way closer to it than I was? Yes, all of those things.

I wheeled around and took off after him, raising dust clouds of my own. The sky was re-darkening fast, although small fires had sprung up here and there. Meanwhile the masked dude proved to be pretty speedy for such a big guy. He glanced back, saw who was coming, and geared up to even speedier. Two can play that game, amigo, as humans like to say, and nobody plays it better than someone you might be able to guess. We raced through the darkness, the masked dude dodging around a burning bush and me leaping over it, at the same time barking my most savage bark. The masked dude reached the ATV, dove onto it, spun himself into the driver's seat, and then the ATV shot silently forward, one of those soundless ATVs that Bernie preferred to the other kind although he still was not an ATV fan. I ramped it up, charged after the ATV, closing and closing all the way down the slope. But when the ATV reached the canyon floor it sped up so much I came close to wondering whether I was actually going to catch it.

Close, though not there, the thought not really happening, not getting free into the open part of my mind, and anything in the unopen part stays there—just my MO in life, no need to make it yours. As for what I did now in the real, physical world, it was all about speed. I ran so fast, faster than I'd ever run, so fast I wondered if I was even still a dog anymore, and not some speedier creature, if such a thing existed, which I did not believe. And this superfast me—chest heaving, throat burning, paw pads raw—caught up to the ATV!

I came right alongside. The masked dude glanced down, saw me, and couldn't believe what he saw. He yelled at me, calling out some nasty names. I growled this growl I have which is all about bad things to come. He twisted toward me and kicked out with a booted foot, kicked right at my head, quick and hard. But out-quicking me is not so easy. I dodged that kick, at least mostly, and if not mostly then partly, and sank my teeth right through that boot and into his ankle.

"AIEEE!"

What a lovely sound! I swung my way right up into the ATV. He punched and punched at me, maybe landing one or two, but if so I felt nothing. Still holding onto his ankle, I somehow got a paw free and pawed at his face, pawing the mask right off and revealing a mean face with a big jaw and a big chin, the scar on the chin now bleeding. He looked at me with hatred but what good would that do? Did I not have him by the pant leg? I was just about to dig my teeth in deeper when he stomped down on the ATV floor with his free leg, in fact stomping on the brake, which I didn't quite realize at the time.

And then I was in midair, high above and ahead of the ATV. For more than a moment or two I thought I still had him by the pant leg, but all I had was the boot. The boot and I landed hard, and all the breath got knocked out of me. All I could do was just lie on my side on the ground. Meanwhile the ATV had zipped around me, careened across the canyon floor, and was now fish-tailing up the slanting trail to the top of the far side, a speeding dark shadow in the night. I bounced up, and if not quite bouncing then at least getting on my feet. I glanced around, saw the boot, pleasantly punctured, lying very near. The ATV was no longer in sight. But out of sight did not mean out of smell. Mean-looking dude with the bloody scar: you're done! I raised a paw, gathering my strength for a run no one would ever believe—and in that slight pause I heard a voice I knew and loved calling from the other side of the canyon, meaning ours.

"Chet! Chet! Are you out there? Chet!"

A light—small and weak—came poking down from our side of the canyon, moving quite fast. The last little fire on the slope blinked out.

"Chet? Chet? Can you hear me?"

I could, and perfectly.

"Chet? Chet?"

My Bernie. He sounded a little on the anxious side, poor guy. I barked.

"Chet! Chet! You good boy!"

And not long after that we were together. He switched off his headlamp, knelt beside me, ran his hands down my back, along my sides.

"You okay? Not hurt?"

My tail let him know the answer to that. I felt, if not tip-top, then quite near the top. He looked into my eyes. I looked into his.

"What happened, big guy?"

Lots. Lots happened. That was the answer.

Bernie rose. He wore only jeans and sneakers, the laces untied. Bernie always tied his laces unless he was in a huge hurry. I came very close to completing a so-therefore! Meanwhile Bernie had switched on the headlamp and was starting in on what he calls a recon, recon being something from his Army days. I joined him, reconning together being one of my favorite activities.

We followed the ATV tracks in the dirt and came to a squashed little barrel cactus. Caught in the spines of the cactus was a black something or other. Bernie pulled it free. Aha! The mask. He shot me a quick glance. I shot him one back, all part of our recon technique. We moved on, Bernie turning his head, shining the light this way and that. The beam passed over a rock with something in the shadow of a rock, paused, returned to that something. We went closer. It was the hiking boot with the thick black sole. Bernie picked it up by the end of one of the laces.

"Have we seen this before?" he said.

My tail, a tail of the encouraging type, started up.

"And what's this?" Bernie took off the headlamp, held it close to the boot. "Some kind of . . . puncture? Or two? Plus . . . plus a reddish smear of . . ."

He put the boot down, careful to touch nothing but the lace end, and felt all around my head, very gently.

"Sure you're all right?"

Perfectly fine. And all this petting was nice. But didn't we have work to do?

He gazed at the far side of Mesquite Canyon and softly said, "What would I do without you?"

What a question? And making no sense—even though Bernie always makes sense—since us not being together, me and Bernie, was impossible. Meanwhile sirens were wailing on our side of the canyon. I barked a bark I have that's not particularly loud but somewhat on the sharp side. It means get on the stick.

"Trouble finds you, huh, Bern?" said Detective Spratt. "And can you get that dog on a leash when I'm in the vicinity?"

We were in our front yard, just me, Bernie, and Spratt, one half of the sky still night, the other part losing its darkness but not actually light, one of those interesting but brief sights you see if you get up early enough, which we hadn't since this was still yesterday to us. Everyone else from Valley PD—crime scene, bomb squad, even K-9, which was kind of crazy but I took care of that with just a look that made Mister K-9 sit right down and go on strike. "Don't know what's wrong with him," said his uniformed buddy as they got back in the K-9 cruiser and rolled off down the street. But where was I? Everyone else. Right. Everyone else was gone, excepting Mr. and Mrs. Parsons watching from an upstairs window at their place, Iggy jumping up and down in his spot behind their front hall window, and old man Heydrich in his front yard making raking motions even though there was nothing to rake.

"No," said Bernie.

"No trouble doesn't find you or no you're not gonna leash 'im?" said Spratt.

"Correct," said Bernie. "Lou still at Disneyland?"

"I got that wrong. Disney World not Disneyland."

"But Disneyland's much closer."

"Land. World. Big difference." Spratt waved his stubby hand in the direction of the canyon. "What makes you think this was all about you? Coulda been just some bomb-building wackos foolin' around in the night. Then this dog of yours gets all excited and everybody's jumping to conclusions." Spratt's face brightened. "No pun intended."

Bernie gazed at Spratt and said nothing.

"Get it?" Spratt said. "Jumping?" He made what might have been the motion of gathering himself to jump.

Then more silence and finally Bernie spoke. "Did you see the ladder by our back gate?"

"Uh-huh."

"How does that fit in with bomb-building wackos?"

Spratt's mouth opened and was still open when a cruiser pulled up and Weatherly and Trixie hopped out. They ran right to us, Weatherly into Bernie's arms and Trixie darting around me at the last instant, somehow nipping my tail on the way by. Really? When I was—I admit it—a bit on the tired side? No matter. I—

After a bit of confusion, I ended up going into the house. We all did, leaving Spratt out front, mouth still open. Not long after that the house was quiet, Bernie and Weatherly in his bedroom, me lying in the front hall, and Trixie sitting by the door, keeping watch. I let her. Daylight came through the windows, but not through my eyelids.

When I awoke it was just me and Bernie. Whoa! How had that happened? Weatherly and Trixie had left the house with me not in the know? Me, in charge of security? That was very bad. I made what Bernie calls a mental note to let Trixie in on what was what the very next time I saw her.

I padded into the kitchen. Bernie was sipping coffee and munching on a BLT, not in his ratty robe, but wearing the good one, let's not say stolen, from our room at the Ritz, where we'd worked a case involving two families of jewel thieves trying to set each other up—well, I never did understand it, and neither did the judge, who sent everyone involved up the river, a story Bernie often tells after a bourbon or two at the Dry Gulch.

"Good sleep, Chet?" he said. "Kibble with fresh bacon bits ready and waiting."

No need to state the obvious, but it was still nice to hear. I was nearing the bottom of the bowl when the phone buzzed.

"Bernie? Jenny Chesnut here. I'm so so grateful."

"Um," said Bernie.

"Thank you, thank you, thank you."

"Ah, that would be for . . ."

"My rent, of course! I got a call from—oh, I wrote it down somewhere—this woman at Kincaid Development and she told me my rent will not be going up after all and not only that but my next six months will be free! Free! I almost fell off my chair.

And when I thanked her she said, quote, You have friends in high places. That would be you, Bernie!"

"Don't mention—" Bernie began, but Jenny talked right over him.

"And why didn't you tell me you were a fellow Chisholm Bear?"

"No real reason," Bernie said. "You found out from the Kincaid Development woman?"

"No," Jenny said. "But I was telling the whole story to a regular customer of ours and she told me. She was also at Chisholm, behind me but ahead of you, I think."

"What's her name?"

"Polly," Jenny said. "Polly Wertz. But back then she was Polly Grace. She says you took her to the Junior Prom. Is that true?"

Twenty-five

I had the feeling that things were going well, except for the possibility of bears. Hadn't bears come up once before on this case? And now again? Anyone with bear experience—and who could forget the time when totally by mistake I got between a mama bear and her cubs, which is why I may have mentioned it already—would now be on the lookout for bears. I sat up high in the shotgun seat, scanning both sides of the street, a very nice shady street in the Horseshoe Hills, one of the nicest and shadiest parts of the whole Valley, the houses all big, the cars all shiny, and no one to see but landscape dudes busy making things even nicer. Not bear country, you might think, but that's the thing with bears: You never knew.

Bernie smiled over at me. "On high alert, huh? Wouldn't want to be a squirrel today."

And just like that, things were going less well. Had Bernie just said he didn't want to be a squirrel today? Could that mean there were days when he did want to be a squirrel? How could all of Bernie ever get stuffed down to squirrel size? And why? Did he understand the life of a squirrel, a life very different from Bernie's? For example, no bourbon. Also no shooting dimes out of the air, no gunplay of any kind, except . . . except for on the receiving end. Where would anyone rather be? On the receiving end or on the dishing it out end, like us? I gazed my closest at Bernie, waiting for the first sign of anything squirrely, long whiskers sprouting on his face, for example, or a sudden tail trying to squirm free.

He shot me a strange look, perhaps slightly alarmed. "What? What?"

I faced forward and minded my own. The message had gotten through. He knew.

Meanwhile we'd turned into a curving driveway paved with bricks, a look Bernie liked and even considered for our place until he found out the cost. Flowerpots lined both sides of the driveway and chimes hung over the door, chiming softly away. A note was stuck on the door. Bernie read it aloud. "'Welcome Bernie! Come around to the back. Polly.'"

I heard a soft splash from behind the house, the sound arriving in time to mix with the chiming in a very nice way, a sort of music. There's all kinds of beauty in life.

We walked around the house, came to a patio with a swimming pool, the whole yard surrounded by a fence and palm trees. In the pool were a big inflatable alligator, its mouth wide open, and a woman in a black bathing suit swimming a stroke men didn't seem to know called the breast stroke, very slow although the head stays out of the water, which is my preference, too. I myself am a rapid swimmer and a big fan of the dog paddle stroke, as you might have guessed.

The woman was swimming to the far end of the pool, not facing us, her blond hair—the kind of blond hair you see a lot in some parts of the Valley, blonder at the ends than the roots—dry, except for the tips, dragging in the water. She reached the end, pulled herself out, turned, and saw us.

"Bernie?" she said.

"Hi, Polly."

"Oh my goodness, you've changed."

"Uh, a lot older," Bernie said.

Polly came quickly around the pool, doing all kinds of things at the same time, like adjusting a shoulder strap, fluffing her hair, and grabbing a towel to wrap around herself even though she was already nicely dressed in her black bathing suit. She held out her hand, the towel pretty much falling away, and they shook.

"It's not that," Polly said. "We're all older, but for you it's working."

Did she seem to be taking the slightest bit too long with the holding hands part that usually ends fast when the shaking's over? Was it perhaps because she was still having trouble with the towel? That was my take.

Bernie gets—I don't want to call it panicky—a look on his face when he's trying real hard to find something to say and coming up with zip. A look you only see, by the way, when he's talking to a woman, and not just any woman but a certain kind of woman. Right then I knew Polly was a certain kind of woman.

"And this," Polly said, turning to me, "must be your beautiful dog. Chicky, is it? Jenny—Jenny Chesnut—was telling me all about her. And you, of course. I had no idea. The two of you were in the news a while back? Something about water rights? The truth is I stopped following the news years ago, but congratulations!"

Where to begin? I sensed that Bernie was struggling with that very same question. At last he spoke, and he began with me. You had to love Bernie, and I did.

"Chet, actually, and he's a he."

"Oh, I'm sorry. Imagine me getting that wrong. Of all people." She gave me a closer look. "What kind of dog is he? It must be one of the really big breeds."

The conversation had taken an interesting turn. I knew that because my ears had gone straight up.

"Well," Bernie said, "he's not just one single breed."

"A mutt, then?"

"I wouldn't call him that. He's some sort of mix. You can

probably guess a component or two, but whatever they were the results were synergistic in a big-time way."

"Synergistic?" Polly said. "You have changed."

"Huh?" said Bernie.

"Back in the day—I'm talking about at Chisholm—you never used words like that. Or any at all, really."

Bernie's eyes darkened the tiniest bit.

Polly reached out and put a damp hand on his shoulder. "Sorry, I didn't mean to be rude."

"Uh, you weren't. It's fine."

"Plus I don't even know what synergistic means." Polly let go of his shoulder and took him by the wrist. "Come sit down and define!"

We sat at a little glass-topped table, Bernie and Polly in chairs, me beside him on the patio, the patio stones cool in the shade.

"All right," said Polly. "Synergistic—go!"

But before any going went on, a slider at the back of the house opened and a woman maybe a little younger than Bernie and Polly looked out. Some humans—almost always women—have a neat appearance, everything just so, as Bernie's mom says. Bernie's mom is what I believe is called a piece of work. For some reason I remember a lot of the things she says, such as "Afraid I've got to eat and run." Where to even begin with that one, and no time now. Back to the woman at the slider, an everything just so type for sure.

"Excuse me, Polly," she said. "Anything to eat or drink?"

"Hey, thanks, Dru," said Polly. "Meet Bernie, high school friend from way back. Bernie, my assistant, Dru."

"Very nice to meet you," Dru said.

"Hi," said Bernie. "This is Chet."

"Wow!" Dru said. "Look at him! I wonder what we'd get if we mated him with Greta."

"Who's Greta?" said Bernie, always ready with the question that needs asking.

"My German shepherd bitch," Dru said. "What do you think, Polly?"

"It's certainly a thought," said Polly. "Green tea for me, please, and what about you, Bernie? Coffee, tea, something stronger? Dru makes a mean Negroni."

"Thanks," Bernie said. "Water's fine."

"Plain or sparkling?" Dru said. "I'll bring plain for Chet, of course."

Bernie smiled. "And for me."

Dru moved back inside the house. My attention wandered, specifically to this mating idea that had come up. I had a pretty good idea what mating was about, but didn't know for sure. Have you ever noticed that wanting to know something for sure can get you in a frustrated mood? My gaze settled on the gator, floating peacefully in Polly's pool. The smell of my gator skin collar grew stronger, taking me back to certain events in bayou country where we'd worked a confusing case of which I remembered only the most watery details, way down deep.

Meanwhile the drinks seemed to have arrived, Dru had gone back in the house, and Polly was saying, "Dru's fabulous. I don't know what I'd do without her."

"What is it you do?" Bernie said.

Polly blinked, one of those blinks that accompanies a little half smile, a combo you see from time to time, the meaning a complete mystery to me. "Do?" she said.

"Whatever it is she assists you with," Bernie said.

"Oh, I get it," said Polly. "Dru's my personal assistant."

Bernie waited for her to go on, but she did not. She sipped her tea and then noticed him watching her. "For example," she said, "Dru discovered this wonderful tea from Nepal. It's the most centering tea on the planet. Care to try some?"

"The most centering tea on the planet?" Bernie said. "Sure."

"As long as you don't mind drinking from my cup?" She held it out.

"Um," said Bernie. Then he drank from her cup.

"Well?" she said.

"Very tasty."

"Tasty?"

"In a mellow way," Bernie said. "How long will it be before I'm centered?"

Polly laughed, a surprised laugh, and delighted.

"Depends where I'm starting from, I suppose," Bernie said.

Polly stopped laughing, tilted her head, looked at him.

"Thinking back," she said, "it was kind of daring of you."

"Sipping from your cup?"

Polly laughed again. "My god! Was all this in you the whole time, or did it come later?"

"Not following you," Bernie said.

"Jenny thinks you were in the army and fought overseas."

"I was overseas."

Polly nodded. "Brave, not daring, is maybe what I meant. And I'm talking about you asking me to the Junior Prom, me a junior, you a sophomore. That was a bit unusual in those stratified days, especially since we hardly knew each other. What made you do it? A bet with one of your buddies?"

Bernie got a faraway look in his eyes and was quiet for what seemed like a long time. Polly's towel slipped a little.

"I guessed right?" she said. "A bet?"

Bernie turned to her very slowly and shook his head.

"Then what? Come on, Bernie. Help me understand my past."

"Is that facetious?"

"Not at all," said Polly. "How can anyone be centered, if you don't mind me using the word again although I can see you do, without understanding the past?"

Bernie glanced at the gator in the pool, at me, finally at Polly. He picked up his water glass, took a sip, paused, then drank it all down. "I remember the moment," he said.

"The moment you decided to ask me?" said Polly.

"It doesn't make a lot of sense. I wasn't in your league. But it happened on the diamond. Can't recall who we were playing, but I hit one over the fence, which didn't happen often, and as I rounded third there you were, sitting with some of the other pretty girls, all of you cheering, and our eyes met, at least so I thought, and—" Bernie shrugged. "That was that. Call it a version of runner's high."

There was a silence, Polly looking at Bernie, Bernie looking down. Then he raised his head and their gazes were on each other.

"Wow," Polly said. "That's just perfect. Baseball high. Too bad I have no memory of it at all."

"You don't?"

"But I'm sure it happened. A bunch of us went to all the games." Polly leaned across the table, her towel slipping a bit more, and the top of her bathing suit somehow slipping as well. "I do have razor sharp memories of that Junior Prom," she said.

"Who doesn't?" Bernie said. "The crazy thing was my mother told me to take dancing lessons but of course I didn't listen to her."

Polly laughed. "It was just like that Wayne Newton song— tore your dress, what a mess." She laughed some more. "I was mortified, of course, and speaking of moms, my mom said it was my own fault for my choice of underwear."

"Underwear?"

"Exactly. There was none. You missed that? No one else did. That was my inner rebel period. But you know something? Now I'm glad it happened just that way. Freedom!" She raised her fist in the air, rings on her fingers sparkling. One of those fingers, ringless, seemed to catch her eye. "Why didn't you ask me out again?"

"Are you kidding? Don't you remember what you said?"

"Something cutting?"

"But deserved," Bernie said.

"Do-over, please," Polly said. "Ha! Strangely enough we were playing the do-over game just last week, me and our therapist. When I say our, I mean mine. Since the divorce Mr. Wertz no longer attends. Makes sense, I suppose."

"Mr. Wertz is—was—your husband?"

"Was is and now just is was," said Polly.

If I hadn't been lost before, now I was for sure.

"Lou—that's Mr. Wertz—is twenty-three years older. Do you know what he said to the therapist on our last visit together? Quote, hey doc, therapist in two words, The rapist." Polly glanced around, her gaze settling on a flowering potted plant on the far side of the pool. "I've been lucky in a lot of things, Bernie—including my settlement arrangement with Lou—but love isn't one of them."

Polly sipped her tea. A slight breeze rose and the gator began drifting my way. I didn't like the look in his plastic eyes, not one little bit.

"The do-over game is just a therapy device," Polly went on. "You think of some event in your life you wish you could do over, and then you have to explain why and that's supposed to lead to some understanding about yourself. At last week's appointment I picked this time when I was in LA and had a one-night stand with a character actor that didn't even last the night. But the appointment came before Jenny's call." Polly took another sip, watching Bernie over the rim of her cup. For some reason unknown to me I felt bad for her. "Jenny's call about you," she added.

"Oh," said Bernie. "Well, what I wanted—"

She interrupted him. "Are you married, Bernie? I notice you're not wearing a ring."

"Divorced."

"Seeing anyone?"

"I am."

"Ah," she said. "Exclusively?"

"Yes."

Polly tugged her towel up higher.

"It's, uh, great to see you," Bernie said, "but—and. I meant and. And I wanted to talk to you about the case we're working on. I thought I mentioned that when I called. Did Jenny tell you anything about it?"

"No," said Polly. "She was all about you and her rent."

"Maybe the best way to start," Bernie said, reaching into his pocket, "is to show you this." He laid the skullhead flip knife on the table.

Twenty-six

The flip knife again? Lately we'd been showing it to lots of folks. All at once it hit me: the flip knife was important. Not only that, but showing it to folks was now part of our MO at the Little Detective Agency. Wow! There's not a perp in the world who can keep up with Bernie. The flip knife was important and . . . and who had actually found the flip knife, buried under Rocket's tent at Padre Doug's encampment in the old rail yard behind his church? Oh, my. That was me! It's nice to feel good about yourself in this world, especially if you've come up big. But even if you've only come up little—or not at all—why not feel good about yourself?

But forget all that, because right now we had Polly—surely not a perp?—gazing at the knife. Her heartbeat—which had been through some interesting changes already in this conversation— sped up, although it didn't get any more powerful and it wasn't one of your powerful heartbeats to begin with. So now we had a real quick thumpitty thumpitty thumpitty, like that. Meanwhile, just to finish up with the heartbeats, Bernie's was its usual slow and steady BOOM BOOM BOOM and mine was exactly the same.

"Oh my god!" Polly said. "Are you giving it to me?" She looked up. "Is that what this is all about?"

I've made a bit of a mistake. Since we were working a case— with a paying client, no less, her name escaping me at the moment although the memory of the severe look in her eyes whenever they were trained on me couldn't have been more clear—what we were having out on this lovely patio was not a conversation but an interview. And in an interview you never saw Bernie look like he was taken by surprise. But now he did.

"Giving you the knife?" he said. "I don't understand."

Polly sat back, her hands on the edge of the table. "That makes two of us," she said.

Actually it made two and one more, namely me, so in fact the number was . . . was . . . Before I could come up with it, Bernie said, "Let's back up a bit. You obviously recognize the knife. From where?"

"You mean where did I first see it?"

Bernie nodded.

"I'll have to think." Polly gazed out at the pool, where the gator was now spinning in a slow circle yet somehow keeping his eyes on me in a very aggressive way. "I guess it was at Aunt Juanita's. But why are you asking?"

"Do you mean the taco place on the corner of Chisholm and East?" Bernie said.

"Yeah," said Polly. "Where the kids went after class. But you didn't answer my question—what's going on?"

"That's what we're trying to find out," Bernie said. "Can you narrow down the date when you were at Aunt Juanita's?"

"We weren't actually inside, now that I think about it," Polly said. "We were parked outside."

"Who is we?" said Bernie.

"Me and my sister Evie. You remember Evie?"

"Of course," Bernie said.

A tiny smile appeared on her face—actually more just in her eyes—and disappeared at once. "Your mouths all dropped when Evie walked by, literally dropped. I'm talking about all the Chisholm boys." Polly shook her head. "My therapist—and the one before, now that I think of it—has this bee in her bonnet about the negative effect of growing up with a flat-out beauty for a sister. Totally wrong, but she can't get past it—reveals more about her than me. I'm referring to the therapist. The truth is I wasn't in the least bit jealous. It was more like having a wonderful family heirloom." A tiny tear rose in the corner of Polly's eye. She blinked it away.

Bernie's face, which can sometimes appear a little on the hard side in interview situations, now softened. Was he starting to like Polly? That was my take. He seemed about to speak but before he could, Polly started up again. When the person getting interviewed wants to talk, we at the Little Detective Agency remain silent, just another one of our techniques.

"I was jealous of her brainpower, which I confessed in therapy without getting a whole lot of interest," Polly said. "I was also jealous of Evie's free spirit. And afraid of it, too. It got more and more prominent after our parents' divorce." She blinked again. "But why am I running my mouth like this? What do you want to know, exactly?"

"You're not running your mouth," Bernie said. "Go back to you and Evie in the car."

"We often drove home from school together. Evie had this cool red Miata my dad gave her in the fall of her senior year. Evie called it his penance for breaking up the family, as in 'let's take his penance out for a spin.'"

Bernie laughed. Before I could even begin to figure out why, a bee came zipping by and buzzed over us real close. Was this the one from the bonnet? Wasn't a bonnet a kind of hat for babies? I looked around and saw no babies, no bonnets, no hats of any kind. The case had taken a bad turn.

"He promised me the same thing for the fall of my senior year, but that was before he lost all his money," Polly went on. "Ever heard of tin futures, Bernie?"

Bernie—no, he did not go pale and even quiver a little. That would not be believable and so I did not believe it. He handled the situation beautifully, simply saying, "uh," and leaving it there.

"Of course not," Polly said. "And you're too smart to get involved with anything like that. But this was before my dad's tin adventures, spring of my junior year. We were sitting in the Miata and Evie opened the glove box and there it was." Polly pointed to the flip knife. "Evie pressed the little thingy that makes the blade pop out. It scared the hell out of me."

Bernie picked up the knife. "Mind if I . . ."

"I guess not," Polly said. "I still don't understand what you're doing."

"I'm not trying to mystify," Bernie said. "Quite the opposite." He pressed the silver button and the blade sprang out.

Polly started, just slightly. Then she frowned. "It wasn't like that, with the point broken off. Maybe it's not the same knife." She reached for it, took it from Bernie's hand, and gave it a close look, ran the tip of her finger very gently over the broken edge. "That skull is so distinctive, and those horrible green eyes, but . . . I just don't know. Here—I don't want it."

She thrust the knife at Bernie, or maybe just thrust it toward him. A jolt went through me and I . . . and I stopped myself when Bernie said, "Easy there, Polly."

"Sorry," Polly said.

Bernie took the knife by the handle and laid it back on the table, pressing the button at the same time, all in one smooth motion, smooth always being Bernie's way with weapons of any kind. We're a team, me and Bernie. The bee came buzzing back. I snapped at it and missed, possibly a good thing. I've been lucky all my life, and if not exactly all then certainly since the day I met Bernie. The days before that day are actually hard to remember.

"Assuming for now that it's the same knife," Bernie said, "what did Evie say about it?"

"First you have to understand that back then Evie was really at her very strongest. She took no crap from anyone. The knife was just one example."

"She used it on someone?" Bernie said.

"Good god, no. She was wild sometimes and a free spirit, like I said, but never violent. It wasn't in her. The point is she stole the knife, not for any violent reason or because she liked knives or thought it was valuable, or anything like that. Do you remember Mr. Kepler, the chemistry teacher?"

Bernie nodded.

"He was a creep."

"In what way?"

"Were you ever in the AP chem lab?"

"No."

"Me neither. But everyone sat on these stools. Tall stools, which is the point. Kepler peeked up Evie's skirt every chance he got, every single chem lab, which was once a week. She hated that. So when he showed off this knife he was proud of—I can't remember why or even if she told me why—Evie stole it. A perfect crime—that's how she put it."

"A perfect crime in what way?" Bernie said.

Polly looked surprised. "No weapons allowed inside the building—a strict Chisholm rule, Bernie. If Kepler had reported the theft he'd have landed himself in the soup."

I remembered Mr. Kepler, of course, an older dude of the roly-poly type. I also knew soup bowls, big as far as plates go, but . . . but that was as far as I could take it on my own.

"How did she steal the knife?" Bernie said.

"Wasn't it locked in a cupboard in the chem lab?" Polly said. "Evie paid the custodian—I can't remember his name—to unlock it. Ta-da."

"Mr. Baca," Bernie said. "Fernando Baca. How much did Evie pay him?"

"I think it was twenty-five dollars," Polly said. "We ran into each other in the cafeteria and she told me her plan. 'Go for it,' I said, and I can remember her reply word for word. It was pure Evie—'Sis, I don't need permission. I need twenty-five bucks.' She never had any cash on her and that day neither did I. But that's how I know the amount."

"Where did she get the money?" Bernie said.

"She must have borrowed from someone else," said Polly.

"Like who?"

"I have no idea."

"What did Evie end up doing with the knife?" Bernie said.

"Kept it, I guess," said Polly. "I don't recall ever seeing it again, after that time in the Miata."

"I'd like to ask her," Bernie said.

Polly looked confused. "Ask Evie?"

"Yes," Bernie said. "The knife's a clue in the case we're working on. We need to know what Evie did with it."

Polly stared at him, her mouth half open. "You don't know?"

"Don't know what?" said Bernie.

"Evie . . . Evie passed away. She's dead." Polly's eyes grew damp. "A long time ago, so there's no reason for me to get up—" She burst into tears, covered her face, and rose, somewhat shakily.

"I'm sorry," Bernie said. "I—"

Polly ran toward the house, stumbling a little and losing her towel. As she struggled with the slider, her back to us, dressed only in her little black bathing suit, there was something about her that needed protecting. But how? She disappeared inside. Were we done with the interview? Hitting the road? We didn't seem to be. Bernie just continued sitting at the table, a faraway look in his eyes.

"Part of me knows she's so different now," he said quietly.

"But when we start talking she looks exactly the same as she did back then. How is that possible?"

I waited for the answer, but it didn't seem to be coming. Have I mentioned that this was the hot time of year, today being particularly hot? I set off in the direction of the pool.

When Polly returned she was barefoot and dressed all in white—white slacks and a white shirt buttoned to the neck. Her hair, a little damp, was neatly combed and she had makeup around her eyes although nowhere else on her face. Also she smelled like some little white flowers you sometimes see by the roadside here in our part of the world.

Bernie pulled out a chair for her as she came to the table.

"Thank you, Bernie," she said, and then looked past him, her eyes momentarily on the pool, where the inflated gator seemed to have fallen on hard times. Let's put it that way. I myself, keeping watch at poolside, trotted over to the table and sat, nice as nice can be. You wouldn't have noticed me, certainly after I'd gotten done with shaking myself off.

Polly sat down. "I apologize," she said.

"No apology necessary," said Bernie.

She took a deep breath. "After all this time to get past it . . . I don't know. Maybe the sight of the knife brought it all back—a memento of when we were so young and . . . and just floating." Polly glanced at the table. "Where is it?" she said.

"Back in my pocket."

"Keep it there, please. I don't want to see it."

"Was it involved in some way with her death?" Bernie said.

"What a strange question!" Polly said. "Of course not. Evie died in an accident."

"A car accident?"

254 | SPENCER QUINN

Polly shook her head. "Hiking. She took a bad, bad fall."

"When was this?" Bernie said.

"It'll be seven years in December."

"Where did it happen?"

"At a canyon up north," Polly said. "Just across the border from one of the reservations."

Bernie went still. "Snakehead Canyon?"

Polly shook her head. "Never heard of that one. I don't recall the name but if you give me a sec I can find it."

"Thanks," Bernie said.

Polly went back inside the house. This time Bernie did not stay seated, but rose and began pacing back and forth. I felt tremendous energy building inside him, although I didn't know why. Tremendous energy began building in me, too, because it was building in him. I wanted to pace at his side but didn't want to interrupt him. I stayed by the table and gnawed the tip of my tail instead.

The slider opened and Polly came back, something in her hand. She set it on the table, a framed photograph of the stand-up kind you'd see on a desk.

"Evie was a wonderful photographer, in case you didn't know," Polly said. "And very artistic in many ways. She even had a successful show at one of the Pottsdale galleries, and who knows where that might have led? This is a self-portrait—and there's the name of the place you were asking about, down at the bottom. That's her handwriting, by the way, so distinctive."

Bernie read aloud. "'Overlooking Amoroso.'" He turned to Polly. "The Amoroso River?" he said.

"Yes," said Polly. "I've never been up there myself, but doesn't it flow through some sort of gorge?"

"The Amoroso Gorge," Bernie said.

"That's the name," Polly said. "About a month after Evie took this she went back again—hoping to get enough material for a second show, if I remember right—and that's when it happened."

"What did?" said Bernie.

"She went too close to the edge, lost her footing, and fell all the way to the bottom." Polly closed her eyes, kept them closed for much longer than a blink. Then they opened, glistening just a bit, and she said, "They never found her. We ended up burying an urn with a lock of her baby hair." Polly's eyes glistened a little more.

"The body was never found?"

Polly shook her head. "They dragged the river for days with no result. Then they went back in the summer when the water level was lower and tried again, but nothing. Well, not nothing. They did find her tripod, totally wrecked. The lack of any . . . remains was apparently not unusual, not with all the animal life in the desert."

Bernie gazed at the photo. A woman, somewhat like Polly but younger and with bigger eyes and a bigger mouth, stood with her back to the edge of a cliff in a way that somehow made my eyes want to keep checking out the emptiness behind her. She was dressed like a rodeo cowgirl—my one rodeo experience, brief but memorable, being how I know about rodeo cowgirls, who dress fancier than the regular cowgirls Bernie and I come across from time to time—with her hat hanging over the back of her neck. The sun was just rising behind her and off to one side, and her face was partly in darkness and partly red gold. The empty space behind her was also dark, as were the cliffs on the far side of the gorge, dark except for the red-gold rim.

"Amazing, huh?" Polly said. "She loved to work at dawn."

Here was where Bernie would normally say yeah, or at least nod his head. Instead he said, "Who was with her?"

"With her? I don't understand."

"When it happened," Bernie said. "When she fell."

"No one," said Polly. "She always went on these photo shoots alone."

Bernie turned quickly from the photo and faced her. "But how do you know what actually happened? Losing her footing, falling into the gorge, all of it?"

"Oh, there was a witness who saw the whole thing," Polly said. "A hiker who'd evidently been camping on the other side of the gorge and was just getting up. He was the one who summoned help. And didn't he actually rope his way down to the bottom first, hoping to save her? He even injured himself, I think, cutting his face quite badly."

"How do you know that?"

"The sheriff from up there was very nice about keeping me in the loop."

"What was his name?"

"Theffles. Gus or Gussie, I think. I could probably look it up if it's important."

"How about the name of the witness?"

"Hmm. Mitchie from California? But don't quote me. And Bernie? I'm not sure what you're doing with all these questions."

"Join the club," said Bernie, which I didn't get at all. For one thing, there was no club, just me and him. For another thing, there never would be. "Did Evie have any children?"

"No. She never wanted them. Neither did I. Then."

"Was she married?"

"Divorced. Just the once. She wasn't the type to keep on making the same mistake. Unlike her sister." Polly's gaze went to Bernie, then quickly away when he noticed.

Bernie went back to looking at the picture. Polly rose, walked over to the pool, stood over the unlucky gator, now sort of tangled in the pool ladder, kind of like a green raincoat. Suddenly she snapped her fingers and turned.

"Whoa!" she said. "Did someone find the knife down in Amoroso Gorge?"

Bernie looked up. "No, it's nothing like—" And then he stopped himself. "I don't know the answer to that question. But maybe you can help me with it."

"How?" Polly said.

"Do you remember Rocket Saluka?"

When humans get nervous their smell changes, and right away. They might as well say, Hey, I'm getting nervous. Which they never do, but it doesn't matter, not when I'm around. In short, Polly got nervous.

She licked her lips. "No. Not really."

"Look, Polly, I don't care if you bought weed from him, or—"

"I never did."

"What about Evie?"

"Absolutely not. She never touched drugs in high school."

"What about after that?" Bernie said.

Polly gave him a long look. "I'm not sure I like this new you after all," she said.

Twenty-seven

A new Bernie? And somehow not likable? I gave his feet, which happened to be close by, a quick sniff sniff, smelled nothing new whatsoever. Same old Bernie feet, same old Bernie sneaks, and it doesn't get any better than that. Bernie's smell is the best human smell out there, standard male of the fresh and clean type—actually not as common as you might think—plus salt, pepper, old leather, a dash of bourbon and a funky layer way down deep. A smell in some ways not too different from my own. But summing up: more likable does not exist, my friends.

Bernie met Polly's unfriendly gaze with a gaze that while not super friendly was still in the friendly ballpark. "It's my fault," he said. "In this business you can get locked into an interrogating sort of routine that ends up nowhere."

"What are you saying?"

"I'm saying I should have started more like this," Bernie said. He cleared his throat, ahem ahem. "We ran into Rocket Saluka the other day. He was unrecognizable, incoherent, down and out. Then before we could do anything for him he went missing. Later it developed that someone else was also trying to help him, and that person also went missing, and ended up dead. I think it was murder although the medical examiner won't sign on for that. My guess is that Rocket's now in danger, too, meaning not only from himself. Chet found the knife under Rocket's tent at the homeless camp in the old rail yard. It's our only clue, which has now led to your sister."

Wow! All that had happened? Why wasn't Polly clapping her

hands? The case was now so clear in my mind, clearer than any I could remember. There was the gator case, of course, and . . . and . . .

Meanwhile the scent Polly had been giving off from the get-go, a woman and man sort of scent, if you see what I mean, was gone. Bernie, too, had been giving off a bit of the same sort of scent although of the man and woman kind, but his was pretty much still there. Women and men and men and women is a huge subject, better left for later, or possibly never.

"Why should I do anything for Rocket Saluka?" Polly said.

"I can't say any more than I have already," said Bernie.

Polly glanced around her . . . her territory! Well, well. I'd never thought about it that way before. We had our territory, too, me and Bernie, our place on Mesquite Road. The whole Valley was also our territory in a way. Only fair to add that. Plus the desert all around. Just so you know. Back to Polly and her very nice, although kind of teeny, territory. Her gaze rested on the gator, now deflated and tangled in the pool ladder, as I might have mentioned.

"What happened there?" she said.

"Um," said Bernie.

"Did Chet do that?"

"Not that I saw. And I'm sure he didn't mean it. I'll replace it, of course."

"Please don't. It's a leftover."

"From what?"

"Hubby number two. Sums him up very nicely." She turned to me. "Thanks, Chet."

Things can change fast in this life, and often for the better. I moseyed over to Polly and sat on her foot. She made a little grunt, kind of surprised and pleased, and stroked my neck, just the once but very nicely. Then, with her eyes still on me, she said, "We didn't know Rocket, either of us, back at Chisholm.

And I never got to know him well, not really. Just through Evie. She believed he had a sweet nature, but there was something a little off about him, in my opinion."

"When was this?" Bernie said. "When did Evie get to know him well?"

"I don't have all the details, not nearly. Evie and I were close when we were together, but there were often these long gaps. Hubby number one and I moved to LA for a few years. He inherited a bunch of money and thought it would be a ticket into the movie business. Before they were done fleecing him I came back alone, and Rocket was in Evie's life."

"In what way?"

"If I tell you will you promise not to go all judgmental?"

"Can something like that even be promised?"

"I don't know. I'd have to think about it."

"The problem is we may not have much time."

Polly took a deep breath and let it out with a sigh. "Please remember the context. Evie was an artist and a free spirit who'd never hurt a living soul." Polly gave Bernie a narrow-eyed look. "You're about to say what about Mr. Kepler."

"You're much quicker than I am," Bernie said. "But didn't he deserve it?"

Polly's scent changed. The woman and man thing was back in play. "If I ever get another chance I'll make it work, so help me."

Bernie looked down.

Polly picked up her cup and took a gulp, like she'd suddenly gotten very thirsty. "Weed was everywhere then—like now, except not legal. Evie got to thinking it might help her see things in a fresh way, artistically speaking. The problem was, given her type of personality, one thing led to another and she got in a bad space." Polly drank what was left in her cup, which didn't seem to be much. Bernie poured what he had left into hers.

"And Rocket was her dealer?" he said.

"At first." Polly sipped her tea. "He did some taxi driving back then, kind of a useful side gig for someone in his business, and one day he picked her up. That was the beginning. He fell crazy in love with her and maybe she even loved him back in one form or other. He was very good looking in that vulnerable way some women like—not your kind of good looking, Bernie."

"Uh, I wouldn't say I, ah . . ."

Whatever he wouldn't say didn't get said. Polly shook her head at some thought she'd had and went on.

"Also he treated her beautifully, like an object of devotion. And the drugs were free—no leaving that out. Evie wasn't poor or anything like that but her divorce settlement wasn't the greatest." Polly smiled a small smile. "My current one's much better, but I've had more practice."

Bernie smiled his own small smile.

"But just from seeing them together as they went down that druggy road," Polly said, "I came to a theory about people getting screwed up on drugs." She glanced at Bernie. "Me running my goddamn mouth. Were you always such a good listener, Bernie?"

"No and still not," Bernie said. "What's your theory?"

"Just that there are two kinds. The ones who are already screwed up and the drugs take them to the bottom, and the ones who simply get screwed up by the drugs. Evie was the second kind and Rocket's the first. So there came a time—this was after one of those weekend mushrooms and moonlight and seeing the face of God and who knows what else binges at that hogan of his—when Evie just went cold turkey. She'd gotten terribly scrawny but now she started putting weight back on and looking more like her old self." Polly pointed to the photo. "Her art got better, too, like a sign she was on the right road. That was taken maybe three or four months into her recovery. Evie was doing so well."

Then came a long silence. Sometimes in one of our interview situations folks break these long silences with something that gets Bernie real interested, but this silence just went on and on, the only sound a soft but somehow pleasant hissing from the direction of the gator. Finally Bernie spoke.

"Did Rocket go cold turkey, too?" he said.

Polly shook her head. "He went the other way."

The other way from cold turkey? That had to be hot turkey! I'd had turkey both ways, loved them the same. My grip on the case tightened like you wouldn't believe. Nothing remained except the grabbing of the pant leg. I inched a little closer to Polly, just waiting for Bernie's signal.

"So they stopped seeing each other?" Bernie said.

"Not exactly. I think Rocket did move out—he'd been living at her place for a year or so."

"Where was that?"

"She was renting a casita at the Gila Hills Resort."

"Where's that?"

"Out past the old Burdette Ranch, where they used to shoot all those Westerns," Polly said. "The resort was kind of run-down then. I don't even know if it's still there."

Bernie drummed his fingers lightly on the table. That meant his hands were helping out with the thinking, always a good sign. "You said something about a hogan?"

"That's what Evie called it. Maybe it wasn't a real authentic hogan, more like—what would you call it?"

"A weekend place?" Bernie said.

"I was thinking more along the lines of a retreat," said Polly. "Why would you call it a weekend place?"

"That's how a witness referred to it," Bernie said.

"A witness to what?"

"That's just our term for interviewees."

"Like me."

"This particular one was not at all like you," Bernie said. "And retreat might be on the money. Do you know where it was?"

"Somewhere without electricity. I had a big lantern Evie borrowed. It held a charge for the longest time." Polly's eyes misted over. "I loved how she borrowed stuff from me." She wiped her eyes with the back of her hand. "I miss that."

Bernie nodded. Meanwhile my gator had stopped hissing and the only sound came from Bernie's fingers, lightly drumming again.

"I'd like to borrow something, too," he said.

"What?" said Polly.

Bernie pointed to the photo.

"Of course," she said.

Bernie picked it up and rose. I rose right with him.

"Do you remember the name of the gallery where Evie had her show?"

"Celare Artem," said Polly. "It's in Pottsdale. Evie thought the name was ironic."

"How so?"

"Celare Artem comes from this old saying about the art is in hiding the art. That wasn't her at all, as you can see from the photo."

Bernie studied it. "You can?" he said.

"Do you know what we're missing?" Bernie said.

I knew the answer to that one. Treats. Snacks. Food of any kind. There wasn't a scrap, a morsel, a tidbit, in the car. Meanwhile we were riding up a long curve with not a single fast food place in sight, just a low sprawling house or two and after that a ranch with weathered fence rails along the road and weathered buildings in the distance.

"A theory of the case," he said, a disappointing answer in

my opinion. "Boots on the ground is one thing. Eye in the sky is another."

Uh-oh. Things were taking a dark turn. Eye in the sky sounded scary. Was this a choice? I was much happier with boots on the ground.

"Got to have both." He smiled at me. "We've been too bootish, big guy. Let's focus the eye in the sky on one little sequence—you dig up the knife, Padre Doug has a strong re-action to the sight, and soon after goes to Snakehead Canyon and whatever happened to him happens. What other moves did the padre make?" He glanced my way. "Can you feel a theory struggling to be born?"

It was then that I began to worry about him. The solution came at once. He was famished and therefore not himself. I gazed outside, hoping my hardest for fast food, the faster the better.

"Interested in the ranch, huh?" he said. Which wasn't it at all. "That's the old Western Studios ranch. John Ford worked there—and so did Wyatt Earp, as a consultant. I wonder if ol' Wyatt ever had a theory of the case, back in his marshaling days."

John Ford? Wyatt Earp? Both new to me. Perps, perhaps? If so they didn't know what was coming.

We drove on, the outside world passing by very fast, the beast gripping the road the way it did, the kind of grip no road would soon forget. The ranch vanished and we entered hilly country with lots of trees.

"Here's the start of a theory. We know Rocket made a con-fession to Padre Doug—a confession in the religious sense. We don't know what Rocket said but we do know from Pepita that the padre was worried about him. Did he go to Snakehead Can-yon to meet Rocket? Or was it to check out some detail from the confession? There's also the possibility that . . ."

Bernie went silent. We turned off the road and onto a long gravel drive with a few small adobe casitas set back in the trees, and stopped before another adobe building, slightly larger, with a sign over the door, one of those thick wooden signs where the writing is made with a branding iron. I've seen that done, and I've also seen—just the once—a branding iron in another sort of action. Just a glimpse, really, since I'd quickly left the corral and crawled way under the Porsche, not the beast but the one before, with the martini glass decals.

Bernie read the sign. "Gila Hills Resort."

We parked and went to the door. Bernie knocked. We waited. He knocked again.

"Hold your horses," called a woman inside.

An old woman, and none too healthy, which my nose and ears knew right away although the information didn't reach my mind at once, on account of the horses issue taking up all the available space in my head. Then came the sound of slow, slippered feet moving on a tile floor, not the kind of smooth, gleaming tile you see in the lobby of the Ritz on your one and only visit to that establishment—a lobby featuring some tall potted trees, behind which who would even dream of lifting a leg?—but the soft and pitted reddish brown tile you find in old ranch houses in these parts.

The door opened. An old woman—just as I'd expected—looked out, but as I hadn't expected she was an old woman of the on-the-ball type. You could see it in her eyes.

"Ten dollar surcharge for dogs," she said. "And you clean up after them."

"Very reasonable," said Bernie. "But we're not customers."

"Then why are you knocking on my door?"

"That depends," Bernie said. "Were you here seven years ago?"

"Who's asking?"

Bernie handed her our card. She reached into a fanny pack she wore on her front, fished out glasses, stuck them on her nose, and peered at the card.

"So damn smeary I can't see a blessed thing," she said.

"Let me help," said Bernie, and he did something amazing, namely removing the glasses, very gently, cleaning them on the hem of his shirt—the one with the surfing palm trees, a favorite of mine on account of the big smiles on the faces of the palm trees—and handing them back to the woman.

Her mouth—those teeth so yellow!—opened like some pointed remark was on the way, but nothing came. She put the glasses back on. "That's better." She examined the card. "A private eye with flowers?"

Bernie shrugged his what-can-you-do shrug.

"Haven't had a private eye here in some time," the woman said. "I used to get lots—working adultery cases—but no more. Are adultery cases not still a thing—" She checked the card and added, "Bernie?"

"Maybe not the cases," Bernie said.

"But adultery marches on?"

"As far as I can tell."

"So what are you doing here? Setting up a touch of adultery of your own or investigating someone else's?"

"Neither," Bernie said. "We're interested in a former renter of yours, from at least seven years back, as I mentioned."

"Why?" said the old woman.

"Her name came up in a missing persons case. We're following the leads."

"Who's missing?"

"Rocket Saluka."

"Don't know him."

"How about a priest named Doug Plumtree?"

"Nope. Who's this former renter?"

"Evie Grace."

"Ah," said the old woman. "Evie."

"I'm guessing you liked her."

"Oh, yes."

"How come?"

"Are you trying to harm her in any way?"

"It's my understanding that she's dead."

"Of course she's dead," said the old woman. "The dead can still be harmed—by gossips and rumormongers and damn liars. If you don't know that you don't know much."

"We have no interest in harming her," Bernie said.

"Who's this we you keep talking about?"

"Me and Chet. We're a team."

"You and the dog?"

"Correct."

The woman turned, took her first close look at me. "Why don't you come in?" she said. "It's hot as hell out here. I'll waive the ten bucks."

Bernie laughed. We went inside.

"Beer?" said the old woman. We were now in the kitchen of the old woman's apartment behind the office.

"That would be nice, uh . . ." Bernie said.

"Stella," the old woman said, her glasses now pushed up on top of her head, her hair white and kind of sparse. "I'm not talking your hopped-up newfangled beer. I'm talking old-fashioned beer."

Stella rose from the kitchen table and opened the fridge, only a few steps away, her kitchen being very small and very cold, an AC window unit blasting away. "The old-fashioned kind of beer that made America great," Stella went on, grabbing two longnecks and plunking them on the table. "Twist-offs but you'll have to do the twisting. My hands aren't stepping up these days."

Hands not stepping up? Some humans can walk on their hands—Weatherly, for example, on a bet at the Valley PD picnic—but had Stella been thinking of twisting off the bottle caps while walking on her hands? How amazing would that have been, but it didn't happen. Bernie twisted off the caps in the normal way and they clinked bottles.

"Old-fashioned beer," Bernie said.

"Down the hatch," said Stella, and she took a nice long swallow. She sat down with a grunt, landing heavily in her chair. "Take a load off."

Bernie sat on the other side of the table. I got myself in between. And what do you know, practically under my paw, a Cheez-It! Did you know we have Cheez-Its and Cheetos in these parts? Who would want to live anywhere else?

Meanwhile Stella was giving Bernie a close look.

"You're good with people," she said.

"I wouldn't say that."

"Course not. Proves my point. But here's the thing." She gestured at Bernie with her bottle. "Some people are good with people cause they're crafty. Others are good with people cause they're just plain good. Which one are you?"

Bernie raised his hands, palms up, and said nothing.

"I grew up on a ranch," Stella said. "Way back when. And we had dogs, lots of 'em. Working dogs, hunting dogs, watchdogs, even a pet or two. I know dogs." She glanced at me. "I look at this big fella and I know the answer to my question."

Stella held out her bottle. They clinked again. "To all the dogs," Stella said.

Bernie nodded. "I think of them as the nation within the nation."

True, but had he ever mentioned that to anybody but me? Not that I remembered.

"The nation within—love it," Stella said, taking another big swallow. She licked her foamy lips. "Misled you just a titch back there."

"Oh?" said Bernie.

"In the matter of Rocket Saluka. Didn't actually lie, mind you. You said you're lookin' for Rocket Saluka and what did I say?"

"You didn't know him."

"Absolutely true. Not in the sense of knowing what makes him tick. Wouldn't even call him a casual acquaintance. But if instead you'd of asked if I knew of him, the answer mighta been different. Supposing I'd decided to own up to the truth, which I might not of. Before I had a chance to size you up, if you're still with me. Follow my drift?"

"I think so."

"Then you're thinking, Bernie, my man, time to brush up on the old interrogation technique."

"I am now," Bernie said. "And I'd like to hear everything you have to say about Rocket. How do you want me to phrase it?"

"Ha!" said Stella. "First I need to know what he's done."

"Done?"

"Musta done something bad. Why else would you be looking for him?"

"He's missing and we've been hired to find him. The only bad thing he's done that we know of is being in possession of a stolen knife that he himself didn't steal." Bernie took the flip knife from his pocket and laid it on the table.

"I'll be damned," Stella said.

Twenty-eight

"God, I hate that thing," Stella said.

"Why?" said Bernie.

"Why? It's a switchblade knife is why. Ever seen one in action?"

"Yes."

"Then you don't need me to explain. A knife is worse than a gun. I'm talking about the pure savagery."

Bernie nodded, just a slight little nod. "Did you ever see this particular knife in action?"

"Of course not," Stella said. "It was Evie's. Evie didn't have a speck of violence in her. She wasn't even sure how to make the blade come out. I remember doing it for her, right here in this room."

Stella reached for it with one of her crooked hands, fumbled around a bit, pressed the silver button. The tipless blade sprang out.

"Whoa," she said. "What happened there?"

"Good question," said Bernie.

She laid the knife on the table, the blade still exposed.

"Back when I was just a kid on the ranch," she said, "when my dad could still afford ranch hands, two of them got into a knife fight in the barn. I saw the whole thing through the window."

"That's pretty bad," Bernie said.

Stella shrugged. She picked up her bottle, found it was empty. Bernie went to the fridge and got two more.

"Plying me with liquor?" Stella said.

"I'd never ply with your own liquor. We supply the liquor when we're plying. That's rule one."

Stella laughed. She had a high little laugh, kind of like Esmé's. Was Stella the Esmé type, just older? Had to be, with that laugh. I yawned in her direction, sending a message. Meanwhile Bernie had twisted off the caps and Stella was downing another big swallow. She gestured at the knife with her chin.

"Do you know the story of this knife?" she said.

"Tell me."

"A nice story, actually. One night—this was after Evie had finally kicked that pretty boy out and gotten straight—I told her about this creep we had in number eight who'd peeked up my skirt that day when I was on a ladder sawing off a hanging branch." She took a quick glance at Bernie. "Some time back, this was, when the sight might still have been a draw."

"Um, I'm sure, uh—"

"Cut the crap," Stella said. "In any case, it reminded Evie of a time back in high school when she'd dealt with a similar creep—a teacher, no less—by purloining—her word, not mine—his prized switchblade away from him. Such a ballsy gal." Stella shook her head. "Do you believe that only the good die young?"

"It just seems that way to the ones left behind," Bernie said. "How did she die?"

"All I really know I heard from Polly—that's her sister—when she came to get Evie's things. Early one morning poor Evie went to some gorge up north to take pictures and fell off a cliff. They never found the body. That's about it."

"Did you happen to see her leave?" Bernie said.

"No. But that wasn't unusual. She was always gone before dawn on picture taking days." Stella's eyes got one of those looks that meant she was taking a little trip inside her head. Bernie was silent till she came back out.

"What was that thought?" he said.

Stella's head went back. "My god," she said. "Now you want to root around in my mind? Is that a private eye thing?"

Bernie nodded, just slightly.

Stella stopped looking so annoyed. Then she sighed. "I was just thinking about not seeing her leave. The thing is I'm not sure she went alone."

"No?" Bernie said.

"This was after she'd thrown Rocket out, but there was a bit of a commotion that night. Her casita's the farthest one, all the way to the back where I butt up against state land, but I thought it came from there."

"What kind of commotion?" Bernie said.

"Shouting. Maybe a door slamming. That kind of thing."

"Did it wake you?"

"Can't say that it woke me. I've never been a good sleeper. I think I started to get up but then things went quiet again, back to normal."

"So you didn't check it out?"

"I would have," Stella said, "but if stuff was going on I was pretty sure I knew what it was. There'd been something similar a few weeks before."

"Like what?" Bernie said.

"Rocket came sniffing back in the night, the way a certain type of man will. I only know because Evie told me a few days later. She let him in on account of how sorry he was and the rest of it—the age-old BS. Evie was doing so well but I knew that if she allowed him in her life again he'd take her back down. I told her she'd be a damn fool and a loser, laid it on pretty thick. Here's something about Evie that made her different from most people. You could get through to her. That very minute—this was out front of her casita where I was making my rounds with the watering can—she took out her phone and told him never to come back and if he did she'd take out a restraining order. So my thought was that on that later night, the night of the commotion, he'd come by again—but this time she'd been strong."

"Can I take a look at the casita?" Bernie said.

"Sure, but there's nothing to see."

We walked on a gravel path that curved through a eucalyptus grove—the lovely smell making me a bit dizzy—and got weedier the farther we went. The path ended at a casita where the door was blue with painted puffy clouds.

"This is it," Stella said. "Number eleven. At one time I was going to give them each a cutesy name but I couldn't come up with eleven cutesy names so I settled for numbers instead."

She took a key ring from her fanny pack and unlocked the door.

"Is anyone staying here?" Bernie said.

"Uh-uh," said Stella. "Slow time of year."

She pushed the door open and we went inside. A tidy little place with tidy little rooms—bedroom, bathroom, kitchen, and a living room with a blackened kiva fireplace. Bernie loves kiva fireplaces, always says we're going to have one built in our own living room as soon as we get some cash. Would that be anytime soon? I sniffed the air for the scent of cash—a papery inky sweaty combo, unmissable—and detected zip. Meanwhile Bernie was gazing up at something dangling on a hook high up on the adobe chimney. At first I didn't recognize it and then I did. I'd seen one before—on a case involving Lake Geronimo, the PD dive team, and an unlucky perp, name of Butchie—although that one hadn't been blackened with fireplace smoke.

Bernie pointed. "What's that?"

Stella looked up. "Evie's snorkel. Polly must've missed it when she packed up Evie's stuff, and it was part of the decor by the time I noticed. No one complains. Maybe it gives off some sort of vacation-type vibe."

"Was Evie a diver?" Bernie said.

"She had been, but earlier in her life. In fact, there's a photo I can show you, if you want."

"I do," said Bernie.

Back in the office, Stella had some framed pictures hanging behind her desk. She took one off the wall.

"I got the feeling Evie had money problems now and then. One month—this was when her work was just starting to sell—I took this instead of rent." She handed the photo to Bernie.

He held it the way he always did at times like this—so I could see, too. And what I saw was a boat out on the water, kind of a big one. Actually just the back of the boat was in the picture. There was writing on it, and lower down a sort of platform hung over the water. A man and a woman, both wearing bathing suits, sat on the platform, diving masks pushed up on top of their heads, with dangling snorkels off to the side. The man was smiling and looking at me. The woman, not smiling, was looking into the distance. Lying on the platform in between them was a big fish with a silver spear stuck right through its head from one side to the other. The woman was the same woman from the dawn photo. That had to be Evie, unless I was way off track—which can happen if there are no smells around—looking a bit younger in this picture. The man—a real big, muscular dude with a deep tan— seemed familiar but I couldn't place him. That was as far as I could take it on my own. Oh, I left out one thing, namely the pool of blood on the platform, not big, to one side of the fish's head.

"Taken off Catalina," Stella said. "She told me she used a camera floating on a buoy. The remote control's hidden behind the fish. I like it but I don't love it—maybe because of the title." Stella pointed to some writing at the bottom. "Catch Slash No

Release. Why would she write out the word slash instead of using the slash sign?"

"I don't know," Bernie said. "Did you ask her?"

"It just occurred to me now," said Stella.

"Was Evie married when she took this?"

"I believe so."

"Is that her husband?"

Stella shook her head. "That's Mitch, her free-diving instructor. The kind of diving where you hold your breath. She loved free diving, could go down eighty feet. Apparently Mitch could do two hundred feet or more."

Bernie pointed to Mitch's smiling face. "There's no scar."

Whoa! The pipe bomb dude? Bernie was way ahead of me. I bring other things to the table so no worries.

Meanwhile Stella's eyebrows, white and thin, rose in surprise, or maybe confusion. "Should there be a scar?"

"Depends on the timeline."

"I don't understand," Stella said.

"Same," said Bernie. "Who was Evie's husband?"

"The name, you mean? She never mentioned it, not to me. Some rich guy, I assume from California."

"How do you know he was rich?"

"That's his boat. Maybe I don't love the picture but I do love the name of the boat. I think it's all about how special this planet is and how we need to protect it, thoughts I've been having more and more."

Bernie leaned in closer to read the gold writing on the back of the boat, maybe not easy to do on account of the gold not standing out much against the white paint of the . . . the stern! Wow! Boating lingo, and it came to me just when I needed it. What if all sorts of things started coming to me, like a fast-flowing river through my head? That actually sounded scary. I decided to stop it from happening at the very first sign or even before.

Bernie, squinting a bit, read the name. "*Rare Earth.*'" His eyes were still on the photo but now they had a distant look, reminding me of Evie's eyes as she sat there on the platform.

"Can we borrow this?" Bernie said at last.

"Sure," said Stella. "Although I don't see what it has to do with Rocket Saluka."

"Same," said Bernie.

We drove away from Gila Hills Resort but hadn't gone far when Bernie pulled over to the side and got on the phone. A voice spoke on the other end, a voice I knew. "Please leave a message."

"Polly," Bernie said. "Call me as soon as you can. We need the name of Evie's ex-husband."

Then we just sat here, Bernie gazing at the photo and me smelling a javelina somewhere nearby. Was there time to hop out and sniff around? I was leaning toward yes—so often the right answer!—when Bernie flipped the photo over and checked the back.

"What's this?" he said.

I saw a bunch of squiggles, all in pencil on a piece of cardboard backing. Bernie checked the front again, and then returned to the back.

"Looks like her writing, maybe after a few drinks, or . . ." He went silent, sort of lost himself in those squiggles. "Whoa! Is it a map?" Bernie began tracing the squiggles with his finger, a finger that seemed to be shaking a bit, which I didn't believe for a single moment.

"What's this number? The writing's so unclear, like she could barely grip the pencil. And why on the back of the photo? Did she just grab whatever was handy? Maybe following some sort

BARK TO THE FUTURE | 277

of instruc—" He went silent, leaned his head to one side, had another look. We do the same head lean in the nation within. I began to feel hopeful about whatever was going on.

"Six six nine?" he said. "And if you follow this line, it comes to a little doodle that . . . that looks like a gas pump?"

He turned to me, eyes widening. I felt his heart beating faster. Mine revved up right away. We're a team, me and Bernie.

"A gas station at a crossroads! Remember that, Chet?"

I did not. And I didn't even try. Bernie was remembering strongly enough for two.

"How did Kepler put it? A miserable little desert crossroads? Something like that. The point is he met Rocket at a gas station near the, quote, weekend place. Weekend place meant ironically, but by Kepler? Or by Rocket?" Bernie made a backhand motion, like he was shooing off something bothersome, and turned back to the squiggles. "Got to be route 669, big guy. And at the crossroads what do we see? This dotted line that ends at an X."

He stepped on the gas. The beast roared like never before, much closer to a howl, and almost left me and Bernie behind.

Twenty-nine

"Does this look like a miserable desert crossroads to you?" Bernie said.

We pulled up to the single pump at a gas station that showed signs of having once been bright blue but now was pretty much desert-colored. The wind does that to everything in these parts. A fattish tumbleweed ball rolled past us as Bernie got busy at the pump. No one was around, not even inside the station. The tumbleweed ball bumped into a rusty oil drum and got stuck. I had the feeling that the poor old tumbleweed was trying hard to keep rolling. There's all kinds of beauty in life, maybe even at the miserable end.

Bernie stuck the nozzle back in the pump, got in the car, spent another moment or two with the squiggles on the back of the dead fish photo, which was how my mind wanted to think about it, the dead fish being very sharp in my memory. "My guess is that this little line will swing around in the direction of Snakehead Canyon. But this line here—" He tapped the map with his fingertip. "—the broken one, leads to the X." He looked up, slowly ran his gaze across the open country. "And I think it starts right about there." He pointed to a small opening in a blackened cluster of thorny bushes, the kind of small opening that always looks promising to me. "What did Esmé say? Pirates always made a map so they could come back for the gold? Something like that."

Gold was suddenly in the picture? I knew right then we were going to be rich. The only question was how soon.

We rolled away from the pump, came to the crossroads, both roads two-lane blacktop, and took the narrower, potholey one a short distance to the thorny cluster. Bernie squeezed us through the small opening, the thorns making tiny shrieking sounds on the body of the beast, very unpleasant to the ears, although maybe noiseless to Bernie's. But then he surprised me.

"Nixon won't be happy about that," he said.

Whoa! Was his hearing suddenly on the upswing? I gave him a close look, saw nothing new, everything like always, meaning human perfection. His eyes were on the road ahead, more of a track than a road, unpaved, stony, rutted, with a tire track or two at first and then none. Bernie's body was relaxed but he had both hands on the wheel. Both hands on the wheel means something's up. I smelled the .38 Special in the glove box and felt pretty good about our chances. At one point we'd taken possession of some perp's .45—a genuine stopper, according to Bernie—but now it was gone, possibly on the bottom of the Gulf of Mexico. Imagine Bernie firing both of them at once! I had myself some fun in my mind with that scene as we bumped our way along the track, up a hill, across an arroyo with a tiny puddle of water in the middle, then along the crest of a ridge where the track gradually stopped being a track and became just like everything around it, meaning plain desert.

Bernie stopped the car and studied the map. Then he popped open the glove box, took out the binoculars, which he hung around his neck, the pocket flash, which he stuck in his pocket, no surprise there, and the .38 Special, which he tucked in his belt, also not a surprise. The surprise would have been if he'd stuck the .38 Special between his teeth, something that had actually happened once, one of the best sights of my whole life.

We walked around for a bit, Bernie peering through the binoculars, this way and that. A tiny human scent rode in on the breeze, the particular human scent that comes when a particular human hasn't taken a shower in some time.

"A weekend place?" Bernie said. "A retreat? A hogan? What exactly are we looking for?"

I waited to find out. At last Bernie pointed at some rocky outcrops, grayish and distant. "How about we try there?"

Brilliant. That was Bernie every time, knowing just what to do. We walked together across rough ground, never flat, and covered with rocks and more of those blackened thorny bushes than seemed right. The sun, behind us and low in the sky, began to turn the grayish outcrops reddish gold, reminding me of the face of the woman at the cliff's edge, meaning Evie, if I was following things right. Our shadows, mine and Bernie's, marched on in front of us, longer and longer. We were huge. The desert was ours. Well, maybe just for now.

"Remember the topic of the sermon Padre Doug was working on?" Bernie said after a while. "Male jealousy."

I had no clue what Bernie was talking about, although I did remember Padre Doug. Was he one of those odd humans you come across from time to time who aren't fans of Bernie? I thought so. Was that fact—him not being a Bernie fan—more important than how Padre Doug had ended up, down under a shelf of rock in the watery pool in Snakehead Canyon? I went back and forth on that, and finally decided it was not more important. But very, very close.

Sometimes out in the desert, small distant sights—like rocky outcrops, for example—turn out to be real big from close up. But not these rocky outcrops, which turned out to be about head height—Bernie's head height, if he stood on his own shoulders. Wow! What a thought! Was there any way that could possibly—?

"Chet? What's with the panting?"

Panting? Uh-oh. If there had been any panting I put a stop to it at once. We moved along the outcrops, which rose and fell like rocky, red-gold waves embedded in the earth. We came to the last outcrop and stopped. Bernie kicked softly at its base.

"It was just a hunch, big guy," he said. "A hunch that made sense, but those can be wrong." He turned back, his gaze on the wall of outcrops, and raised his voice. "Rocket! Rocket! Are you here?"

Ah. We were looking for Rocket? How nice to be in the picture!

"Rocket! Don't be afraid! We're here to help! Rocket!"

We listened. There was no sound but the evening breeze starting up, plus a plane somewhere way way up in the sky. Bernie turned to me.

"Smell anything?"

A tough one. The answer was I smelled everything there was to smell, which was plenty. Where to begin? At that moment I remembered something very important. I was a total pro. And where does a total pro begin? Not with the smell of dried-up flowers on the breeze, or a tortoise somewhere not too distant, or even the snaky smell under one of those thorny bushes, just steps away. No. A total pro begins with a smell he'd been smelling since we'd first driven onto the track, and was now much stronger: the smell of an unshowered human. I trotted back along the rocky outcrops, stopped in front of the largest one, where the unshowered human aroma was strongest. Not an unpleasant smell to me, although I'm pretty sure humans have a different take. Sometimes you'll see humans sniff under their arms and make a face or say, yikes. Imagine not liking your own scent! Where would you go from there?

But none of that's important. What's important is what I did next, namely sitting in front of the outcrop in the exact right spot from the smelling point of view.

Bernie glanced at me and went still. Then he moved to the face of the outcrop and began running his hands over it. This particular outcrop wasn't the flat wall kind, at least not completely.

It had stones sticking out from it here and there, some big, some little, like they'd somehow gotten caught. Scrawny plants grew in the wall as well, mostly around those sticking out stones. Bernie tugged at one of those plants. It didn't budge. He tried another, somewhat bigger, and got nowhere. He stepped back, checked the wall again, and moved to another scrawny plant, this one maybe the scrawniest and quite small. Bernie grabbed hold and gave it a mighty pull.

The plant turned out to be bigger than I'd thought and maybe not so scrawny. Also it wasn't really stuck at all and came out easily, Bernie staggering and almost falling. A few small stones came with it, and then a bigger one, all bumping down to the ground and revealing a dark hole in the face of the wall, right at my head height.

Bernie leaned forward and peered into the hole. I did the same, the two of us peering side by side. There was nothing to see but darkness. As for smells, the unshowered smell was now like an enormous balloon of aroma growing and growing. A weak red-gold beam of light from outside found the entrance and made a sort of swirling tunnel of red-gold dust. At the end of the tunnel two red-gold eyes were waiting. Then came a voice.

"You're dead men."

Rocket? No doubt about it. Once I hear your voice it's mine.

"D-E-A-Double D. Dead. Shoulda woulda coulda been dead a long long time ago. I shoulda woulda coulda done it personal. So how about—NOW!"

That NOW, so high and loud and piercing, was the scariest sound I've ever heard come out of a human, and I've heard plenty of scary human sounds, comes with the territory in this business. It seemed to echo back and forth across the desert, like it was coming from everywhere at once. And then, silence. Bernie put his hand on my back. Deep in this hole or cave or whatever it was, the red-gold eyes disappeared. Bernie stepped in front of me. A grunting sound came out of the darkness. Still facing the hole, his hands behind him, if you can picture it, Bernie pushed me down. A rock, baseball size, came flying out. Well, not flying, more like looping out, too slow to do any harm. It plopped down beside us.

"Rocket?" Bernie said. "No one's going to hurt you."

No answer came from inside. Bernie raised a leg and climbed into the hole. I passed him on the way. He switched on the pocket flash and swept the beam back and forth.

I've had lots of experience in caves and abandoned mines, but I'd never seen anything like this . . . retreat? Weekend place? Hogan? What had Bernie called it? I couldn't remember. The point is that inside this hole in the side of a rocky outcrop out in the loneliest part of the desert—although we ourselves are never lonely, me and Bernie—we had a comfy little den, with Indian-type rugs on the floor and on the walls, a mattress covered with an Indian-type blanket, a beanbag chair—those beans being remarkably easy to get at, by the way, although this probably wasn't the time—plus lanterns, not turned on, hanging from ceiling hooks, and a special camping toilet of a kind we'd tried out ourselves, Bernie doing the actual trying. What else? Empty food wrappers, empty bottles, and needles, all scattered around. A comfy little den, except for those things, especially the needles.

The flashlight beam found Rocket and stayed on him. Rocket looked the same as before, only worse. He was on his hands and knees on the floor, feeling around in a strip of dirt between two rugs, and muttering to himself.

"No more rocks to throw, you lucky bastards, no more rocks."

"Why would you want to throw rocks at us?" Bernie said.

Rocket began digging frantically, jabbing his fingers into the hardened dirt. "You know you killed her. You know, I know, he she it knows."

"Who got killed?" Bernie said.

"Who got killed? For the love of god!" Rocket looked up,

raising a handful of dirt, but not to throw at us. For a bad moment I thought he was going to eat it. Then his eyes fastened on Bernie. "Can't take your money, Bernie," he said. Then he toppled over and lay still, curled up in a ball, hands between his legs, eyes glassy, heart beating wildly.

We got Rocket out of his hole, mostly by dragging him, Bernie at the front and me sort of pushing from behind. The sky looked like it was on fire. Bernie hoisted Rocket on his shoulders and under that fiery sky carried him all the way back to the car. Everything darkened toward the end, finally leaving just a burning trace in Bernie's eyes.

"Drink," Bernie said.

Rocket, slumped in the shotgun seat, opened his eyes. "Can't take your money," he said.

"This is water," said Bernie.

He sat Rocket up, held a bottle to Rocket's cracked lips, tilted it. Rocket made some gurgling sounds. His eyes closed. He slumped back down.

Bernie glanced over at me. I was still standing beside the beast, waiting for the seating plan to get straightened out before we hit the road.

"Chet?" Bernie said.

The little shelf in back? No. Absolutely not. Out of the question. I made myself immovable.

Bernie smiled at me, just a tiny, quick smile, the color of the stars that were starting to spread across the sky. I hopped onto the little shelf in back.

We rolled through the crossroads, the gas station dark, no lights showing anywhere around. The beast sped up, not roaring, but just letting everyone know that roaring was possible. Rocket sat up, opened his eyes. From where I was—at least my head, wedged between the seats—I had a good view. Rocket turned to Bernie.

"I caught that damn ball."

"A thing of beauty."

"Forget beauty. Beauty gets it in the gut. I saved your ass."

"True. How can I pay you back?"

"Can't take your money. How come that don't get through?"

"There are other ways for paying back."

"Like?"

"Think of something you want. Maybe we can make it happen."

"Who's this we?"

"Me and Chet."

Rocket gazed down at me. "Lucky son of a bitch."

"I am," Bernie said.

"Not talkin' about you," said Rocket. His eyes closed. He slumped down.

"Did you have dogs growing up?" Bernie said.

No answer.

"When you were a kid," Bernie said.

Still no answer. We took a ramp onto a freeway and the night got brighter. The beast demanded the passing lane. We passed everybody. Once, over the roar, I thought I heard Rocket, his eyes still closed, say, "He kicked doggies."

Sometime later my own eyes closed. I heard Bernie on the phone, heard Weatherly, and after that the beast, and later: nothing.

Back in the Valley it was still night when we pulled up in front of a small lemon-colored house with a lemon tree in the yard.

The porch light turned on right away and Weatherly stepped outside, followed by Trixie. Not followed, exactly, Trixie somehow squeezing through the doorway first. Right there was the kind of thing that makes her so annoying. Squeezing through doorways first was my thing, not hers, but how do you get something like that across?

Rocket's eyes opened again. His head turned slowly to the porch where Weatherly and Trixie were standing.

"Am I dead?" he said, very softly.

"Very much alive," said Bernie.

"Bad news," said Rocket. He gazed at the small lemon-colored house. "Let me into heaven. This is the very last day."

Bernie got out of the car, walked around to the other side, helped Rocket with the door, with standing up, with walking to the house, with everything. I helped from the other side.

"Same what I told the padre," Rocket said. "Let me in."

"And what did he say?"

"Blah blah blah."

"What else did you tell him?"

"All my sins. Confession, for god sake. Didn't you use to be smarter?"

"Why did you come back from Mexico?" Bernie said.

"Got a free ride," said Rocket, and then his legs went out from under him. Bernie carried him in his arms the rest of the way, like a baby, Rocket's scraggly, tobacco-stained ponytail hanging down from the back of his bald head. Bernie's real strong of course, but Rocket, all bones and leathery skin, didn't look heavy.

There were two bedrooms in Weatherly's house, hers and a small one at the back. We took Rocket in there. Everything was neat and tidy. Bernie laid him on the bed. Weatherly switched off the light. She and Bernie left the room, but what was this?

Trixie seemed to be staying? Why? Was anyone more annoying? In short, I stayed, too.

Rocket lay on his back, at first with his eyes open, and then closed. His scrawny chest rose and fell. He had a funny way of breathing, with a faint whistle at the end of every breath. This little bedroom was dark, except for a weak light stream that flowed in through a slight gap in the curtains of the only window, the dark pink light of the Valley at night. Trixie sat on the floor at one end of the bed. I did the same thing at the other end. Her eyes, dark pink, were on me every time I checked. I waited for Weatherly to call from down the hall: Trixie, come to bed.

That did not happen. Instead, in a slow, deliberate, annoying way, Trixie yawned, stretched, and then climbed right up on the bed and lay down beside Rocket. Was this really happening? In my mind I went over my choices and found none. There was only one thing to do. I climbed onto the bed and squeezed my way in.

We all just lay there and breathed, Rocket with that faint whistle, and me and Trixie for some reason in the exact same rhythm with each other. I'd never met anyone as bothersome as Trixie, not even close. For example, after some time Rocket shifted in his sleep and one of his hands slipped down and rested on my side in a very nice way. But did that last long? Oh, no, far from it! Somehow—I have no idea how! I'm a hundred-plus pounder!— Trixie managed to inch me aside so that Rocket's hand ended up resting on her. Inching aside a hundred-plus pounder! Can you imagine? I was about to do something about it and in no uncertain terms, when Rocket spoke.

"Don't kick the doggie, Pop. The doggie's nice."

Then came more breathing, the faint whistle at the end growing fainter. After a while I realized that Trixie's rhythm was no longer with mine, but had changed so now it was right in time with Rocket's. Was that just one more bothersome thing or not? I was still going back and forth on that question when it hit me that the rhythm of my own breathing had changed, switching over to Rocket's rhythm, just like Trixie's. So therefore: not bothersome. And as a bonus I'd come up with a so-therefore—always Bernie's department—on my own.

We lay on the bed in the small back bedroom in Weatherly's house, breathing together in the dark pink night. It was all very peaceful until Rocket groaned, not at all loudly but somehow very scary, and I'm not the type who scares easily, if at all.

"Don't, Pop," he said. "That hurts Mama. Stop. Oh, god, oh please god."

Rocket's hand curled into Trixie's fur. She got scared. I could smell it. Trixie eased herself away, climbed down off the bed. I stayed where I was. Rocket's hand curled into my fur. Maybe it wasn't comfortable, but . . . but the poor guy. His grip on me strengthened and he groaned again, this groan ending in a little sob. Rocket's eyes stayed closed but dark pink tears appeared on his cheeks.

"Evie, oh, Evie," he said. "I can't help you. I'm sorry, love-bird. I did wrong. It's the same again, and I can't . . ."

Rocket went silent. His scrawny chest rose and fell. His cheeks got damper.

Bernie spoke from the doorway. I hadn't even known he was there. That wasn't me at all. I turned my head slightly. Bernie stood in the darkness of the hall with Weatherly slightly behind him, two shadows but somehow so solid.

"What couldn't you do?" he said, his voice very soft.

Rocket shook his head, just the tiniest movement. "Protect her. I couldn't protect her."

"From who?"

"One on one, no problemo. But what about when that god-damn driver comes bustin' in? Two against . . . against . . . Maybe if I take off it all mellows out? I'm Rocket. I run."

"But it didn't mellow out?" Bernie said.

"She grabbed the knife." Rocket groaned again.

"Who burst in?"

"I ran." He clawed at his face. "Rocket! Stop! Go back! Help!"

"Did you go back?"

His clawed hand froze in the air. "Too late. They're in the car." His voice sank to a whisper. "Snakehead."

"Snakehead?"

"Mitch said so."

"Mitch the diving instructor?"

"Inside is all nice and clean," Rocket said, "like nothing happened." His eyes opened. He sat up in a sudden way, his body, against mine, feeling for a moment like the body of a much stronger man. He twisted around toward Bernie. "But they dropped the knife in the grass and who finds it?" Rocket had still been whispering but now his voice rose to a shriek. "MVP!"

It was silent for a moment, although the remains of the shriek still seemed to linger in the air. "Who was with Mitch?" Bernie said. "Who was the other person?"

Rocket's mouth opened wide, a dark pink hole, but he didn't speak. Instead he let go of me and began to wail, a terrible wailing that grew louder and went on and on. He collapsed back on the bed and after a long time went quiet, just like that, all at once. Bernie came in and felt Rocket's chest. Then he took off Rocket's sneakers, horrible filthy laceless sneakers, full of holes. Weatherly tucked a pillow under his head. Rocket's scrawny chest rose and fell. We left the room, all of us. Weatherly closed the door.

Thirty

"We've got the Mitch who taught Evie to free dive," Bernie said, "the Mitch who was in on what sounds like her murder at Gila Hills Resort, and the Mitchie from California who witnessed her falling to her accidental death at the Amoroso Gorge, no remains ever found."

He poured coffee for Weatherly and for himself. We were in Weatherly's kitchen, the night still dark pink through the window, Trixie curled up at Weatherly's feet, Weatherly at the table, and me in the doorway, listening to Rocket breathing steadily if not strongly in the back bedroom down the hall.

"One and the same?" said Weatherly.

"Maybe I'm just thinking that because otherwise we'd be nowhere," Bernie said.

"Nope," said Weatherly. "My money's on you."

Good to know. I waited for her to pull a nice wad from her jeans pocket and hand it over, but that didn't happen, at least not right away.

"Have we got a last name?" she went on.

"There should be records from the Amoroso Gorge search." Bernie checked his watch. "That's now Fritzie's territory. I'll call him first thing."

"I got that," Weatherly said.

Their eyes met. Something very good was going on between them. I didn't know exactly what it was but I liked being around it.

"Is life plain crazy all the way down?" Weatherly said.

"You're talking about Fritzie's rise?" said Bernie.

"Yeah."

Bernie circled the table, stood behind Weatherly's chair, leaned down and kissed the top of her head. She smiled.

"I hear you," she said.

Whoa! Stop right there. I hadn't heard a thing from Bernie and Weatherly had? I checked her ears, normal human ears, even on the small side. Crazy all the way down. I began to get it.

Bernie patted Weatherly's shoulders. "You good with Rocket here for a bit?"

"Of course."

"I've got a hunch."

"What kind?"

"Geometric."

"Doesn't sound promising."

"More like a circle," Bernie said. "A circle closing."

"That's better," said Weatherly.

And not long after that we were out of there. The last thing I saw was Weatherly opening a drawer and taking out a box of ammo.

We drove through what was left of the night: Bernie, me, the beast, and the .38 Special, not in the glove box but tucked in Bernie's belt. What else? We'd borrowed Weatherly's mask and snorkel. Bernie has a mask and snorkel of his own at home—I'd carried them for him the day we went to the beach in San Diego, where we'd surfed, me and Bernie!—but we didn't swing by to pick them up. Were we in a hurry? That was my take. I leaned forward in the shotgun seat, my muzzle touching the windshield.

Bernie glanced at me and smiled. He was opening his mouth to say something when the phone buzzed.

"Bernie? It's Polly. Sorry to call at this hour but I just got your message. The one about Evie's husband. Her ex-husband. She divorced him years ago. He was a cheater of the indiscreet kind, which Evie thought made it even worse. We disagreed about that, and I was the expert. I'd dealt with both."

"The name, please," Bernie said.

"Luke Kincaid."

"Luke Kincaid from Chisholm?" Now Bernie, too, was leaning forward.

"Right," said Polly. "Kind of unusual—they weren't high school sweethearts or anything even close, hardly socialized at all back then. But a couple of years after Evie got out of college—she'd been living in one of those artsy Hudson Valley towns—she came back here and they got together. He went to a showing of hers in Pottsdale and bought something. That's how it started. I was so happy for her. And gradually not. He tried to give me a hug at Evie's funeral and I wouldn't let him."

"Luke went to her funeral?" Bernie was sitting back now, his face very hard.

"He cried," Polly said. "But why are you asking about him?"

"Tell me about Mitch," Bernie said.

"Mitch Inwood?" said Polly.

"I don't know his last name—the guy who taught free diving to Evie."

"Yes, Mitch Inwood. He works for Luke, or used to, doing what I'm not sure."

"How did he get the scar on his jaw?"

"I don't remember him having one, but I haven't seen him in years."

"Does Luke own a boat called *Rare Earth*?"

"I don't know if he still does. He kept it at his place in Catalina. Evie loved the boat. She said it almost saved the marriage.

Luke was aware of that, by the way. When he came crawling back he promised an even better and bigger one in her own name."

"He came crawling back?"

"A few years later. Meanwhile Evie had been through so much, gone down and was coming back up. She was a different person, beyond his reach. That didn't stop him from being quite insistent."

"Insistent how?"

"Showering her with gifts. Calling all the time. Even coming to her place uninvited."

"Her place at Gila Hills Resort?"

"I think so. My take was that he'd matured and finally realized what a special thing he'd lost. Evie just thought he couldn't bear rejection. But I don't get it. What's going on?"

"This works better if I ask the questions, Polly. You mentioned a witness at Amoroso Gorge—Mitchie from California."

"I think that's what Sheriff Theffles said. He knew the man—a hiker familiar with the territory."

"The hiker being Mitchie from California."

"Yes."

"Did the sheriff mention Mitchie's last name?"

"Not that I remember."

"Did you ever make the connection to Mitch Inwood?"

There was a long silence. Then very quietly Polly said, "Oh my god."

We stopped at the end of a rough track, parked the beast between two rotting gateposts with no gate between them. Bernie switched off the headlights and I saw a faint pale glow over in one corner of the starry sky. The glow seemed to have driven away all the nearby stars, leaving a blankness up there. In fact, more and more stars seemed to be dimming out. Big doings were going on high above. They came close to making me feel small. I hopped out of the car—a very energetic hop—and went right back to feeling like myself.

Bernie grabbed a few things—mask and snorkel, pocket flash, .38 Special—and walked with me through the gate toward those two enormous rocks, one black and round, the other red and burger-shaped, not touching but joined at the top by the coiled rock with a wedge-shaped head, a sort of rocky snake waiting up there. His phone buzzed.

"Hey," said Weatherly. "I spoke to Fritzie. He checked the records—not him personally, the actual checker being, quote, a firecracker little gal in the back office. Turns out there are gaps, probably the result of Gussie Theffles covering his tracks, although no one knows for sure. Bottom line—the report on the Amoroso Gorge investigation is MIA. Is that where you're going?"

"No." Bernie gazed up at the rocky snake. It seemed to have eyes. I shifted sideways and they were gone. "Amoroso Gorge is the alibi."

"Ah," Weatherly said. And then, after a pause, "Are you carrying?"

"Yup," said Bernie. "See you later."

"Holding you to that," said Weatherly.

The tip of the curve of the sun popped into view and the milky glow turned all sorts of colors, spreading slowly across the sky. An unusual sky with an enormous dark and foggy ball growing in the distance. Bernie spotted it, took another look, had some sort of quick thought. An odd smell was in the air, a smell I hadn't smelled in some time, a hard to describe smell, like dusty water. Monsoon? Yes, that was it. Monsoons brought a strong smell of dusty water, even from far away.

We moved on, out from under the rocky snake, up the easy slope to the cliff face, along it to the entrance to Snakehead Canyon. A sign hung on yellow tape crisscrossing over the opening. Bernie read it aloud. "'Closed for repair. Danger. Do not enter.'"

We entered, one at a time as before, Bernie in the lead as before, me taking over almost right away as before, as before so often being the way to go. The only difference was that then we'd had daylight beaming down from the top of the slot and now night was still lingering on. Bernie switched on the pocket flash, giving us glimpses of the sheer rock walls, the hard dirt path, the stray rocks, those odd red sand piles like rounded traffic cones. Somehow I felt way more closed in than I had the first time. I didn't need the flashlight, of course, could make my way perfectly well in darkness. But if Bernie wanted the flashlight then that was that. He was in a hurry, although we didn't seem to be moving any faster than we had the first time. The hurry was going on inside him. I could feel it.

Something glinted up ahead. Bernie steadied the light. A wheelbarrow, then another. Beyond them rose the rubble from the landslide and the big round boulder crashing down. Bernie pointed the beam up, revealing the steep canyon walls, our little light getting drowned in the brightening daylight at the top. A shovel poked out the side of the rubble pile. Bernie grabbed it. We worked our way over and through the rubble—me in no time, Bernie in plenty of it—and continued on the path, now sloping down and down. I smelled water, actually two kinds of water—normal water from farther down the trail and that strange dusty water from above. We rounded a corner and the blue pool appeared, now black.

At the edge of the pool Bernie put on the mask in one easy motion, like putting on dive masks wasn't at all new to him. He glanced over at me.

"Feel like a little dip?"

My tail started up right away. It felt like a little dip and so did I. Bernie kicked off his sneakers and tucked the barrel of the .38 Special into one of them. We were leaving the .38 Special behind? I felt a bit uneasy about that. Bernie switched off the flashlight and tucked it in his belt.

"Guaranteed waterproof, so we'll get our money back if it fails," he said.

Good news! My uneasiness vanished just like that.

We slipped into the water and began swimming side by side, perhaps not as fast as before, now that Bernie had the shovel in one hand. But we'd be fine as long as I didn't start steering him back to shore.

"Chet?"

I put a stop to it at once and swam on, minding my own, a total pro. How lovely the water was! Whoa! Not the right thought, Chet. This was work, not play. I tried not to feel so good, perhaps not with total success.

We bumped up against a flat rock at the far end of the pool, taking us by surprise in the darkness. Bernie raised himself and switched on the flash. We had light! He made a little grunt, the surprised kind, and then swept the beam along the rocky wall, stopping at the spot where we'd gone down and found Padre Doug. He set the flash down on the flat rock. Then he stuck the breathing end of the snorkel in his mouth and still holding onto the shovel swam along the light beam, me right beside him and slightly in the lead.

We reached the steep wall. Bernie sucked in a big breath through the snorkel. Then we dove down together, the light failing fast. But here's something interesting you learn if you work a lot at night or in abandoned mines, which of course I do: from just a murky clue or two your mind will fill in the rest, the mind being quite useful at times. So my mind could see the rocky slab, and under it the underwater cave where we'd found Padre Doug, tucked behind those basketball-size stones. Bernie rolled one aside, and then another. They sank slowly down to the bottom of the pool. We swam into the cave.

Thirty-one

At first, in the cave, I couldn't see a thing, not even with my mind helping out. But the next thing I knew I could. A milky kind of light was slipping in all around us, like a second dawn. Who's luckier than us, me and Bernie?

Meanwhile he was swimming deeper into the cave, which proved to be much bigger than I would have thought if I'd thought about it, which I hadn't. I was actually thinking that another breath of air would be nice, but if Bernie didn't need one then neither did I. I swam up next to him and . . . and what was this, way at the back? Some sort of longish canvas sack, the kind you might stick a tent inside when you had it all folded up. Tied to one end of the sack with a thick rope and lying on top of it was a big and very rusty barbell, the heavy kind you see in musclehead gyms. Bernie dropped the shovel. He took the skullhead switchblade knife from his pocket and pressed the silver button. The blade sprang out. He sawed through the thick rope. The two ends fell away. Bernie took hold of one end of the sack and began dragging it out of the cave. Not a very heavy sack: it seemed to be trying to float.

We got the sack out of the cave and swam toward the surface, Bernie kicking real hard and me—in a bit of a hurry now myself—helping from below. After what seemed a little too long, in my opinion, we burst through the surface and just breathed and breathed, side by side.

"You all right, big guy?"

Never better. We swam back to the other end of the pool,

Bernie towing the sack. Silvery morning light from above shone on the .38 Special, sticking out of Bernie's sneaker.

We climbed up on dry land. Bernie knelt by the sack. I got as close as close can be. He untied the line at the opening of the sack and peered inside. I did the same. There was a skull in that sack, a skull and some bones. Bernie removed the skull and then the bones, one by one, laying them gently on the hard-packed red earth at the edge of the pool. We'd seen skulls and bones before, comes with the job, but that doesn't mean you get used to it. I myself was ready to leave this place and take the beast on a long spin, but Bernie wanted to gaze at this skull and at these bones so I did the same. And what was this? Stuck in the top of the skull was a small piece of metal, somewhat toward the back, which was maybe why I hadn't spotted it right away. I barked my low rumbly bark.

Bernie leaned closer and saw what I saw. He skipped a breath, or maybe two. Then something very strange happened. A white bird flew down from above and landed on a ledge close by, a ledge sticking out from the canyon wall—not so sheer in this spot, and sort of supported by an unsteady-looking pile of boulders. The white bird folded its wings and gazed down at us. Birds have angry eyes, in my experience, but this one did not. I felt a little quiver under my paws.

Bernie took out the flip knife and pressed the silver button. Then he touched the little metal piece stuck in the skull with the broken end of the blade. The two parts lined up perfectly. I heard distant sounds that reminded me of surfing in San Diego. Bernie pocketed the knife and was rising when a voice spoke behind us, up the trail.

"You do good work, Bernie. I could have used someone like you in another scenario."

We turned real quick. Two men, both big, came out of the shadows and moved toward us. The real big one had a scar on his jaw and carried a rifle, the barrel pointing down. I caught a whiff of his minty mouthwash smell and so much came back to me at once: the pipe bomb, the horrible fish photo, and our first meeting, outside this very canyon. Mitch the diver. I was all set.

The other man, not quite as big, had just done the talking. He wore khaki pants and a wrinkle-free blue shirt, like he was on his way to brunch at a nice restaurant. It was Luke Kincaid.

Bernie didn't wait one more second. He dove for the .38 Special, sticking out of the sneaker. Bernie can be real quick when he has to be but Mitch was—not quicker, I won't go there, but before Bernie could grab the .38 Special, he'd raised the rifle and fired a round that blew the sneaker to bits and knocked our weapon into the pool where it sank with a tiny splash. Tiny, but somehow the surf sounds got louder. The white bird spread its wings and flew up and away.

Luke and Mitch came closer. Bernie rose, stood right beside me, gripped my collar. Luke gazed at the skull and the bones. Mitch's eyes were on Bernie and the rifle barrel was raised.

"You're the curious type or you wouldn't be doing what you do," Luke said. "So I suppose you want to know why."

"Because you're twisted inside," said Bernie. "Beyond redemption."

Mitch didn't like that one little bit. A muscle bulged in his face, rippling his scar, not quite hidden by the beard he was growing.

But Luke didn't seem to mind. "That's not very understanding. Put yourself in my place. I'd done some—what do they call it?"

"Self-analysis," Mitch said.

"Self-analysis," Luke said. "Not easy for aging jocks like you and me, Bernie. But I came to understand that I'd let Evie down in our marriage, maybe even been the unintentional cause of later troubles in her life." He raised a finger. "More important, that

I'd do better if she gave me a second chance. But she wouldn't listen, wouldn't even give me a chance. So I went up to her place in Gila Hills one night to try one more time."

"Sounds good," Bernie said. "But why bring Mitch along on such a loving expedition?"

The expression on Luke's face changed, got a little misshapen, more like Mitch's. "What makes you think Mitch was there?"

"Wasn't he?"

"See, I'm guessing your information comes from Rocket. Meaning you know where he is."

"Wrong," Bernie said. "My information comes from the scar on Mitch's face."

Mitch took a step forward. Luke put a hand on his arm and stopped him.

"Which one of you killed her?" Bernie said.

Luke and Mitch exchanged a glance. Luke spoke. "I'm the leader. But just imagine, Bernie. I show up to bow my knee and beg—leaving Mitch in the car, by the way. My intentions were good. But what do I find? She's with that lowlife nonentity. Lowlife and a coward. He ran off and then she just went crazy like women do, and grabbed that stupid knife. Which I lent her the money for, so many years before! Irony of ironies."

"You handed the money to Baca yourself?" Bernie said.

"Correct. Just innocent high school fun."

"Maybe. But it came back to bite him."

"Old Mr. Baca was greedy. He bit himself. And I'll have the knife, pretty please."

"Then you'll have to go downtown," Bernie said. "I turned it in to PD headquarters yesterday." Had we been downtown yesterday? Perhaps I'd been napping.

Luke's eyes shifted. "I don't believe you," he said.

"Want me to search him?" said Mitch.

"It'll be easier when he's dead," Luke said. He turned to Bernie. "You're dead, of course. I don't see any other way. But your dog here can live. All I need in exchange is Rocket's whereabouts. Maybe not a sweet deal, but at least a deal."

"The same deal you offered the padre?" Bernie said.

Luke looked surprised. "How could it be? He didn't have a dog. But it wouldn't have made a difference. Imagine my surprise when he called out of the blue and asked if—how did he put it?—my wife or former wife was still alive."

"You must've panicked," Bernie said.

"Never," said Luke. "So what's it going to be? Deal or no deal?"

All at once the surf sounds were much louder and the quiver in the earth was back, stronger and not stopping.

"I have your word about Chet?" Bernie said.

"I swear," said Luke.

"That's a relief," Bernie said.

The expression on Luke's face changed in a bad way, like something very nasty was coming up from below.

"Just having a little fun with you, Luke," Bernie said. "No deal."

Fun? Was this really a good time for—

"Mitch?" Luke said. "Shoot the dog."

Mitch pointed the barrel at my head.

"Move a bit thataway," Luke told him. "So it falls in the water."

Mitch took a few steps sideways. "Sure thing. No mess, no—"

That was when Mitch realized—and maybe Luke did, too—that they'd made a big mistake, namely taken their eyes off Bernie. He let go of my collar, whipped the flip knife from his pocket, freed the blade, and threw backhand style, all in one single blur. The knife spun once and then that broken blade sank deep in Mitch's neck with a ripping sound that was going to be hard to forget. Mitch looked kind of shocked and then had no look at all, sinking down and lying still.

Luke dove for the rifle. We all did, but Luke was closest and got there first. He rolled over, got his finger on the trigger, and—

And at that moment a frothing cliff of water burst through the trail opening at the other end of the pond, the sound drowning out everything. Luke cried out and scrambled away from the pool. I bumped Bernie my very hardest, bumped him toward the unsteady pile of rocks beneath the white bird's ledge. Then we were both clawing our way up. Well, me more like bounding and Bernie clawing. In no time I was on the ledge. Bernie! Faster! But he didn't seem able to go faster and meanwhile that wall of water was almost upon us. I got my front paws to the very edge and leaned down. Bernie looked up, feeling for a handhold. The water hit, like a tremendous river, wrapping itself around him from the waist down. Our eyes met. The look in his I'll keep to myself.

Bernie! Grab my collar!

He grabbed my collar. I felt the force of this river trying to pull my Bernie away, and fought with all my strength to stay on that ledge. Backward, Chet! Dig in! Back! Back! I pulled and strained and pulled and—and all at once Bernie popped up onto the ledge and lay facedown. I sat on top of him, which seemed like the right move at the time.

Meanwhile this river went boiling by, carrying all sorts of things with it—boulders, tree trunks, a telephone pole. But quite quickly it began to lose its force, and soon we had just a trickle, and then nothing, just silence.

"They say that's how it is with flash floods, and now we know for sure," Bernie said. "So we never have to do it again."

Bernie: they don't come any smarter.

We walked back out of Snakehead Canyon, finding Luke's body wedged in a very narrow part and leaving it there. Outside a sheet of water was spreading over the land, but very thin, not even up to hubcap level. Birds came down to take a sip or two, birds and more birds. Bernie and I sat side by side on the hood of the beast, the big red SUV parked nearby. Sirens were on the way. Bernie gave me a big hug and kissed the top of my head. His feet were bare and I gave one of them a quick lick.

"That tickles," he said.

I did it again.

"Who's this?" Rocket said.

He lay on his back in a nice clean bed in a nice clean room with a window view of a flowering bush, bees buzzing softly around it.

"Meet Francesca," Bernie said. "She hired me to find you."

"Where was I?" said Rocket.

"Nice to meet you," Francesca said. She was dressed in bright colors and had a bright smile on her face but her eyes were dark and deep. "How are you liking this place?"

Rocket looked around a bit, although without raising his head. "The bed's all right."

"There's nothing like a well-made bed," said Bernie.

Rocket nodded. "You always had brains."

I knew right then that Rocket was good to go, or just about.

"Francesca was Padre Doug's closest friend," Bernie said. Her eyes shifted toward him. He looked right at her and added, "He was lucky to have her." Her eyes came close to misting up—I smelled the tears but they never arrived.

"When's he coming?" said Rocket. Bernie and Francesca exchanged a glance, like maybe they were deciding who would answer. Before either of them could, Rocket said, "I confessed the whole thing to him. But don't ask. My lips are sealed. God's rules, Bernie, not mine."

"I get it," Bernie said. "But it might help you to know that Luke Kincaid and Mitch Inwood are both dead. A monsoon came through and they got caught in a flash flood."

Rocket thought about that. "God's rules," he said again.

"Also I lost your knife," Bernie said.

"Not mine," said Rocket. "Evie's."

"Why did you bury it under the tent?"

Rocket seemed surprised. "So it would live on when I was gone, of course." He put his hands together in the prayer position. "I told the padre I killed my poor lovebird."

"Why did you do that?" Bernie said.

"I ran. That killed her."

The door opened and a nurse looked in. She tapped her wristwatch.

Bernie leaned in and touched Rocket's bony shoulder. "Get some rest."

"I'm not tired," Rocket said. "See you at the ramp."

Fritzie took us out to lunch. He ordered champagne.

"My consultant'll be along in a minute," he said. "You're gonna be impressed."

"What kind of consultant?"

"Political. It was Rayette's idea." Fritzie leaned forward and lowered his voice. "My consultant says that if we play our cards right, come the cycle after next the statehouse isn't beyond the realm of . . . something or other."

"Possibility?"

"Bingo," said Fritzie. "So thanks for what you did, Bernie. It's a real feather in my cap. I've figured out the whole case, by the way."

"Oh?" Bernie said.

"Easy peasy. After the murder Kincaid looked for Rocket for

a while but eventually figured he was home free. Then years later Rocket shows up with a story for the padre and the padre calls Kincaid to check it out. Not naming Rocket, of course, but where else was the info coming from? So he and his muscle guy Mick—or is it Mitch?"

"Mitch," Bernie said.

"So he and Mitch go hunting for Rocket. Rocket gets spooked and disappears in his hole. Mitch tails the padre up to Snake-head Canyon, tries to shake Rocket's whereabouts out of him—that's how Rayette put it, shake out the whereabouts—but things go south. And that's all she wrote."

"She meaning Rayette?" Bernie said.

Fritzie shrugged. "She's one hell of a wife, Bernie. What can I say?"

We were out in the front yard, Bernie rearranging some of the rocks and me and Charlie digging for pirate treasure, when Esmé and her mom showed up, her mom driving and Esmé saying something to her. Esmé's mom got out and approached Bernie. He straightened up, seemed to realize he was holding a big rock, and dropped it.

"I've done some rethinking," Esmé's mom said, "and I owe you an apology."

"We're good," said Bernie. He held out his hand, quickly withdrew it and wiped it on his jeans, tried again. They shook.

"Esmé," Charlie said. He made a come here motion with his skinny arm.

Bernie and Esmé's mom exchanged a look.

"Fine with me," Bernie said.

"I could run some errands," said Esmé's mom. "Say an hour and a half?"

"Sounds good."

Esmé got out of the car and her mom drove off.

"Race you around the house," Charlie said.

"Three two one, blastoff," said Esmé.

They raced around the house. I went with them, loping along from in front. It was a pretty hot day, so after the race we all had drinks, water for me, beer for Bernie, and lemonade from little boxes with straws for the kids.

"What's rethinking?" Charlie said.

"When you think over something you've thought about before," said Esmé.

"Yeah?" said Charlie. "What's thinking?"

"What's thinking?" said Esmé.

"Yeah. What's thinking?"

Charlie started laughing. There's a kind of human laughing you don't often see but it really is the best. That's when the laughter takes over and the laugher falls down laughing. That's what we had going on now, Charlie rolling around and laughing in the yard and Esmé watching him with a kind of strict expression on her face. But then Charlie's laughter spread to her, wiping away that strict expression, and she fell down laughing beside him.

"What's so funny?" Bernie said.

At halftime of the Chisholm Bears' first game of the season they had a little ceremony. We stood at midfield—me, Bernie, Coach Raker, Ms. Chen, Danny Feld, and a kid from the team, his uniform pants grass-stained from play and a bit of blood on his jersey. The stands were packed. I left out that we also had with us what I believe is called a mascot, in this case a human dressed as a bear. I . . . not an actual bite, no, not at all. I admit I nipped him on his not very bearish ankle and he got himself quickly over to the sideline where he belonged, no one noticing the slightest thing although something funny must have happened around the same time since there was laughter in the stands.

Ms. Chen took the mic and introduced everybody and when she came to "and let's not forget the amazing Chet," there was lots of cheering. My tail cheered right back, if that makes any sense.

"Now for something that touches me very deeply," said Ms. Chen, placing her hand over her heart. "Thanks to the generosity of our distinguished alumnus, Danny Feld, I'm proud to announce a new scholarship that will provide full college tuition, room, board, and expenses to a deserving Chisholm athlete every year. It will be called the Bernie Little Scholarship, after our other distinguished alumnus here beside me, and our first recipient is Raheem Wills, wide receiver, number eighty-two. Chisholm folks! What do you say?"

The Chisholm folks clapped and cheered and stomped.

"And now, if Coach Raker will hand the game ball to Mr. Little, we're going to have a ceremonial first pass, symbolizing the connection between the generations in the Chisholm community. Bernie? Raheem? Are you ready?"

They both nodded. Coach Raker flipped the football to Bernie. He caught it the way he catches everything, his hands folding softly around it. Then he smiled at Raheem and gave him a little nod.

Raheem took off. My, how fast he was! Bernie reared back and threw. The ball soared into the bright blue sky. What a beautiful sight! Maybe I should have mentioned that Raheem was fast for a human. But there's more than one kind of fast, my friends. What happened next couldn't be helped.

ACKNOWLEDGMENTS

Many thanks to Kristin Sevick, my superb editor; to Libby Collins, who has handled publicity so smoothly in these unsmooth times; and to Linda Quinton for her support of Chet and Bernie.